MW00893965

LOVED MARS HATED THE FOOD

WILLIE HANDLER

KYANITE
Publishing

In memory of my late parents who would not have had the ability to read this book but would be have been proud just the same.

PB: 978-1-949645-46-0

HB: 978-1-949645-47-7

EB: 978-1-949645-48-4

Design by Sophia LeRoux

Editing by Sam Hendricks

CHAPTER ONE

Mars
Earth calendar: 2039-09-02
Martian calendar: 45-11-582

I'm sure I'm a dead man.

I'm seated on a large red boulder next to my rover, overlooking the gaping crater that was once the first permanent Mars colony, Futurum. The silence of Valles Marineris is broken only by my heavy breathing. My throat feels sealed off and I'm steaming up my face mask.

Beyond the dense smoke spewing from the crater, the colony rubble spreads over a wide radius, metal debris glittering against the red sand and rocks. My head spins, and I'm sweating despite my suit's cooling system. I hope it's a hallucination brought on by the weed brownie.

Maybe I died in the explosion. Maybe I'm having an out of body experience. What was I thinking when I signed up for this mission? I'm a thirty-two-year-old chef from Toms River, New Jersey. I don't know anything about surviving on a barren planet. I just prepare meals.

I stand up and yell at the top of my lungs, "IS ANYONE ELSE ALIVE?" and wince as my voice bounces off the inside of my helmet.

With my source of food, water, and oxygen gone, I don't think I'll be living on this planet much longer. Or anywhere else for that matter.

The quiet is interrupted by the clunk of shifting rocks. As I turn toward the sound, I notice two figures standing just beyond the fringes of the colony blast radius. I spring to my feet and squint. I'm not the only survivor.

I take a few steps forward and squint harder. It looks like they aren't wearing spacesuits.

I try to shake off the marijuana haze as I climb into the rover, reaching for the power button to turn on the vehicle. After shifting the gears, I carefully press on the accelerator pedal, slowly approaching them. The bouncy ride and the clouds of red dust kicked up by the tires make it difficult to see.

The two figures are the size of preteens, although one is several inches taller than the other. They each have two arms, two legs, and coppery, wrinkled skin.

Either I'm more messed up than I think…or these guys aren't human.

The taller Martian has larger feet and the shorter one has a sizeable belly. Both wear tunic tops and loose-fitting trousers made from metallic orange and silver, like they're wearing Harley Davidson duds.

I brake about twenty feet away. The aliens step toward me. I'm convinced that they either intend to vaporize me with a ray gun or make me into a slave. I wet my spacesuit. Not my best day.

Their large heads bobble as they shuffle. Their big, black, pupil-less eyes are fixed on me. A flat nose and no ears make them look like Shar Peis. I climb out of the rover, raise my right hand, and wave. They glance at each other. Mission training never covered this.

I raise my hand again to wave and shout, "Live long and prosper. Dif-tor heh smusma."

Then I try the Vulcan salute, spreading my four main fingers into two sets to form a V. Though I'm positive they can't tell because my hand is in the glove of my spacesuit.

No reaction. This is going well.

I try again. "Klaatu barada nikto."

I remember the line from a movie my dad made me watch when I was a kid, *The Day the Earth Stood Still*. It's the first thing that pops into my head. Again, they look at each other.

A strange voice resonates in my head. *Klaatu barada nikto, are you intact?*

At first, I think I imagine it. I hear it again. *Klaatu barada nikto. What transpired here?*

I watch the two aliens closely, but don't see any mouth movement.

Klaatu barada nikto, can you comprehend? says the voice.

"Yes," I respond in a shrill voice. "Please…please, don't kill me."

Klaatu barada nikto, says the voice. *We intend no harm.*

"How am I hearing you?" I ask, pointing to my ears. "And I'm not Klaatu barada nikto. I'm Dixon Jenner."

The two Martians amble over to the rover. The short one with the big belly walks around the rover before stopping and placing a hand on the side of the vehicle. *Good wishes Dixon Jenner. I am Bleeker and this is my partner, Seepa. What then is Klaatu barada nikto?*

I shrug. "No clue. How are you communicating with me?"

The voice in my head changes. *Through telepathy. How else would one communicate?* It must be the tall Martian, Seepa. She wears a dozen bracelets up and down her arms.

"So, you understand the English language?" I ask.

We transmit and receive thoughts from one being to another, says Bleeker. *I do not comprehend the concept of 'English language.'*

"Are you kidding?" I try to climb back into the rover but miss a step and fall over.

I don't know why, but I laugh hysterically. It might be the brownie.

What are brownies? asks Seepa. *Did they cause you to topple over?*

"How did you hear that? I never said anything?"

Yes, you did, says Bleeker. *I also heard you.*

I grimace. "I don't like the idea of you hearing my thoughts."

You can block your thoughts whenever you wish, says Seepa. *I just think of a black wall or something analogous.*

I stand up, shaking my head. "Yeah, I'm going to have to work on that."

We picked up shockwaves from the detonation, she continues. *That is why we journeyed to the surface to investigate.*

She was opposed to investigating, says Bleeker.

A shrill voice cuts him off. *That is not accurate. I did not want to interrupt my activities to probe what shook our dwelling.*

It is constant negativity from you, says Bleeker.

I step aside as they argue. Great. I travelled over a hundred million miles to listen to a couple bicker.

We are not bickering, replies Seepa. *We just have dissimilar perspectives.*

She breaks into a smile. Well, I assume it's a smile. The corners of her mouth move horizontally.

What type of structure was constructed here? asks Seepa, creeping closer to the edge of the crater.

I kick at a small stone in front of my boot. "I came from Earth with twenty-three other people. We had a colony here."

You are an Earth-being? asks Bleeker, reaching out to touch my spacesuit. *And why are you wearing that strange outfit?*

"I...I would die outside this suit. The environment is too harsh for Earth-beings...I mean Earthlings."

Your community was precisely above our dwelling, says Bleeker. *What happened to it? There is only this large depression.*

My voice wavers. "I don't even know where to start, man. I was part of a mission to establish a permanent colony on your planet." I gaze at the canyon walls in the distance. "In Valles Marineris."

We call this, Brootah. But why here? asks Seepa.

"We were told the canyon walls would provide protection from the winds," I say.

Looks like the winds should not have been your primary concern, says Seepa.

And how permanent could this community have been, if it is gone? asks Bleeker.

I feel as though there are weights on my shoulders. "It was permanent. I don't get it. I was setting up tonight's dinner and was having trouble with the nuclear oven."

Nuclear? chirps Bleeker. *We are not acquainted with this.*

"Me neither," I respond. The buzz from the brownie makes it difficult to focus. I wish these aliens would stop interrupting. "I needed our mission engineer to look at the equipment. She was out with a group collecting rock samples."

That seems like a pointless endeavour, says Seepa. *The surface is littered with rocks.*

"The point I'm trying to make," I say, frowning, "is that while I waited for them to get back, I hopped into this rover to, um…" I feel the two remaining brownies in my suit pressing against my ribcage, the ones I had been planning on sharing with Tammy. "To kill time."

What about the brownies? asks Seepa. *You continue to mention them.*

Are brownies another type of Earth-being? asks Bleeker.

"No, I didn't say anything."

Is this Tammy-being a brownie? asks Bleeker.

I pick up a stone and toss it toward the crater. "Tammy was part of the crew. She radioed me to let me know she was back at the colony, so I headed back," I say. "Then I heard this explosion and when I got here . . ."

Images of Tammy spin in my head. I look back at the crater and sob like a baby.

How unfortunate, replies Bleeker, waddling closer to the crater. He carefully avoids several pieces of debris that are still smouldering. *Not that you survived, but that the other beings did not.*

"I can't survive out here alone," I spurt out, my voice quaking. I grab Bleeker by the arm. "Can you help me?"

No need to be alarmed, says Bleeker, pulling his arm away from my grip. *You will come with us. We will assist in sustaining you.*

Bleeker, be sensible, snaps Seepa, stepping in front of her partner. *We cannot have this Earth-being reside with us. What will the other citizens say?*

"Holy crap," I say, dropping to my knees. "You can't just leave me here. Please help me."

We cannot leave this unfortunate Earth-being to expire here, says Bleeker, patting Seepa on the back. *Do not be distressed, Seepa. I have formulated a strategy.*

I scramble back up, letting out a huge breath. Then I stop exhaling.

"Wait—there are more of you?"

They look at each other, smirking in their straight-mouthed way. Their heads bob from side to side like turtles. They must be mocking me.

Yes, says Seepa. *There are sixty million beings, under the surface.*

Seepa, that is an antiquated tally. There are sixty-three million.

Do you have to be persistently correcting me?

I just want to ensure our visitor possesses the most current statistics. Stop being so sensitive.

I am not being sensitive.

These two Martians are creeping me out. I could be dying, and they would be having a hissy fit.

We aren't creeping anywhere, says Bleeker. *You are not being lucid. It could be the brownie objects you keep mentioning.*

Bleeker, maybe the Earth-being is ill, says Seepa.

Then I look down at the oxygen indicator on my chest.

"I'm a little bit desperate," I murmur with a shaky voice, even if the Martians can't pick up the sound. "I'm not going to survive much longer in this suit. When I run out of oxygen, I'll be dead, too."

Bleeker turns and plods toward the closest canyon walls. *Follow us. We will resolve your depleting supply of breathable air.*

He stops and turns to his partner. *That is, unless you have an objection.*

No, says Seepa. *I concur that we cannot leave this Earth-being alone on the surface. It would be cruel. Can we return to our dwelling? I detest the surface.*

I abandon my rover and follow the two Martians on foot, glancing back at the portable 3D printer lodged in the back of the vehicle, its red power button blinking on and off. I know it might come in handy, but it can't produce oxygen.

Valles Marineris is much like the Grand Canyon but deeper and with no vegetation. Massive rock formations tower over us from all sides. Overhead, the sky is hazy from big clouds of dust, blowing well above the canyon floor. I can't see the Earth through the red swirling sand.

A few steps ahead of me, the bow-legged aliens waddle like a pair of penguins. I have difficulty keeping up in my suit and space boots, stumbling over the rough terrain whenever I pick up my pace. Five times, I trip and fall onto my hands and knees. They waddle ahead.

Bleeker turns to look at me, his head cocked to one side. *What does it mean 'things are so fucked up?'*

"Crap, you've been reading my mind," I say. "I've got to get a hang on this blocking shit."

Apologies, but I had the impression you were having uncertainties about coming with us.

"No. No. Not at all."

We continue to hike across the rough terrain until we are almost at the red cliff face. As we are about to walk around a shallow crater, I hear voices that don't belong to Bleeker and Seepa. The two Martians freeze. Then Bleeker grabs my arm and shoves me behind a large boulder.

I peer around our shelter to see what has them so alarmed. There is a group of blue Martians standing over a chubby one who is stretched out naked on the ground. Like Bleeker and Seepa, he is reddish—well, more of a reddish orange, like an underripe tomato or an Oompa Loompa.

"Who is that?"

That is Cheyhto, our Grand Leader. He controls our government and many Martian enterprises. He is a very powerful being.

"What is he doing out here?"

He takes pleasure in going to the surface to lie in direct sunlight, says Bleeker. *It turned his outer membrane that unusual hue.*

"Who are those other Martians around him?" I ask.

He is an exceptionally important being, says Bleeker. *They take direction from him or are assigned tasks to complete.*

"Oh, an entourage," I say. "And why are they blue?"

There are two distinct Martian classes, says Bleeker. *About one-third of Martians are Machers, which is the class we belong to. The remainder are from the Arbiter class and have the blue pigmentation—*

Bleeker, this is not a suitable occasion for a sociology lesson, say Seepa. *We need to journey past Cheyhto without him discovering Dixon Jenner.*

"Is it bad that he sees me?"

Affirmative, says Bleeker. *How can we explain why you are wearing that space outfit? And he might send us to one of our social re-education centers.*

"What the hell are those?" I ask.

You do not wish to know, replies Bleeker, looking in the direction of the Grand Leader. *I have an idea. Seepa, I will distract Cheyhto and his entourage while you sneak Dixon Jenner past here.*

I am apprehensive about this, she says.

Do not be, says Bleeker. *This will work.*

He grabs my arm. *Keep your thoughts silent.*

Before I can respond, Bleeker steps from behind the boulder and walks toward the group of Martians. *Greetings Grand Leader.*

One of his henchmen steps in front of Bleeker. *Why have you journeyed to the surface?*

Our dwelling shook from a detonation, replies Bleeker. *So, I traveled here to investigate.*

Still lying on his back, Cheyhto turns his head to look at Bleeker, frowning. *We felt no vibrations.*

Cheyhto jerks up into a sitting position. *What is that voice I hear? Who is with you?*

He points to one of the Arbiters. *Did you hear it?*

No, Grand Leader.

I did, says Cheyhto, shoving an underling in the direction of the voice. *Go see who is there.*

Grand Leader, I am here alone, says Bleeker.

We will see, says Cheyhto, his eyes fixed on Bleeker. *What is this about vibrations?*

It was short, but very distinct, says Bleeker, pointing in the opposite direction of the colony site. *It turned out to be an object from space that had crashed onto the surface.*

The Arbiter returns from his search. *I found no one, Grand Leader.*

Well, you have completed your investigation, barks Cheyhto, as he returns to lying on his back. *Proceed back underground. You are disturbing my sunning session.*

While Bleeker creates his diversion, we double back and take an indirect route to the canyon wall. We arrive almost at the same time as Bleeker.

Did you have any problems? asks Seepa, rushing to hug him.

He was more concerned about being disturbed than why I was on the surface, says Bleeker. *We should return to our dwelling before another incident occurs.*

Bleeker lumbers toward the wall of rock in front of us. When he is about ten feet away, he steps onto a black metallic mat. The ground around us rumbles.

A part of the wall in front of us separates from the rest of the cliff and slowly slides down into the ground. I hadn't noticed the entryway because it was the same color and composition as the rock around it. I step several steps forward to get a better look. I don't see any track or mechanism operating it. The vibrations kick up dust and sand, and the Martians cover their faces with their arms.

In less than a minute, a portal opens. It's large enough for me to step through without stooping.

Bleeker motions to me with his hand. *Earth-being, please descend these stairs with us.*

I look back through the portal. If I follow them down, will I ever get out again? No one is going to find me down there.

CHAPTER TWO

```
Mars
Earth calendar: 2039-09-02
Martian calendar: 45-11-582
```

"Um, are you sure this is safe?" I ask, stepping forward to the edge of the stairs, allowing my eyes to adjust to the darkness. My gaze follows a long set of stairs made of polished black stone. As much as I try, I can't make out what's at the bottom. Vertigo strikes me as I look down and step back from the edge. Okay fuck it, I'm going.

Affirmative, Dixon Jenner, says Bleeker, trying to nudge me forward. *We used these stairs to ascend to the surface.*

I swallow. "And you can call me Dix."

Bleeker lumbers over to another metallic mat. When he steps on it, the portal entrance slowly closes.

As the Martians begin their descent, my legs shake. I'm not accustomed to doing stairs in low gravity and I try to keep from straight-up cartwheeling down these creepy dream-sequence steps. After every dozen, the landing reverses direction, winding down into this cavernous space. I look down at the oxygen indicator and discover I have less than thirty minutes left.

I feel like a hamster on a wheel. All that's missing is the water bottle. There is no railing, so I keep to the center. It's well lit, but when I look up at the reflective ceiling, I can't make out the original source of the light. When we get to the bottom ten minutes later, the top is no longer visible.

I'd imagined a windowless medieval torture chamber, but when I reach the bottom, I'm standing in an elaborate city of reflective colored stone that stretches as far as I can see. Taking the final step from the stairs, my feet hit a red roadway made from a hard, rubbery material. It has a lot of give when you step on it.

"What is the surface made from?" I ask, bending down to touch it.

Bleeker grabs my arm to get me to continue walking. *The surface is made from dismoul,* he says. *Do you not have it on Earth?*

I kick the road surface with the toe of my boot. "No. Nothing here looks familiar."

I follow the Martians down the road and we stop at a silver-domed vehicle without wheels. When Bleeker touches a small panel on the door, the entire thing lights up with a pale pink glow. The doors lift, sliding above the vehicle's curved roof.

Bleeker points at my suit. *You can remove your protective clothing,* he says. *The atmosphere below the surface has a substantive quantity of oxygen. Put it in the rear of my transporter as it will attract attention.*

I hesitate. "Are you sure I'll be okay?"

Our atmosphere is thirty percent oxygen. I hope you do not require more.

"That's way more than on Earth."

I unsnap my helmet and pull it off. The air is cool, but not cold like on the surface. I breathe.

Nothing weird happens. Well, aside from breathing on fucking Mars without a spacesuit.

Bleeker and Seepa watch me remove the rest of my suit and patiently wait as I fold it up. "I don't get it," I say. "How are you able to breathe up on the surface and down below when the conditions are so different?"

Our systems adapt to multiple environments, says Bleeker.

Our civilization abandoned living on the surface because it is too windy, says Seepa. *We have no sandstorms here, and we can cultivate provisions because of the warmer temperatures and the presence of water.*

I walk around the Martian's vehicle, examining it. "How do you drive this when it has no wheels?"

Before Bleeker can answer, something hurtles into me and I'm thrown onto the ground. I look up, rubbing my elbow to find two blue Martians in a heated argument right next to me, pushing and shoving each other. A perfect time to try out telepathy. *Why don't you idiots watch what you're doing?*

They stop their fight and look down at me. *What did you call us?* one of the Arbiters says.

You knocked me over, I say.

Dix, please get into the transporter, says Bleeker.

I do not appreciate your attitude, says the second Arbiter. *You were in our path.*

I get up onto my feet. I tower over them. *I was not in your way. I was standing here, minding my own business. You morons ran into me.*

They rush at me, swinging. One fist lands in my midsection, another a little lower. I drop to the ground, clutching my crotch. The two Arbiters jump on top of me, pounding me with their fists.

Get off of him, shouts Bleeker, as he tries to peel them off.

The four of us roll around on the ground, a big ball of arms and legs. I get a couple of good shots on the heads of my attackers. Seepa scrambles into the transporter to contact security services.

Several minutes later, two transporters arrive with four Arbiters wearing uniforms. They pull us apart and drag the morons to one of the vehicles. One of the security agents remains to get a statement from us. He is staring at me. *Why are you so pale?* he asks.

I look over out of the corner of my eye to Bleeker and Seepa.

Bleeker jumps in. *My cousin has a rare medical condition, glaberism.*

The agent continues to stare. *I've never heard of that ailment. Can each of you please provide me with your birthing pod records?*

Bleeker and Seepa pull a token out of their pockets and hand it to him. I pretend to be searching for mine in my pockets.

Dix, are you not able to find your birthing pod record? asks Bleeker.

Um, no.

Perhaps it fell out during the scuffle, suggests Bleeker. *We can search for it.*

It will not be necessary, says the agent, handing back their documents. *I do not have time. Make sure you find or replace it.*

I laugh. Are all Martians this gullible?

The security agent turns and glares at me, his eyebrows furrowed. *What do you find so humorous?*

I... I didn't say anything. Oh, crap. The telepathy thing again.

I heard you, he says. *Are you a social deviant? We have social re-education centers for beings like you.*

Bleeker steps between me and the uniformed Martian. *I am not just his cousin but also his physician. He has been suffering from erratic and transitory thoughts.*

The officer retreats, scratching his chin. *I have never heard of that condition either. Get this being out of public space or I will have to detain him.*

Affirmative, says Bleeker, as he grabs my arms and pulls me toward his transporter.

We scramble inside. I look behind us and see the officer fly off in his transporter. I attempt to find a position in the backseat where my knees aren't in my face. Bleeker passes his hand over a screen on the front panel, and the vehicle lifts off the ground and hovers.

Dix, you must control your thoughts, says Seepa. *You have already created chaos for us.*

"Sorry, but this telepathy stuff is so new to me."

The transporter zips between houses and down a main thoroughfare. The space above the main road is bustling with flying cars, and we slip into the stream of traffic without slowing down. Apparently, the transporter has some form of artificial intelligence as Bleeker does nothing with the controls after activating it. Just like Earth cars, only these ones fly.

"Can this be operated manually?" I ask, shifting around to find a comfortable position in the puny backseat.

Affirmative, but I don't know how the manual operating system functions, says Bleeker. *If my transporter fails, I notify a mechanical engineer to retrieve it.*

I strain my ears to pick up the sound of an engine but hear nothing. "Does your transporter run on some sort of battery?"

Transporters operate by accessing the planet's magnetic fields, says Seepa, shaking her head.

I look at the roadway beneath us. "Well at least you don't have to deal with pot holes."

What is a pot hole? asks Seepa.

"They are small craters in the road," I say.

Why would you construct roadways with craters? asks Seepa, her head cocked to one side.

Seepa, you saw the vehicle he left on the surface, says Bleeker, *it was primitive. Their roadways must also be primitive.*

It must be an exceedingly rough journey to travel directly on the surface and over those craters, she says, her brow furrowed as she looks at me.

I hold my head in my hands. "Never mind."

Seepa turns away, still frowning and I glance out the curved window at scenery flashing by.

"You have a great view of the city from up here," I say. "What is it called?"

Elysium, responds Seepa.

I gaze out the transporter windows at the miles of shiny stone buildings. Some practically reach the cavernous ceiling. I try to make out what type of activity takes place inside them, but we are moving too quickly and it's all a blur. Around us, hundreds of different sized transporters dart in every direction, never colliding. It doesn't feel much different than the streets of New York except for the Technicolor residents.

But not everyone is traveling in transporters. Some Martians wander the roadways on foot, darting between buildings. From the air, they look like rodents scampering around in search of food. There are lineups in front of several buildings and some of those waiting in line try to push past others.

"You have flying cars, so obviously you have advanced technology," I say. "But why are there just stairs to the surface?"

The government wishes to discourage citizens from venturing to the surface, says Bleeker. *Therefore, the only means to reach the surface is by foot.*

"Where is the light coming from?" I ask, staring up at the ceiling several hundred feet above the road surface.

The upper surface is constructed out of luminite, which radiates light, says Bleeker.

The transporter touches down behind an aquamarine stone building, perhaps two stories high, with what looks to be a flat stone roof. Its arched front door is made of the same polished stone as the building exterior, but in black.

We have arrived at our destination, says Bleeker.

We step out of the vehicle into a large open space made up of red dirt and stones, which connects to a similar space behind the homes of their neighbors. The lot is about a half acre, with nothing on it. There's no fencing separating the properties. Most of the houses have a similar transporter parked in the identical place.

They lead me to an entrance that is high enough for the Martians, but not me.

"Nice looking place you have here." I bang on an outside wall with my fist. "Solid."

The door thickness is not much more than the width of my thumb and Seepa easily swings it open. We file in. I duck.

This is our dwelling! Seepa proclaims.

As I look around, I sense an annoying humming sound in my head. I can't tell if it's an actual sound. The two Martians give each other worried looks.

A citizen is at the door, says Bleeker, biting his lip.

CHAPTER THREE

```
Mars
Earth calendar: 2039-09-02
Martian calendar: 45-11-582
```

As Bleeker scurries out of the room to answer the door, I grab my NASA communication cap and pull it over my head just in time for another Martian to bound in. Like Seepa, this Martian is tall with large feet, so I assume it is another female.

Well, who is this immense exotic being? she inquires.

This . . . is Bleeker's cousin, Dix, Seepa stammers. *He originates from . . . Nilosyrtis and is staying with us for a period of time. Dix, this is our neighbor, Plinka.*

Very pleased to have encountered you, Dix, says Plinka. *Why have you travelled to Elysium?*

If she had eyelashes, she'd be batting them. I concentrate on using telepathy and not thinking about shit I don't want her to know. I remember Seepa's suggestion about the black wall.

Um, just visiting family and stuff.

Bleeker jumps in. *As you may observe, Dix appears quite dissimilar. He has a rare medical condition. I plan to administer some tests on him during his stay with us.*

Plinka grabs my arm and rubs her hand up and down my skin. Her touch sends tingles down my spine and other places. These Martians aren't much to look at but there's no denying this Plinka has a magic touch.

Your smooth membrane is exceedingly stimulating both emotionally and physically, she says.

Oh, yeah? I say, smirking. *Are you attracted to smooth skin?*

Positively, she replies. *Dix, are you partnered?*

Seepa pulls Plinka away from me. *Plinka, don't be discourteous.*

Plinka gives me one of those weird Martian grins. *I am just attempting to become acquainted with your cousin.*

I give the neighbor a smile. *As a matter of fact, I'm single.*

Dix, be cautious with this being, declares Seepa. *She is desperate for a partner.*

I am not, says Plinka, crossing her arms. Her mouth drops, which I take it to be a pout.

Plinka, thank you for your visitation, says Bleeker, directing her to the front door. *Dix will be here for an extended period. There will be ample opportunities to become more acquainted.*

Plinka remains where she is standing with her hands on her hips. *Have you forgotten about the sling match?*

Bleeker slams his hand on his forehead. *Um, I had forgotten about the match with Dix's surprise visit. But where is your social partner?*

That social relationship no longer exists, says Plinka, pouting. *Your cousin should come with us.*

Dix does not enjoy—

Yeah, I would love to come along, I say.

Bleeker gives me a death stare.

Plinka, we still have ample time, says Bleeker, grabbing her by the arm and dragging her to the door. *We will enlighten you when it is time to depart.*

He slams the door shut.

Truly, that Plinka is exceedingly impertinent, says Seepa, flopping back into a chair.

At least she accepted the story, says Bleeker, revealing a small smile.

"Yeah, what was that about?" I ask, frowning.

Bleeker takes a seat and leans back in his chair, his hands folded on his skinny lap. *There is a rare Martian ailment which causes a white smooth membrane that resembles yours,* he says. *The most recent case was encountered more than a decade ago.*

We will communicate to citizens that you are a cousin on a visit from Nilosyrtis. But to keep from raising suspicion, you must only utilize telepathy in the presence of other citizens. Your mouth movements when you speak will attract attention.

"Sure," I say. "I can go along with this, but my plan is to get rescued as soon as possible."

That will be marvellous for you, say Seepa, waving her hands in the air. *You never revealed that other Earth-beings are coming to rescue you.*

Or that they know you are still alive, adds Bleeker, nodding in agreement.

"Um, well, I don't know," I say. "But I'm sure that they will come save me. Mission control is manned by the smartest people on Earth. NASA is full of rocket scientists."

How much time would it take for your planet to send a spaceship to Mars, asks Seepa.

"It's hard to say. It only takes a month to travel here, but a crew needs to be picked and trained," I say. "Actually, I was wondering whether someone on Mars would happen to have a spaceship?"

They both shake their heads. *Why take the risk of interplanetary travel?* asks Bleeker.

"To go where no Martian has gone before?"

Seems futile, replies Bleeker, shrugging. *We are content here.*

"Oh, great," I say, my shoulders sagging. "So, what's this disorder called again?"

It is termed glaberism, says Bleeker. *But you should be aware that there exists one complicating factor.*

I sigh. "I should have known."

Bleeker looks at my legs. *We need to come up with an explanation for your stature.*

I bend my gangly legs at the knee. "Can't you find another condition to explain my height?"

We will advise other citizens that you are here for medical research purposes to ascertain the origin of your atypical stature, as well as to study your glaberism.

I grin, scratching my chin. This Martian could work in public relations at NASA.

"Okay, but are you really a doctor?"

Yes, I am a physician and Seepa is a sociology educator, says Bleeker.

Seepa corrects him. *I work in the field of qualitative analysis.*

As you can see, says Bleeker, *she is sensitive about how her vocation is described.*

I am not being sensitive, Seepa replies, her tone acidic. *How would you like me to depict you as a medical technician?*

I cringe.

We are not arguing, says Seepa, scowling at me. *We are engaged in a common couple's discussion.*

Just one more thing, says Bleeker. *You need to do something about the growth sprouting from the top of your head.*

"My hair?" I say. "Not a problem. I can cut it off."

That would be acceptable, says Seepa. *Please do the same with those flaps on the side of your head.*

I jerk my head back. "Um, those are my ears. I'm not cutting them off."

Affirmative. We shall tell others that the other abnormalities, the ear flaps, eyes, and unusual membrane are related to his glaberism disorder, says Bleeker.

"I'm still not clear why we need to make up this dumb story," I say. "Why can't I just say I'm from Earth?"

We cannot have you soliciting unwanted attention, say Seepa.

"Why not?" I ask. "Will I get arrested? Killed? What am I up against here?"

We do not know. But we would prefer your identity be kept secret so that our study is not compromised, says Bleeker.

"Study? What are you talking about?"

Why do you reason we resolved to assist you? asks Bleeker.

I smirk. "Because you are both humanitarians and were concerned about what would happen to me?"

They respond with blank stares.

What is a humanitarian? asks Seepa. *Is that someone who grows humans?*

Earth-being, says Bleeker as he picks up a tablet from a shiny green side table. *We are intellectuals and there is nothing altruistic about our motives. You are an extraordinary discovery and present a unique professional opportunity for us. We would like to study you. Seepa is interested to learn about the social structures that exist on Earth. I am interested in your anatomical and physiological systems.*

I take a step back. "Holy crap," I say. "Do you plan to dissect me?"

Bleeker wrinkles his nose. *Do not be ludicrous. Our inclination is to keep you alive.*

* * * * *

That evening, I climb into the back of the transporter with Plinka while Bleeker and Seepa sit in the front. When the doors close, the vehicle elevates and flies in the direction of Arsia Hall. According to Bleeker, it's the headquarters of the Martian Sling League.

Bleeker wears a red and yellow sling jersey to the game; Elysium is his favorite team. Plinka wears a top that sparkles in the light. I assume she's wearing the Martian equivalent of sequins. Although there is plenty of room in the back of the transporter if you're under five-feet, Plinka presses against me.

I consider tall beings to be very appealing, says Plinka.

Yes, back home they refer to me as Stretch, I say.

Bleeker indicated your stature was the result of a medical disorder, says Plinka, *but I never realized you have been stretched.*

Plinka, that was a joke, I say.

I am not familiar with that form of humor, she says, but at least she smiles.

The transporter swings onto a broad avenue that ends at a large oval building about thirty feet above the road with steps that lead up to several wide, gated entrances. When we exit the transporter, the vehicle lifts above the hall on its own. There are hundreds of transporters hovering there in a massive, floating parking lot. We climb the steps to one of the entrances, where hundreds of big, black eyes turn to stare at me. I'm nearly two feet taller than everyone else.

When we reach the gate, Bleeker hands the attendant a black disk that he scans with a device that looks to me like a wand.

The attendant looks up at me, a little startled. *What happened to you?* he asks.

I have a rare medical condition, I say.

I'm his physician, adds Bleeker.

I hope there is a cure, responds the attendant.

These Martians aren't so hot looking either. They're as wrinkled as my ninety-one-year-old grandmother.

The attendant glares at me. *What do you mean I look like a grandmother?*

Um, I wasn't referring to you, I sputter, quickly moving past the gate.

We shuffle into the main concourse and make our way to our seats. It's so crowded that I get pushed and elbowed. People gawk.

What is that?

Where did that being come from?

Parental-being, I am frightened.

Jumping a little, I glance to my left at the Martian child. He is a smaller version of the grown-ups, but with huge eyes that widen as he stares at me. He grabs his mother's arm.

Holy shit! That thought is mine. I'm getting a little creeped out. I stoop over, trying to be inconspicuous.

We climb a set of stairs to our seats, which are close to the center of the court and about a dozen rows up. When I try to sit I nearly crush my legs. Now I understand why Dorothy ran down the yellow brick road and out of Munchkinland.

I try to cross my legs at the ankles, my knees hang over the front of the seats. Plinka smiles when I touch her leg.

Don't you find the seating to be a little too cozy, I ask.

I do not object, says Plinka. *I appreciate the intimacy.*

I feel my pulse rise, and my face flushes. This Martian is quite the minx. I wonder if all Martian women are like this.

What does that mean? asks Plinka, wrinkling her nose up.

What does what mean? I respond.

You referred to me as a minx, she says.

Um, yeah, I sputter. *Where I come from um… it means you're attractive.*

She smiles and wraps her arm around mine.

As fans take their seats in the stands, I notice that only Machers attend the game.

Bleeker, why are there no Arbiters?

You are amusing, Dix, says Bleeker. *Arbiters are not permitted here, except as participants. That would be an outrage.*

That doesn't seem right, I say.

You could be sitting next to an Arbiter, says Seepa.

I would be fine with it, I say.

Well I would not be, she says, wrinkling her flat nose.

I scan the arena, taking in the atmosphere. For such a large facility, the crowd gives off little sound; it's more like what you would expect attending a classical music concert rather than a sporting event. Instead, the cacophony of 'voices' bounces around in my head. It's a little unnerving.

Plinka snuggles up to me. Her wrinkled and leathery skin feels like a rawhide handbag.

Dix, do you not have a sling squad in Nilosyrtis? asks Plinka.

Um, yeah, we do. I just never went to games.

Are you familiar with the regulatory provisions?

No, but I should be able to figure it out. Do you come to many games yourself?

No, I have no attraction to witness Arbiters running about on a court creating such bedlam, says Plinka. *But I imagined you would appreciate the company.*

I turn my attention to the court, as the players make their appearance from the dressing rooms. Some players are banging into each other while other are jumping off the players' benches onto the court surface.

Bleeker, what are the players doing out there? I ask. *Is that how they warm up?*

Warm up? he asks, rubbing his chin. *You mean prepare for the match. Yes, that is what is taking place.*

The court is made from a rubberized material judging by how the players bounce on it. One half is red, and the other yellow. I assume these reflect the team colors of the home squad, Elysium. The court is larger than a basketball court but not as large as a hockey rink.

A giant slingshot stands at each end. The sling itself is attached at the ends to something like football uprights, and a scoreboard unlike anything I've ever encountered hangs high above the center of the court. It isn't a physical object, but rather a virtual scoreboard, consisting of light images.

I can identify the home team by their red and yellow jerseys. The Cerebus team wear green and black, but all the players are blue Arbiters. I count twelve on each team but only six on the court. The others sit on benches along the sidelines.

When the match begins, the defensive team lines up in a row at the far end of the court. The offensive team gathers right behind their sling. One player mounts the sling while two teammates, whom I mentally name launchers, pull him back. The players' faces strain as the tension in the sling builds, and then they let go. The player in the sling—the launchee—sails at a least hundred feet across the court. At the same time, the defensive players run forward. About half way into the defensive zone, the airborne player collides with the defense and knocks several players backward. Players limp around the court, holding a twisted arm or a dented head. It's like a bizarre version of red rover.

I wince with every collision, but no one reacts to the injuries, occurring with almost every play. In the silence, I can clearly hear a sling player bouncing across the rubbery surface. I get the impression the crowd will not do the wave.

Someone taps me on the back. *Hey, friend,* he says. *How am I to follow the match with you obstructing my view?*

I turn around and find a pudgy Martian glaring at me with those big, bug eyes. *Sorry, buddy,* I say. *Can't help that I'm tall.*

Apologies do not resolve my situation, he says. *I cannot see unless you move. Where on Mars are you from? Nobody is this large.*

He happens to suffer from a rare condition, glaberism, says Bleeker. *I'm his cousin and a physician. Dix, exchange seats with me.*

I unfold my legs and move to Bleeker's seat. That calms the little red snot behind me but gets a frown from Plinka. As I turn my attention back to the match, another launchee flies through the air. He soars higher, but not quite as far. He lands just short of the line of defensive players and takes a big bounce off the court, which carries him over the heads of the defense and lands him behind them. The play gets quite a rise from the crowd with many of the fans raising a fist in the air.

After several launches, the offensive team goes on defense and the other team launches players at them.

I soon pick up why you need bench players. Not every player makes it to the end of the match. One launchee goes a little too high and sails right through the virtual scoreboard into the arena roof. He drops like a shot duck and lands with a thud on the playing surface. A group of Arbiters with white uniforms run onto the court to carry him off. He doesn't make another appearance.

The launchers release the next player too early and he gets no height at all. He bounces across the court like a stone skipping on a lake, never making it to the defensive line. His arms and legs are twisted as he is carried off the court. I have to look away.

When the play resumes, a rather stout player in the center of the Elysium defense catches my attention. Airborne players bounce off him without knocking him over. After a while, the Cerebus team attempts to aim players toward the sideline to avoid this guy.

The match progresses quickly despite the many delays to carry off the injured. At half-time, the players leave the court, no doubt to be scanned for fractures and concussions. We get up and stroll around, which I appreciate. My legs are getting cramps.

Bleeker, I think Dix might be uninterested in the match, says Plinka. *Do we need to remain for the second half?*

I try to be nonchalant, ignoring the stares as we walk through the concourse. *This is not what I expected,* I say. *It is much more violent than any sport on Earth, but I don't want to be the reason for ending the evening early.*

Plinka, I think it is you who is disinterested, says Bleeker.

You know my opinion of sling, says Plinka.

I am enjoying the match, says Seepa. *If anyone is interested in knowing.*

Good. The majority elects to stay, says Bleeker. This elicits a pout from Plinka.

In the second half, the teams change sides. The Cerebus team miscalculates when it attempts to direct a launchee toward the sideline. The player sails out of the court into the crowd. Spectators scramble out of the way, and he lands head first in the stands. His head becomes wedged in a seat with his little arms and legs waving wildly in the air. This is brutal.

This brings out a group of Arbiters attendants who take several minutes to dislodge him. They return him to the sidelines, where he sits dazed, several indentations clearly visible in his head.

By the time the match ends, each team is down to only one substitute player. Elysium wins the match by a score of 52-38. No doubt the home crowd is delighted, but I can't feel my legs anymore.

We stand up and inch toward the arena stairs, shuffling along with the crowd. Since I'm taller than everyone else, I can see the exit at the bottom of the steps. The stares and comments from the Martians around us distract me, and I become separated from my group in the concourse. I retrace my steps, hoping to locate the right exit out of the building or that the others will notice me towering over the crowd.

Then I run smack into that Cheyhto dude and his entourage who come out of a room on the concourse level. Before I can react, two of his henchmen grab me by the arms and pin me up against a wall.

I'm...um...going to miss...my ride home, I say. *Please let me go.*

Cheyhto steps toward me, his arms folded against his chest as he gives me the once-over. His Arbiter cronies hold me so tight that my hands start to feel pins and needles. These Arbiters are tiny, tough dudes.

What creature do we have here? Cheyhto says with a sneer.

My heart races, and my mind goes blank. *I'm . . . eh, not a creature,* I say. *I'm Dix from Nilosyrtis.*

Has anyone told you that you are grotesque? says Cheyhto as he pokes at my nose. *What a mess.*

I can't help the way I look, I say. *I suffer from glaberism.*

I've never heard of that ailment, says Cheyhto, as he continues to size me up through squinting eyes. *It sounds like something fabricated.*

I hope they don't notice my knees knocking. I take a deep breath. *I can assure you that it is the real deal.*

You do not resemble a Macher or Arbiter, says Cheyhto, staring at my ears. *And what are those flaps on the side of your skull?*

They are membrane growths related to the glaberism.

They are horribly disturbing.

I bite my lip as he continues to stare.

Something about you is not right, he goes on. *I should have you thrown into one of my social re-education centers, but you appear to have enough to deal with.* He grimaces, then turns his back to me. *I cannot bear to look at you any longer.*

His Martian flunkies snicker. Cheyhto grabs the arm of one of them and tosses him against a wall.

Take down his information, says Cheyhto, *and have someone probe into his background to verify his story.*

With that he waddles in the other direction. His henchmen scurry after him. I provide information to one of his subordinates on where I'm staying and take off in the opposite direction. Gulping air, I wipe a shaky hand down my face and blow out a breath.

I weave through the crowd to where we got separated. Catching Bleeker's eye, I wave my arms in the air.

He pulls me aside. *Where did you depart to?* he asks.

I got lost and ran into Cheyhto, I say. *I . . . I gave him your address.*

Bleeker's head drops. *What else did you tell him?*

That I was visiting from Nilosyrtis.

Dix, there is no record of you in Nilosyrtis, says Bleeker.

Then why did you tell me to say I was from there? I ask. *What's going to happen now?*

I do not know.

Bleeker is unusually quiet as we exit the building. Once we are outside, our transporter glides down from the airborne lot, and we pile in.

It's quiet on the ride home. Seepa tries to start a conversation. *What are your thoughts on the match, Dix?*

I'm surprised that this type of exploitation exists on Mars, I say.

What are you implying? asks Bleeker.

I've seen violent sports before, but this is beyond what I consider acceptable, I reply, tapping a finger on my window. *Having the lower class batter each other for your entertainment is nuts.*

We regret that you feel this way, says Seepa, *but they are merely Arbiters.*

Plinka remains quiet on the subject. When we are close to home she nuzzles up to me.

Dix, it is not nearly time for restoration mode, says Plinka. *Would you like to come to my dwelling where we can learn more about each other? You can tell me about your glaberism and I can show you my orb collection.*

I like the sound of this. Plinka is cheeky.

But then I look at Bleeker who shakes his head like a chaperone at a school dance.

Plinka, I'm pretty tired, I say. *I'm going to have to pass. Another time.*

After we drop Plinka off, Bleeker turns around, glaring at me. *I hope you have not jeopardized our study as a result of your careless encounter with Cheyhto. I am concerned that there will be repercussions.*

I swallow hard but say nothing. I have no interest in finding out firsthand about Martian social re-education centers. They don't sound educational to me.

CHAPTER FOUR

Johnson Space Center: Houston, TX
Earth calendar: 2039-09-03
Martian calendar: 45-11-583

"Dr. Farley," says his assistant on the other side of the door. "The executive team is waiting in the hall."

"I'll be right out."

Farley looks over his notes one last time. He then folds and stuffs them into the left breast pocket of his suit. He takes a deep breath and wheels his chair back to get up. As he walks to the door, he glances over to the wall covered with photos of him posing with former astronauts. He wonders what some of them are thinking right now.

Farley continues out of his office and into the reception area to join the others senior NASA officials who are standing in front of the reception desk. The conversation stops as soon as he appears.

"Is everyone ready for the dog and pony show?" he asks.

The group nods in unison. Farley marches out of the executive wing of the Johnson Space Center, with the others trailing behind and down the corridor. The executives look like they've been cloned with identical dark suits, red ties, and graying hair. The portraits of his predecessors look down at him. He wonders how soon he will be joining them, passing silent judgement on his successors.

When they arrive at the entrance of the press center, Farley peeks into the packed room. The front rows are filled, and late arrivals roam up the aisles looking for a vacant seat, tiptoeing around the large, electrical cables running toward the back of the room. It seems that every reporter is on their phone, straining to hear over the collective roar. A cart carrying equipment topples over, which sets off a stream of shouting and profanity.

Farley pushes the door open and steps into the melee. The crowd falls silent.

His executive team members find a place at a long table that has been set up at the front of the room. Farley stands next to a podium emblazoned with the NASA logo just to the right.

He nods to the others and steps behind the podium. He pulls notes from his jacket pocket and peers down at his prepared remarks through a pair of metal-framed glasses that rest on his long, thin nose. He grips the podium with pale, veiny hands and blows a strand of his patchy, salt-and-pepper hair out of his face.

Farley takes several quick breaths, then looks up from his notes. "Good morning, ladies and gentlemen. I'm Dr. Charles Farley, the NASA Administrator responsible for the Mars Colony Mission. I'm here to read a short statement and after that I will answer a few questions.

"The Mars colony has been up and running for thirty-two days with twenty-four mission specialists. Yesterday evening, mission control lost contact with the Mars colony. Initially, we believed it to be a communications problem. After further investigation, we now know the colony has suffered a catastrophe."

Gasps spread throughout the room. He pauses to allow those present to absorb the news, looking around the room. The crowd is motionless and silent.

"Our investigation will carry on, but our initial findings suggest that all crew members have been lost. We will continue to provide updates as we know more. I'll take some questions now."

This triggers the journalists. A sea of waving arms and a chorus of incoherent shouts compete for his attention. Farley scans the room for a familiar face, one that might go easy on him. He points to a woman in the second row.

She stands, clutching a notepad and pen. "Can you tell us what led you to believe this was a disaster and not a communication breakdown?"

Farley runs a hand through his thinning hair and clears his throat. "All our crew members wear monitors to measure heart and respiration rates and other vital signs," he says. "We stopped receiving signals at the same time the communications terminated, except for one crew member, Dixon Jenner, the Culinary Specialist on the mission. A Mars orbiter picked up his vitals, but the signals stopped several hours later. This suggests he may have survived the disaster, only to run out of oxygen afterward."

The shouting resumes, arms thrust into the air. He points at another reporter.

She pops to her feet and uses her pen to poke the photographer in the next seat who is looking down at his phone. "Can you speculate as to the type of disaster that might have taken place?"

He looks over at the other NASA officials seated next to the podium, their faces expressionless. He clears his throat. "Until we have more information, we are going to avoid any speculation."

Farley peers down at a reporter in jeans and a Dallas Cowboys t-shirt in the front row and nods.

The reporter gets to his feet, dropping his phone while he fumbles with his notes. "Have you got satellite photos of the colony, and would you be able to share them with the media?"

Farley removes his glasses and digs a tissue out of another pocket. He wipes the lenses, but they don't need cleaning.

"Several hours ago," he says, "we positioned a satellite to take photographs of the colony. We are still reviewing those photographs, and all I can say at this moment is that they confirm the colony has been lost. We will make those photographs available to the public once we have finished analyzing them."

A young reporter in the third row stands up and shouts, "Dr. Farley, Dr. Farley!"

He looks over at him, scowling as he nods.

"How does NASA respond to the critics who argued this mission was too dangerous in the first place?"

Farley shifts his weight from one foot to the other. "This question always comes up whenever we have a failure in space, in particular when lives are lost." He fiddles with his notes again, ruffling the pages. "We are driven to explore the unknown, discover new worlds, push the limits of science and technology.

The intangible desire to explore and challenge the boundaries of what we know – and where we have been – has provided benefits to our society for decades, even centuries."

He raps his index finger on the podium. "Columbus attempted to find a trade route to Asia and ended up in America. Magellan attempted to circumnavigate the globe. Captain James Cook pushed even further when he reached Australia. Explorers are aware of the risks they take."

He scans the room and points again.

"A growing number of Americans are opposed to the billions of dollars being spent on space exploration. They want to know why their government is focused on colonizing some distant planet when there are so many more pressing problems at home. They would like to see NASA shut down. What do you have to say to these hard-working taxpayers?"

Farley grips the sides of the podium as he stares down the reporter. "Our agency has had a long history of successes. Our scientific experiments lead to discoveries that benefit everyday Americans. We have strong support in Washington and Main Street, USA. I can take one more question."

"What about you, Dr. Farley?" asks the same reporter. "How concerned are you about your job security in light of the disaster?"

He moves his hand to his glasses and stops himself. "Here at NASA, we are a results-based organization. I am accountable for what goes on here. There are bigger issues at stake than my job security."

He looks to the back and points to the last questioner, a burly man with wild, curly hair and a bushy beard.

"Since your monitors picked up that Dixon Jenner survived the catastrophe," the man says, in a deep booming voice, "is it possible that he is still alive but no longer connected to his monitor?"

Farley shakes his head. "Unfortunately, that isn't possible. Those monitors are built into his spacesuit and he can't survive without his suit." He steps to the front of the podium. "It's not like he was picked up by Martians."

CHAPTER FIVE

```
Mars
Earth calendar: 2039-09-04
Martian calendar: 45-11-584
```

I wake from a deep sleep brought on by a second brownie. I dreamt that the crew members were yelling at me for blowing up the colony. I tried to explain that it wasn't me, but no one was listening. Tammy had called me a pothead. Talk about the pot calling the kettle black.

When I open my eyes, I'm in a strange, little room.

I imagine myself going weird like *Castaway* Tom Hanks. I'd have conversations with the helmet of my EVA spacesuit – "Good morning, Eva. Yes, it is a lovely day. Would you care to go for a walk?" – and pine after my pathetic apartment over old lady Carter's garage.

The Martians' bed is too short for my frame, and my legs dangle over the end when I stretch out. Pins and needles shoot through my legs. I move them until I get the feeling back.

I get up and stagger past my spacesuit, sprawled out in the corner of the room like a passed out drunk. I stumble to a window. The Martian cityscape looks the same as yesterday; I assume it's morning, but who can tell without a sky?

In the common room, I find Bleeker and Seepa. One- and two-seater chairs are scattered around the space, as well as dining room furniture. The walls have framed artwork, displaying landscape and strange looking creatures that move. The motion makes me nauseous and I have to look away.

In the center of the room is a large red stone table with six chairs around it. Two of the chairs are occupied by the red, wrinkled Martians.

Morning greetings to you, Dix, says Seepa. *How was your restoration mode?*

"Um, yeah." I rub my eyes. "Morning."

Seepa directs me to one of the empty seats. *Come join us and consume some nutrition,* she says. A tray sits on the table, covered with what I presume to be food.

You must require replenishing.

I eye the platter of what looks like sponge toffee cut into little cubes. "I am a little hungry."

I gingerly work my way into a chair. It's too small for my legs and I have to pull my knees up to my chest to avoid banging them into the table. This place is a Toys "R" Us showroom.

"What is this?" I ask Seepa as she passes me the food.

You have never consumed dimosh? asks Bleeker, gaping.

"Nope, we don't have this on Earth." I pick up a piece to examine before biting into it. Working it around in my mouth, it has the texture of chalk and tastes like chalk.

"Wow. Look what I've been missing my whole life."

Bleeker picks one of the spongey cubes up with his spindly, red fingers and pops it into his mouth. *A very popular form of nutrition on Mars, he* says, passing the platter back to his partner. *We normally commence most days with a serving of dimosh. It contains many vital nutrients.*

Watching him eat reminds me of a camel. He doesn't chew, he chomps. Some flies out his mouth, landing on the table.

Looks like I'll be taking over the food prep.

When we are almost done eating, I notice a blur in the corner of my eye. I turn to my left in time for a red, ugly creature to jump onto my lap. It resembles a gecko covered with spikes.

I jump to my feet and it tumbles to the floor.

"What the hell is *that*?"

The creature runs over to Seepa, who scoops it up.

Seepa looks up at me. *This is our pet lappa, Poof. Do you not think she is appealing?*

I roll my eyes. "Oh yeah," I say, "appealing. Does it bite?"

Do not be ludicrous, Seepa says, still hugging the creature. *She is very gentle. She just wants to snuggle.*

I eye the spikes again. "Let's try to avoid the snuggling part."

As Seepa clears the table, I pull Bleeker aside. "I need to speak to you about something."

You cannot go, says Bleeker. *It is not safe.*

"You read my thought again," I say, scrunching my face. "I need to go to the surface. The 3D printer we left will be handy during my stay here. There may be other stuff that survived the explosion."

Then I am offering my assistance. I cannot have you journey up alone.

I walk toward my room to retrieve my spacesuit. "Is that so? Why the sudden change of heart?"

Seepa and I are concerned that if you were to incur a mishap, it would terminate our proposed study before it even begins.

I shake my head. "Nice to know you're so concerned for my welfare. I'm concerned that any useful equipment that survived the explosion might get buried by blowing sand. So, my plan is to go today."

Bleeker leaves my room and returns several minutes later with a green jar. He lifts my EVA suit. *Where does your oxygen supply originate from?* he asks.

I kneel and remove a panel in the back of the suit to expose the oxygenator. "Right here."

He opens the jar and removes a green crystal and drops it into the chamber of the oxygenator. *Your suit should be functional now.*

"Gee, thanks, but what are those?"

Crystalized oxygen. I use them in my medical practice. I will leave you with this container for future use.

"Oh my God, that's awesome."

I am prepared to leave now if you are.

"Lead the way."

I follow Bleeker to their backyard of their house, my spacesuit slung over my shoulder. Bleeker touches the keypad to his transporter, causing the doors to lift. *Deposit your suit in the back so it won't be visible,* he says.

I stuff the suit in the back and climb in the front with Bleeker where it's only slightly less cramped. It's early in the day and the transporter zips through the light traffic to the foot of the staircase leading to the portal. We unload my suit from the vehicle and Bleeker sends it back into the air to hover until we return.

I throw the suit over my shoulder, take a deep breath, and begin climbing the stairs. Bleeker scampers up behind me. It takes about twenty minutes to reach the top. After dropping the suit to the ground, Bleeker helps with the clasps to the boots. I check the gauges on my chest to confirm everything is operational. Chilled air on my face tells me the cooling system has kicked in.

When we are ready to exit, I step on the mat that opens the portal. The ground rumbles. Bleeker protects his eyes from the flying dust with his hands. There are no sandstorms today and the sky is the usual butterscotch color. As we walk through, Bleeker steps on the outer mat. We hike in the direction we had come from two days earlier with the sound of the portal closing behind us.

It doesn't take long to locate the rover, which from a distance resembled a slumbering buffalo. Aside from a light layer of red dust, it's otherwise just as I left it. Within a few minutes, we are driving back to the crater. The rover is much roomier than the tiny Martian transporters, with lots of leg room in the front. The flat bed in the back can carry a lot of equipment and hardware.

Almost immediately, Bleeker whines. *Dix, I find this vehicle excessively uncomfortable.* He is bouncing about like a pinball in the passenger seat. *Why would one choose to journey directly on the ground? This mode of transportation is primitive.*

This is how we travel on Earth, I say, steering clear of a small mound of boulders. *We could have used your transporter, but you were against taking it up to the surface.*

My transporter is not designed to be taken to the surface. Please do not interpret my comments as an attempt to be obstinate.

Then stop whining, I say.

I stop the rover when we reach the colony site. Just two days ago, it was a small but thriving outpost, an oasis in this vast, red desert. Now, it is a graveyard and a pile of space junk. I could easily have been there when the explosion took place. My eyes well up. Tammy was in there.

Who is this Tammy? asks Bleeker. *Was she your partner?*

I reach to my face to wipe away the tears, then realize I'm wearing a helmet. *Someone who was with me at the colony,* I say. *Someone I will really miss.*

Bleeker puts his hand on my shoulder. *That is distressing,* he says. *Dix, your error was not in coming to Mars. It was in constructing your community on the surface. You subjected yourselves to numerous perils.*

That wasn't my call, I say.

Bleeker steps out of the rover to get a better look at the debris. *Dix, what objects are you searching for?* he asks. *You had indicated you were retrieving the device in the back of your vehicle. What else?*

I have no idea.

I cannot ascertain what you expect to discover in this debris, he says, kicking aside part of a table leg.

He is probably right. The landscape is littered with twisted pieces of charred metal and white ashes.

Bleeker gets back into the rover.

This is the plan, I say. *We will do circles around the site. Each one wider than the previous one, so we don't miss anything.*

The rover lurches forward, jostling Bleeker. *I regret not bringing cushions to sit on,* he says.

I complete my first few circles and only find unidentifiable, blackened metal fragments lying on top of the red sand. Fortunately, we don't encounter any body parts. After about thirty minutes of circling, we come across a large, shiny object among the smaller debris. I pull up and hop out of the rover. It's a metal case with multiple dents, but it's still intact. The metal has a gray-bluish tint from the heat of the blast.

Bleeker leans out of the rover for a closer look.

Looks like one of our food lockers, I say. *Can you help me put that on the back of the rover?*

Are you sincere? he says. *You want me to elevate a weighty object?*

Yes, I say. *I can't lift this on my own. It's larger than I am.*

Bleeker hesitates before climbing out of the rover. I grab one end of the locker and he does the same with the other end. As we lift the object, Bleeker's arms shake. He drops his end and the case nearly lands on him.

This object is far too weighty for me, says Bleeker.

Bend your knees when you lift, I say, bending slightly to demonstrate the proper form.

We try again. He struggles but manages to lift it high enough to slide onto the flat bed in the back of the rover.

From there, we continue circling. Other opened metal cases are scattered across the landscape, their contents destroyed. I can make out twisted pieces of bed frames, airlocks, and rover parts.

About an hour and another supply locker into the search, we reach the end of the debris field. I'm ready to head back when we almost drive over a metal object, partially buried in the sand. I jam on the brakes, creating a cloud of red sand that has Bleeker coughing. I scramble out of the rover and drop to my knees.

I can't believe this survived intact.

Bleeker is behind me, peering over my shoulder. *What is exceptional about this object?*

Each person in the colony was assigned a metal locker just like this. Strange how these are the only items that are salvageable. And this one's mine.

How do you know that one is yours?

It has my name on it, I say, pointing to the side of the case.

Oh, that is what those markings are.

Let's get this one loaded onto the rover with the other, I say.

Dix, my arms and back are getting fatigued, says Bleeker. *How are we going to get them down the stairs?*

I haven't figured that out yet, but let's get them to the portal first.

Bleeker struggles to help load the last case onto the rover, and we head back to the stairs.

Within minutes of our return trip, Bleeker tugs at my arm. *Stop,* he shouts, pointing to prints in the sand. I slow down to look more closely. They are the shape and size of a barefoot human print.

I slump back in my seat. This doesn't make sense. Could another crew member still be alive after two days? Wandering around in bare feet?

Are you envisioning that these prints might be from another Earth-being? asks Bleeker.

Possibly, I say, driving slowly along the trail. *But the foot prints are too small for a human wearing big boots. And they can't be made by a Martian.*

I suggest that we continue to the underground portal, says Bleeker. *We should not risk an adverse encounter.*

I press my foot on the accelerator. *No. I need to know who made these.*

We pick up speed and continue to follow the trail. The prints must be fresh because the blowing sand would cover them within a day. I glance down at the rover's GPS. We haven't been traveling in a straight line.

I believe we should resume the trip back to the portal, says Bleeker. *I do not have a positive feeling about this.*

Then, in the distance, I make out a figure that looks human. The person we've been trailing is not wearing a spacesuit, just a jumpsuit. It is tall and thin, arms swinging back and forth as it plods across the barren landscape.

By the time we are about fifty feet away, I recognize it is as one of the Sementric robots that accompanied us to Mars. Somehow, this one appears to have survived the explosion. The bots are just over five-feet tall and covered with a flesh-colored metal alloy, which make them look lifelike.

Is that another Earth-being? asks Bleeker.

No, it's a robot.

What is the function of this robot?

It has been programmed to do construction work, I say. *They helped us build the colony.*

We have Arbiters for that, Bleeker replies. *They have greater physical strength than Machers.*

As we pull up next to him, the bot stops and looks at us. He resembles a full-sized Ken doll in a NASA jumpsuit, except for his large eyes, like prisms that only give off red light. He is barefoot and walking normally, despite the low gravity. Bots adjust quickly to changes in the environment.

"What are you doing out here?" I ask him.

The bot stops and puts his hands on his hips. "Thank heavens you showed up," he says. "Two days ago, I was doing maintenance work on the spaceship when I felt tremors and the ship toppled. I could have been crushed. I've been wandering for fifty-one hours and eighteen minutes, looking for someone."

"I'm certainly glad to have found you," I say. "It looks like you and I are the only survivors from the colony."

He frowns, with his red eyes fixed on me. "Well then, it's fortunate that we crossed paths. Hopefully, you have a replacement battery for me." The bot leans against the rover with his hands on the roof. "My battery only has three hundred and twenty-four days, eleven hours, and forty-one minutes of power left. I'm quite concerned."

"Sorry," I say. "I don't have any batteries."

"Oh dear," says the bot. "It is imperative that you inform Mission Control that they need to send another battery."

"Listen, Todd," I say. "I have no way to communicate with Earth. Mission Control probably thinks we've been vaporized."

"My, aren't we full of good news today," says the bot. "And I'm not Todd. I'm Sementric 3."

"Hop in the rover, Todd," I say. "We're going to need your help with the lockers in the back. That's Bleeker."

Why do you call the Sementric 3 a Todd?

I smirk and give them a shrug. "Todd is my brother's name. I like the idea of ordering around a Todd."

Greetings, Todd, says Bleeker.

The bot stares at Bleeker as if he's not entirely certain what to make of him. "Good Lord," says the bot as he climbs into the rover. "Aren't you a hideous creature? And the name is Sementric 3."

"Todd, don't be rude," I say. "Wait, how can you hear what he's saying? The Martian is using telepathy."

Fortunately, I've been designed with a fully functional artificial brain that can transmit and receive thoughts, explains the bot.

"I'm just a chef and don't know much about this kind of stuff," I say, "but why would NASA design telepathic robots?"

"Let me explain it so that a chef can understand. Our robotic engineers decided that the Sementric robots should communicate with each other without speech. They developed an advanced form of Bluetooth technology for that purpose."

Bleeker, our lovely Martian host. The bot reaches out to put his hand on the Martian's shoulder. *You wouldn't happen to have access to a Sementric battery pack?*

Good God, I say. *The empathy function in the upgraded bots is so creepy.*

My apologies, but I do not possess one, says Bleeker, cautiously eyeing the bot. *Dix, I am astonished that this machine is capable of telepathy. It is extremely advanced.*

I wasn't even aware that it had this function, I say.

"What a nightmare this is turning into," says the bot, plopping back into his seat.

"I just thought of a great idea," I announce.

I turn the rover around and head back to the colony site, where I instruct the bot to gather up metal debris and lays out the pieces to form a giant SOS.

"Do you actually believe NASA will be able to see that feeble distress signal?" Todd asks later. As the rover crawls across the surface back to the portal, the bot chatters away. "It would be easier to spot an African Pygmy in Times Square."

CHAPTER SIX

Two and a Half Years Earlier
Toms River, New Jersey

I was lying on my bed, trying to decide if I should get up when my cellphone vibrated. The drilling sound bounced around in my head. I reached across the bedside table.

"Hello," I answered, my voice still hoarse from sleep.

"Good morning," came a female voice on the other end of the line. "I'm looking for Dixon Jenner."

The frigid air coming through the old Victorian-style windows made my teeth chatter. "That's me."

"I'm Sue Grady from the Madison Consulting Group. We're an executive search firm based in New York. Is this a good time to chat?"

It was almost ten in the morning and I hadn't gotten out of bed. I wasn't ready to answer a bunch of questions, not without some coffee first. But I didn't want to give the impression that I was a slacker.

"Yes," I said as I cleared my throat. "Of course."

"You applied online for an executive chef position several weeks ago, and I'm doing some initial telephone screening," she said. "I have your application in front of me, but there are a few things I would like to cover that weren't included in the application."

"Sure, I remember the job ad," I said, still rubbing my eyes. "It was kind of vague. Something about a government agency and an opportunity to travel?"

"Yes, that was our posting," she said. "Mr. Jenner, are you married? Do you have a family?"

Her abrupt tone taxed my already-lagging brain. "No," I stammered. "I'm single."

"This position will require you to be away from home for an extended period," she said. "This might be more difficult for someone with a family."

"I'm okay with traveling," I said.

"How do you feel about space travel?"

"Huh?"

"My client is the National Aeronautics and Space Administration, NASA," said Sue. "They are recruiting a team for a permanent colony on Mars. You must have heard about our mission in the news?"

My mouth dropped. "Holy moly!" I said. "I mean, sure, I've heard about the Mars mission. But I'm a chef, not an astronaut."

"The team NASA plans to put together will include specialists to support a permanent colony," said Sue. "They have identified a chef, a culinary specialist in NASA jargon, as one of those positions. Are you still interested in the opportunity?"

I was thirty-one years old and never had a relationship that lasted more than six months. I looked around at the dilapidated apartment. It contained mostly Goodwill rejects: a dresser with no handles, a wobbly table, mismatched IKEA chairs. Would I give this up to cook on Mars? Give up living in a dull town on the Jersey shore? Where I'd been out of work for months? To live in a pod instead of a rented apartment over a garage in a house owned by a widow with six cats?

"Yes, I'm still interested," I said.

"Good," said Sue. "Are you available to come into New York later this week for some tests and an interview?"

I looked across the room to the wall with last year's Sports Illustrated Swimsuit Calendar. "Let me just check my calendar."

Miss April was giving an approving wink.

"Yes," I responded. "I can juggle a few things."

"Alright, my assistant will get in touch with you and set something up. I look forward to meeting you, Mr. Jenner."

"Thanks," I replied.

After the call ended, I peered into my closet and pulled out my only suit. It badly needed a trip to the cleaners, judging from the wrinkles and stains. I wondered if it still fit.

* * * * *

On the morning of the interview, I got up at six with the intervention of two alarms set to "shock therapy."

As I pulled myself out of bed, the smell of bacon drifted up from my landlady's kitchen, making my early morning experience that much worse. Who eats at this hour? I crawled into the bathroom, where the cold ceramic floor chilled my bare feet.

I shivered as I waited for the hot water to make its way up from the main floor water heater. When I finally stepped under the spray, the early morning haze had drifted away.

I opened the mirror vanity to search for some toiletries. My bathroom essentials were largely 'donated' by various hotel chains. The soap and shampoo were Marriotts, the towels and terry-cloth robe were Hiltons, and the drawer full of disposable razors were Hyatts. Hotels have made contributions throughout my apartment including cutlery, mugs, a coffee maker, a microwave, linens, two pillows, and a sex toy found in a drawer at a Best Western.

By the time I showered and shaved, there was just enough time to get dressed, but no time for a coffee. I'd have to pick one up on the way to Manhattan. To get to the city, I hired a Google car. It cost three times as much but would provide an extra two hours of sleep.

The robot-driven car had already arrived by the time I stepped out of the house onto the landing. Shore houses can have a weathered look but this one looked like it had squatters living there. I carefully made my way down the dilapidated front stairs. The overnight snow crunched with each step. Pulling my collar tight, I opened the car's back door and got in. A recorded voice reminded me to buckle my seat belt. As the vehicle accelerated, I leaned back and closed my eyes.

When I opened them again, we were in Manhattan. The car turned north on Madison Avenue and I gazed at the famous branded stores, Hermès, Cartier, Prada. We merged into the right lane with all the other autonomous cars. It was less chaotic to travel in Manhattan since manual vehicles were banned. No traffic jams, collisions, or jerks leaning on their horn like they owned the road. Now cars travel in uniform lines as if they were connected. A few minutes later, the car stopped in front of the offices of Madison Consulting Group just below 45th Street.

The robot thanked me for riding with Google as I stepped out onto the chilly Manhattan street. No sign of the snow that fell in Jersey, but the cold wind whipped between the buildings. The other pedestrians pulled down their hats and tugged on their coats to hold in their body heat. I scurried inside the humongous glass and steel office tower that housed Madison Consulting.

Since I'd arrived early, I had just enough time to grab a coffee and a pastry from the Starbucks in the lobby before heading up the elevator for my interview. It's a good thing I picked up that coffee because I spent the next two hours answering mind-numbing multiple-choice test questions.

When they ran out of questions for me, I was escorted to a meeting room on the thirty-second floor to meet the interview panel. Most of the space was occupied by a large table that could easily have accommodated thirty people. The table top was made of black glass and was smudged from the fingerprints of the thousands of applicants who had already been interviewed. On the walls hung ads from their clients' marketing campaigns, including a few NASA posters. As I sat down, I glanced out the floor-to-ceiling windows. I thought I could make out the East River. Opposite me sat a forty-something woman, wearing a navy-blue power suit and a double strand of Tahitian black pearls. She seemed jittery. I imagined it was from that fifth cup of coffee she downed on the way into the interview room.

On her right sat a guy about the same age, temples greying, hair thinning on top. He wore a garish plaid jacket with almost no lapels, a bright yellow shirt, and a distracting tie covered with

LOVED MARS, HATED THE FOOD | 49

orange, green, and blue bicycles. He was somewhere between a used car salesman and pro wrestling manager. On the left of the twitchy woman was a man about my age, buff with a square jaw and close-cropped, blond hair. He had grey-blue eyes and a disarming, warm smile. Unlike his two colleagues, he dressed casually.

The woman stood up and walked over with her right hand extended. "Mr. Jenner, I'm Sue Grady. We spoke on the phone." The other two people did the same.

I rose and shook their hands. "I go by Dix."

"Dix it is," said Sue as we sat down again. "Thank you for coming into the city to meet with us. Let me introduce the panel. I'm a partner here at Madison Consulting Group."

Sue looked at the executive with the gross jacket. "This is Tyron Blacker," she said. "He's Associate Director of Human Capital Management at NASA and responsible for recruiting the team for the Mars mission."

I tried not to smirk at the official-sounding, bureaucratic title. She then looked over at the buff guy. He was either an astronaut or a former linebacker.

"This is Tom Jonas," said Sue. "He will be the mission commander."

Bingo.

"Do you have any questions before we start the formal part of the interview?" she asked.

I shook my head.

"Great," said Sue. "Then let's get started. We are very excited about this mission. The U.S. government and NASA consider Mars to be the next frontier. We've successfully landed men on the planet and the next step is to establish a permanent settlement. But a Mars colony will be more like Antarctica than the New World of the Europeans. You won't be able to live off the land. Everything will be a challenge in self-sufficiency.

"So, let's talk about you. Now that you know the position is with NASA, tell us why you are attracted to this opportunity?"

I wish I had prepared instead of taking a nap. I cleared my throat.

"I enjoy challenges," I blurted out. "What bigger challenge is there than to prepare meals on a barren, cold planet?" I looked her in the eyes. "I don't have illusions that this will be some type of adventure. I realize I will work under some very unusual conditions."

Mr. Macho jumped right in. "Tell us, what are the harshest conditions you have ever had to endure?"

I once survived without Internet for a month because I forgot to pay the bill.

"My family was poor when I was growing up," I said. "I was determined to attend the Culinary Institute of America, but we couldn't afford the $40,000 tuition. I worked all types of jobs to pay for it. I drove a taxi, worked as a roofer, collected road kill, worked on a pig farm."

All that was bullshit. But *good* bullshit. My dad was a Wall Street hedge fund manager. He'd paid for everything until two years ago, when he'd finally cut me off.

"Thank you, Dix," said Tyron. "It is impressive that you attended the Culinary Institute. But your employment history following graduation is inconsistent for someone with such credentials. I see from your application you worked at Bertha's Diner, Nick's Place, Olympic Grill. Can you explain?"

I was ready for this one. I gave him my most serious look.

"I could have started my career apprenticing at a top restaurant," I said. "But I prefer to learn the business in the trenches. I chose to work in small establishments, where real Americans eat. Where you are free to experiment and personalize the menu. I've created dishes like creamy burrito casserole, Spam sushi, fried Kool-Aid, and trailer park hash. That may not impress you, but it's the dining experience that most Americans are comfortable with."

The interviewers nodded their heads. "Fried Kool-Aid," remarked Sue. "That sounds um…unusual."

I was about to describe the dish, but Sue followed with another question. "You've taken a non-conventional route," she said. "Which I can appreciate. You seem like a man of conviction. Tell us what your careers goals are. What do you see yourself doing after this mission has ended?"

I leaned back in my seat to collect my thoughts. "I would love to be running my own restaurant. It wouldn't need to be anything fancy. I'm passionate about food. Maybe an underground supper club, where I can create innovative and interesting menus."

"We appreciate your enthusiasm for your work," Sue said. "Let's move on to another topic. On Mars, you would be in a small and restricted environment with twenty-three other individuals. Survival will partly depend on cooperating with others. Tom may have some difficult and unpopular decisions to make. How do you feel about that?"

I was on a roll now.

"I don't know anything about space travel. I'll leave those decisions to the specialists. I don't expect Tom will tell me how to bake bread. We'll get along fine."

Sue passed around some notes to the group, which temporarily held their attention. After this awkward pause, Tyron stared me down, lips pursed. I fidgeted in my seat until he finally spoke. "Dix, one of the tests you completed was the Hare Psychopathy Checklist-Revised. Your score was twenty-seven, which is just below the threshold for a sociopath diagnosis."

"Um, is that good or bad?" I asked, biting my lip.

"Normally, it is not good," responded Tyron. "However, in this case we want people who can remain calm in scary or dangerous situations, and who are capable of disregarding the feelings of others in these circumstances."

"We think you would be a good fit for NASA's Mars Colony Mission," added Sue.

CHAPTER SEVEN

Two Years Earlier
Johnson Space Center: Houston,
TX

On the first day of mission training, I took a seat in the back of a small NASA lecture hall with my mug of coffee. The room was nearly full. Everyone wore astronaut jumpsuits. Several discussions took place, but I was more interested in my coffee.

The walls were the color of sun-bleached sand, as if the harsh lighting had worn them down over time. About fifty pedestal seats with writing tablets were set up theater-style. A large TV monitor mounted from the ceiling dominated the front of the room, with a small lectern to one side. At exactly 0830 hours—a time I was still getting used to—a military-type with the obligatory buzz cut marched up to the podium.

"Good morning, ladies and gentlemen. I'm Colonel Billy Baumleiter, the Director of the Astronaut Training Program at the Johnson Space Center. First off, I'd like to congratulate you on making it through our four-round screening process and for being selected for this very important mission. The twenty-four men and women ultimately selected to live on Mars, along with the six alternates, will undergo an intensive eighteen-month training program, in which you will learn every aspect of the mission.

"You will learn how to cope under harsh conditions, operate and repair all equipment, and deal with a wide range of possible health issues. The first phase will involve personal training, so that you will be able to tolerate the harsh conditions of life in space and on Mars. Each of you will be assigned two technical specialties for the mission, which you will receive training on during the second phase. The final phase will have the group train together to simulate what you will be up against.

"NASA will pioneer several innovations on this mission. The new Hermes rocket will cut the time to get to Mars from 248 days to as few as thirty and since they are fusion-powered, they will carry a much lighter payload without all that rocket fuel. A shorter flight means the crew will be exposed to fewer health risks, as there will be far less exposure to cosmic radiation leading to possible brain damage. The colony will be nuclear-powered and won't need to rely on solar power, which will be more reliable since Martian sandstorms can block the sun and . . ."

About five minutes into the introduction and orientation, I drifted off. At first, I had loved the blue NASA jumpsuit with my name sewn on it, but now it was hot and made me sleepy.

I looked around at the others in the room. In the front row was Mission Commander Jonas, poker straight, eyes locked on the speaker. He looked like he had overdosed on the purple Kool-Aid. Behind him sat a small, Asian man, the opposite of Jonas, his eyes darting around the room. My guess was computer specialist. I found out later he was Okuma Nikko, the mission's exobiologist. Next to me was a attractive, redheaded woman. Every so often, I caught her looking at me.

At one point, I leaned toward her. "Dix Jenner," I whispered.

She glanced over and smiled. "Tammy Spanner."

"I'm the chef . . . or I should say the Culinary Specialist."

"Really?"

I nodded. "What about you?"

"Mechanical engineer and geologist."

"Do you want to grab a coffee at the break?"

Tammy flashed a stern look. "Shhh . . . sure."

Less than an hour later, I sat opposite Tammy in the center's cafeteria. With my elbows on the Formica table top and my hands supporting my head, I leaned forward, staring into her baby blue eyes. After ten minutes, I wanted to marry her.

And have five children.

"So, you're a cook?" she said in a mocking tone that was honey to my ears.

I wince, pretending to be hurt, "Ouch. I'm a trained chef from the Culinary Institute of America, thank you very much."

She laughed.

Make that six children.

"Is that like the MIT of cooking schools?"

"Something like that," I said. "So, where are you from, darlin'?"

"Norman, Oklahoma," she said. "You?"

"Toms River, New Jersey." I leaned closer and whispered. "You know it can get very cold and lonely on Mars."

"Is that so?" she said softly, tilting her head forward. "What are you suggesting?"

"Park somewhere romantic, look up at the Martian night sky and keep each other warm."

"A warm sweater works just as well, Romeo," she replied with a mischievous grin.

"So, what training have you been assigned to this week?"

"I'll be working on the water and oxygen production systems," she said between sips of coffee, "but I don't start until later this morning. What about you?"

"They plan to show me how the cooking equipment works," I said. "I'm not sure what else."

I glanced down at my watch. I had my first training session in less than ten minutes and I didn't know where the room was located. "My first session is in a few minutes. Do you want to tag along?"

"Do you think it'll be alright?"

"Don't worry about it," I said. "It'll be fine. Have you seen the mock up colony they've built here?"

"Not yet."

"Then you might as well tag along."

"Sure. Why not?" She flashed me a smile that could trigger a smoke detector.

I got up and hustled toward the exit, looking over my shoulder to make sure she was following me. We hiked down several corridors looking for the training room. The Space Center was huge and littered with security checkpoints. This wasn't anything like Bertha's Diner. I kept looking over at her. Even in an unflattering jumpsuit, she looked striking. Her flowing red hair swayed across her back, in step with her hips as she moved.

About ten minutes later, we arrived at an area the size of a warehouse. Construction crews were still building sections of the fake colony, sophisticated hardware set up just as I imagined it would look at our base. We stood at the entrance, mesmerized.

"Wow," said Tammy. "Look at this place."

"Awesome."

My mental picture of the colony was a village built under a dome: instead, I was looking at a group of hard and inflatable pods, connected to each other in a long row.

"I hope they send these guys to assemble everything for us," I said as we wandered around.

"Not a chance, cowboy," she said. "But NASA's Jet Propulsion Laboratory has designed robots to help us put this place together. I understand the robots will be sent ahead with the other cargo."

"Come on, let's take a look inside some of the pods," I said, grabbing her by the arm.

"Sure."

As we approached a cluster of modules, the construction noise made it difficult to hear. I walked up to one of the modules that looked completed and push on a wall with my fist. "It looks like I could poke a hole through this with one of my kitchen knives."

Tammy slapped the wall with her hand. "I don't think you have anything to worry about," she said. "They're made of hybrid materials. They'll withstand everything Mars has to offer, including cosmic radiation and extreme temperatures. Your puny knives won't do anything to this stuff."

I turned the wheel to the pod's exterior airlock and pulled the door open. "Let's take a look inside."

"Okay," said Tammy, following me into the airlock.

I closed the door behind us. The outside noise was just muffled sound. We stood in a chamber that provided just enough room for the two of us. I could feel her body pressed against mine.

"Isn't this cozy?" I said, rubbing my butt on her.

"Hey, don't get any ideas," she said. "Open up the other side of the airlock."

I cranked open the door and we stepped through to the other side.

"Um, so what's this cosmic radiation everyone keeps mentioning?" I asked. "It doesn't sound good."

"Cosmic rays are high-energy radiation that originate outside the solar system," she explained. "While space is full of radiation, the Earth's magnetic field protects us from these particles. However, once we leave the Earth's orbit, we'll be exposed to a constant shower of various radioactive particles."

"You know a lot stuff," I said, staring into her dreamy eyes. "No one can see what we're doing in here."

She laughed and gave me a playful shove. "Slow down cowboy, we just met."

"Actually, this is what I was thinking of," I said, pulling out two wrapped brownies from my pocket. "We can get baked on some baked goods."

"Oh my God! Is that what I think it is?"

I waved the brownies just below her nose. "They are."

"We could get in big trouble."

"Who is going to know?" I said, taking a bite out of one.

She took the other brownie out of my hand and slowly bit into it. "Yum, this really tastes good."

"Thanks. You may not want to eat the whole piece. It's pretty potent."

Tammy handed back what remained of the brownie. She walked over to the next airlock at the far end of the module and turned the wheel. "Let's see where this goes."

We began making our way through a series of modules and airlocks. The inflatable pods contained bedrooms, working areas and recreational space. I sat on a bed in one of the units. "Wouldn't you like to try them out?"

"I'm not tired," she said, giggling. "Come on, let's get out of here. And where the hell is your trainer?"

We continued to the end of a row of modules and step into a large space. Inside was this fantastic kitchen with stainless steel industrial appliances. I stepped back, and my mouth dropped. "Wow, this is one of the nicest kitchens I've ever seen."

Tammy pulled open one of the fridge doors. "This blows away the galley kitchen in my condo."

I approached the oven to examine it. It looked state-of-the-art. I flipped some of the switches and turned a few knobs.

"Hold on there," shouted a deep gruff voice over at the airlock. "Don't play around with the equipment until we've gone over how to operate them."

I spun around and spotted a plump, middle-aged man in a grey jumpsuit lumbering toward me. Bald except for a small fringe of short-cropped hair, his scalp shone with perspiration, and dark stains were noticeable in the armpits of his jumpsuit.

"Take it easy," I said. "I know my way around a kitchen."

"This ain't no ordinary oven," he replied. " It's nuclear powered and functional. If you don't operate it properly, you could blow us up."

"Oh, shit! Don't want to do that," I said, turning the switches and knobs back to the off positions.

CHAPTER EIGHT

```
Mars
Earth calendar: 2039-09-05
Martian calendar: 45-11-545
```

According to my internal clock, it's my third "morning" waking up in tiny town. I still feel like I'm in a remake of *Gulliver's Travels*.

As I stretch to shake loose the cobwebs, I remember the lockers. I get up and slip into the common room, where the bot had dropped them off. The scorched cases are covered with dents and scrapes. I open the latches to the first locker and tug at the top until it flips open. It's a supply locker. Inside, I find an assortment of fruits and vegetables, stored in Ziploc bags, flash-frozen by the frigid Martian temperatures. I hope they can be salvaged for cooking.

I turn to the next locker and after a couple of hard yanks, I'm able to wrench it open too. Inside is more frozen produce. I didn't notice any Brussels sprouts in either of the cases. My experience in the colony was that Martian-grown Brussels sprouts are green balls of hell, nothing like the ones at home. Not going to miss them. I dig down to the bottom of the second locker and pull out bags of seeds. I plan to put them to good use. Anything to compensate for Martian food.

The top of the remaining case won't budge, no matter how hard I pull.

Judging by the amount of potatoes in both cases, the first meal I prepare for my Martian hosts will be mashed potatoes. As I settle in to peel them, the bot strolls into the room.

"Todd, would you mind helping me peel potatoes?"

"I'm not a culinary bot, I'm a construction bot," says Todd.

"Then how about you construct some peeled potatoes for me?"

"Absolutely not," says the bot. "The next thing I know you will have me doing laundry and dusting."

"Come on, Todd, you've got to be flexible enough to take on a few more jobs," I say. "There aren't many construction opportunities here."

"You will need to take the matter up with my programmers. And while you're at it, you can inform them that I require a replacement battery."

"You're just busting my balls," I say, picking up one of the potatoes. "Watch me and I'll show you how it's done."

"I'm a Sementric advanced intelligence robot, not a monkey," says the bot, crossing his arms. "I need to be programmed to execute tasks."

While I argue with the bot, Seepa and Bleeker wander into the room.

I detect you have accessed your cases, says Bleeker. *Have you discovered anything beneficial?*

"No," says the bot. "There are no Sementric battery packs."

"Don't listen to him," I say.

Bleeker stoops to look at the bags of produce. *Can you enlighten us on the contents of the cases?*

"These two lockers are loaded with food,"

What is this form of nutrition? asks Seepa as she pokes at one of potatoes. She reaches in, pulls out a potato, and takes a bite out of it.

I grab if from her hand. "You don't eat them raw."

There is no justification for being agitated, Dix, she says, frowning. *What harm is created by consuming them raw?*

I grab another unpeeled potato and a knife. "It's just that they taste much better cooked."

I enjoy the taste of this nutrition in this form, says Seepa, picking up another potato. *How do you refer to this Earth nutrition?*

"They're called potatoes. I'll make mashed potatoes tonight. Trust me, you'll love them."

Bleeker and I look forward to this nutrition you call mashed potatoes, she says.

"And don't expect me to participate in this culinary extravaganza," says the bot, waving dismissively.

I pick up several small bags and hand them to the Martians. "I also found some Earth seeds. I'd like to set up a farm."

Bleeker peers at a bag of seeds. *I have no knowledge of cultivation techniques. Can you establish one?*

"One of my responsibilities in the colony was to maintain a farm," I declare, picking up another potato to peel. "I hope I could reconstruct one here."

Bleeker toddles over to the unopened locker. *What does this one contain?*

Bleeker, do not be intrusive, says Seepa with a scowl.

I was merely inquisitive, responds Bleeker.

Perhaps it contains personal property that he would not want to divulge, says Seepa.

Well, that is the point of asking.

"Calm down," I say. "Yes, that one has my personal belongings, but the case is so dented, it won't open. I will need something to force it open. Bleeker, do you have any tools?"

No. Why would I require devices associated with physical labor?

"Never mind," I say, walking to the corner of the room where we left the printer. "Good thing we dragged the 3D printer from the surface."

"I believe I carried the printer," says the bot. "You two just watched."

Bleeker wobbles over to the printer. *How does it work?*

"I'm not sure," I say. "I was only half listening during mission training. I do remember it runs off its own energy supply."

The 3D printer is about the size of an average office photocopier. I find the power switch and flip it to the on position. The display screen lights up.

"I hate to be a bother," says the bot. "But can you produce a battery for me with the printer? My battery only has three hundred and twenty-three days, nineteen hours, and seven minutes of power left."

"Hmm, let me see," I say, scanning the memory directory. "Sorry, Todd, I don't see batteries in the printer memory."

"So, what good is it?"

I find the tools I want in its inventory of digital designs, but it's going to take a couple of hours to produce just a hammer and chisel. Instead, I bang away at the top of the locker with my fists.

Careful with your digits, says Seepa. *I do not believe Bleeker can repair them if damaged.*

I am certain that I am capable of repairing them, says Bleeker. *I am an accomplished physician.*

How many alien life forms do you have in your clinic? asks Seepa.

That is not relevant, says Bleeker. *My training has prepared me to address new and unforeseen conditions.*

What are you planning on next? says Seepa, giving her partner a glassy stare. *Will you secure the Earth-being to a gurney and dissect him?*

I bang away harder to drown out the bickering. These two would argue over the color of water.

"I can't stand to watch this feeble effort," says the bot, bending down and giving the lid a hard tug. The case lets out a loud creak, and the top springs open and comes off its hinges.

Todd, says Bleeker, beaming. *You certainly are powerful.*

"What a surprise," says the bot, stomping away. "No battery packs. I can see that I'm doomed."

I rummage through my personal belongs and locate what I hoped would be here—a small bag of marijuana seeds. I slip the bag into my pocket.

The two Martians edge forward to peer into the case.

Appears to be a collection of refuse, says Bleeker. He picks up my basketball from the case. *It's too bad you exerted so much effort to transport that here.*

I snatch the ball from his hands. "This is an official NBA basketball. It's signed by Knicks star Bry'n DeMatwah."

What is basketball and how is this sphere used? asks Bleeker.

The bot takes the ball from me and palms it. "Basketball is a limited-contact sport played on a rectangular court. The objective is to shoot a ball through a hoop eighteen inches in diameter and ten feet high that is mounted to a backboard at each end of the court. The game was invented in eighteen hundred and ninety-one by Dr. James Naismith."

"Thank you, Todd," I say.

Is your basketball valuable? asks Bleeker.

"You're darn right it is," I say, cradling the ball in my arms. "I would guess it's worth thousands of dollars. DeMatwah is a big star now."

I don't understand why you brought it with you, says Bleeker. *What do you plan to do with that sphere?*

"This happens to be my most prized possession," I say. "I wasn't about to leave it at home. Maybe I'll set up a basket outside and shoot some hoops."

It is an exquisite looking sphere, Dix, says Seepa.

Bleeker takes the ball back from me. His hand runs across its pebbled surface. *Oh, I forgot to advise you,* he says. *I invited Plinka for dinner.*

Well, she invited herself, adds Seepa. *She is so aggressive. I hope you are agreeable with her company.*

I bounce the ball onto the floor and dribble it around the Martians. "Sounds like fun."

* * * * *

The Martians are seated around their teeny table when I march in with my famous mashed potatoes. Well, they aren't quite the same as my famous mashed potatoes, which normally contain mascarpone cheese. Since I haven't run across any Italian dairies, I improvised. The food lockers contained powdered milk and cheese, thanks to the good folks at NASA.

The aroma of the steaming platter of potatoes fills the room, though I wonder if the Martians notice, or if they can even smell. I place them down on the table before plopping onto a pillow.

Here you go, I say. *My decadent mashed potatoes.*

They look at the platter as if there's a heap of dog poop on it. Seepa picks up the serving spoon and passes it to her neighbor.

Go ahead, Plinka, she says. *You are the guest. It looks...well...appetizing.*

Plinka cautiously takes the spoon from Seepa and puts a small scoop on her plate before passing it on to Bleeker. *Where did you learn to make this nutrition?* asks Plinka.

Dix has always experimented with new nutrition, says Bleeker. *He is exceptionally enterprising.*

Yes, I have a reputation, I say as I put some in my mouth. *Mmm. These are good.*

But the others are gagging.

They tasted much better before you crashed them, says Bleeker.

They're mashed, not crashed, I say.

Dix, it was a very good effort, says Seepa as she gets up from the table. *Let me find additional nutrition to serve with your smashed potatoes.*

Mashed! I say.

I think these mushed potatoes look attractive, says Plinka. *I am impressed that you created it.*

Poof scampers from a corner of the room and hops onto my lap, her spikes chafing my thighs. She leans up on her hind legs, reaching up to the table to nibble on the mashed potatoes. Right now, I prefer Poof to the Martians.

CHAPTER NINE

National Transportation Safety
Board: Washington, D.C.
Earth calendar: 2039-09-22
Martian calendar: 45-11-601

Farley hears his assistant call out through his open office door, "Dr. Farley, the limo has been waiting out front for twenty minutes. You don't want to be late for the first day of hearings for the Commission on the Mars Colony Accident."

"I'm just getting ready," he shouts, grabbing his coat and briefcase.

He rushes past his assistant, out the office and down the corridor. He doesn't wait for an elevator. Bursting into the stairwell, he takes the steps two at a time, reaching the lobby in less than two minutes. By the time he's outside, he's breathing heavily and damp from the rainfall. He pulls open the limo door and clambers inside. NASA's General Counsel, Abe Tuff, is already in the limo. He's the Agency's senior lawyer, and Farley is always more comfortable in these situations with Tuff by his side.

It's a short distance to the hearing, and the town car pulls out into traffic once they confirm their destination on the passenger touch screen. Farley removes his glasses to wipe the rain drops off the lenses.

"Abe, let me give you a quick rundown on the Commission Chair," he says. "As you know, Senator Ted Harper was also Secretary of Transportation during the Buttle administration. He was a key supporter of the President during the primaries, which is a big reason why she appointed him to chair her Commission on the Mars Colony Accident."

Tuff uses his hand to wipe away some of the condensation on the side window as he glances at the traffic on New Jersey Avenue. "I've heard he's not easy to get along with."

"He was known for being a prick back then," he says, grinning. "No doubt, that hasn't changed. And he's pissed about NASA's Board of Inquiry. He's also suggested I be fired on number of occasions."

"Well that's not his call. And don't worry, I'll back you up in any way that I can."

Farley wipes a few remaining droplets of rain from his forehead with his hand. "He believes this was a flawed mission and someone has to pay for it. I expect him to give me a rough ride."

"Chuck, let me handle any questions about our Board of Inquiry," Tuff assures him. "We need to push back on any challenges regarding jurisdiction."

"For this initial session, we'll primarily be asked what we know about the disaster," says Farley. "I expect they won't be happy with my answers."

"Holding the Board of Inquiry must be pretty awkward for you, since you report directly to the President and she created this Commission."

"I spoke to President Bondar and she understands what we are doing," says Farley. "The Commission is political, while we're looking to science for the answers to our questions."

The car stops in front of the offices of the National Transportation Safety Board. Farley peers out at the plain steel and glass building that is so typical of government buildings in Washington. Despite the rain, there are a cluster of reporters, photographers, and news cameramen, and about forty protestors with placards in front of the building. The signs of the Christian groups read, "Christians Against Space Exploration" and "Jesus Hates Martians." A few anti-poverty protesters carry signs which proclaim, "Feed The Poor On Earth." One protestor in a Star Trek outfit holds a sign that reads "Colonize Vulcan." They exit the car, back into the rain, and dash past the protestors. Fortunately, the protestors are unaware of their identity and ignore them as they weave through the motley assembly. They scamper up the steps to the revolving doors of the front entrance, jutting out from the building.

After they sign in at the security desk and get their visitor's badges, they file down a corridor where the hearing room is located. Portraits of former Board Chairs stare down at them. When they reach the doors to the hearing room, they show their badges to the guard who ushers them inside.

In the front of the room, there is a long table on a riser where the Commission members sit, with a nameplate situated before each seat. Rows of tables and chairs for those attending the sessions cram the remainder of the room with a single table in the first row reserved for witnesses. People filter into the room from the outside corridor, and the seats fill up. To one side are Commission support staff. Some hand out documents to the Commission members while the rest tap away on their phones.

Commission members enter the hearing room through a side entrance near the front. The Chair, Senator Harper, is one of the last to arrive, taking his seat at the center of the table. He has a short, wiry frame with a craggy face, large ears, and a small mouth. He looks up through the pair of thick, framed glasses and notices the NASA people seated in the front row.

Harper looks over at the clerk. "Let's get these witnesses sworn in and get this show on the road," he says.

They step up to the witness table where they are met by a clerk with a Bible. After swearing an oath, they take a seat.

"Gentlemen," says Harper, wearing his usual scowl, "welcome to the first session of the President's Commission on the Mars Colony Accident. For the record, can you state your name and position within the space agency?"

Farley leans forward toward the microphone on the table. "I'm Charles Farley, Administrator of the National Aeronautics and Space Agency."

"Abraham Tuff, General Counsel at NASA."

"Great," says Harper. "You both know who I am. The President formed this Commission earlier this week to review the accident that occurred on the Mars colony on September second and to determine its probable cause. I'm expected to get back to her in 120 days. Let's not waste time and get right to it."

"Can I suggest something, Mr. Chair?" says Tuff.

Harper grimaces. "What's that?"

"Dr. Farley has a statement that he would like to read to the Commission members."

"That won't be necessary," says Harper as he waves a hand in the air. "We can dispense with speeches and get right down to the questions."

Tuff nods his head. "Yes, Mr. Chair." He looks over to Farley who shrugs.

"Dr. Farley," says Harper. "The Commission understands that NASA has established a Board of Inquiry to investigate the Mars colony explosion. I'm concerned about a second investigation taking place while this Commission is operating. Can you explain to us why your Board of Inquiry is necessary and whether your agency is prepared to share any findings with the Commission?"

The NASA lawyer grabs the microphone.

"NASA's mandate includes learning from mishaps like these," says Tuff. "Learning is critical to NASA's success. We never sweep our findings under the rug, Mr. Chairman. NASA's policy is to conduct a review following each mission and share those findings. Our goal is to reduce the occurrence of future adverse incidents and build a more resilient agency. We will fully cooperate with this Commission, which is why we are here today."

"Thank you, Mr. Tuff," Harper clears his throat and continues. "Dr. Farley, for the record, please tell us, in as much detail as you can, what happened on Mars on September second."

Farley shifts closer to the microphone.

"Good morning," he says. "This incident has had a devastating impact on the Agency. We don't have a lot of facts right now, just theories.

"On September second, at 2115 hours Central Time, controllers in the Johnson Space Center Mission Control Center stopped receiving communications from Futurum, our Mars colony. The colony had been inhabited by a twenty-four-member team since August first. At the same time, we stopped receiving signals from the monitors worn by twenty-three members of the team. We continued to receive signals from Culinary Specialist Dixon Jenner until 0122 hours Central Time on September third, which then resumed on September 4th from 1340 hours until 2012 hours. And nothing since.

"On September third, we positioned a Plymouth satellite over the site of the Mars colony to take images. These images have already been shared with the Commission. The images show that the colony was destroyed. Based on the wide field of debris, a massive explosion appears to have leveled the colony. Our satellite also picked up an intact rover that was about one or two miles from the colony."

One of the members of the Commission interrupts Farley's response. "Mr. Chair, may I ask a question?"

It's Sam Bush, a Texas senator and the senior Republican on the Commission. He's a large man with big thick fingers and a ruddy complexion, visibly perspiring despite the room's cool temperature.

Harper rolls his eyes. "Go ahead Senator Bush."

"Thank you," says Bush as he looks down at Farley. "I would first off like to say that I am deeply saddened about the twenty-four brave American men and women who lost their lives on this mission. Y'all know I've been a strong supporter of space missions while in the Senate."

"Thank you, Senator," says Farley.

Bush pauses then his face forms a smirk. "But a culinary specialist?" he says. "Ain't that a cook?"

"Yes, it is."

The Senator clasps his hands and leans forward. "Dr. Farley, how could you have picked up a signal from this here Jenner fellow when the colony was destroyed?"

"The transmission tower is some distance from the colony site and survived the explosion. It runs on solar power, which has turned out to be unreliable. As it turns out, one of our orbiters circling Mars picked up the signal."

Bush mops the sweat off his forehead with a handkerchief. "Are you suggesting that the cook survived the explosion?"

"Yes, we have made that conclusion," says Farley.

"How?"

"We believe he wasn't in or near the colony at the time of the explosion. That would explain why a rover also survived, in addition to the signals we received."

"Then, you haven't picked up any signals from Mr. Jenner since September fourth?" asks Harper.

"That is correct."

Harper glares down at Farley. "Then you are certain that he is no longer alive?"

"Yes. There is no scenario we can come up with that has him surviving this long. He would have eventually run out of oxygen and—"

Harper interrupts. "Do we know what caused the explosion?" His foot tapping under the table can be heard throughout the room.

"No, we don't at this time."

"Well you must have some theories? Your billion dollars worth of space technology must tell you something?"

"There are several possible explanations, but right now we have no physical evidence to go by," he says. "However, the main source of energy for the colony is a small nuclear reactor, which was developed—"

"Excuse me, Dr. Farley," says Harper. "Why the hell would NASA put a nuclear reactor on Mars?"

Farley pauses to maintain his composure. "Mr. Chair, the reactor was developed several years ago and has been included in numerous NASA reports. We long ago determined that relying solely on solar energy would be messy. The number of panels to support so many people and this much equipment would be prohibitive, not to mention dealing with brownouts during sandstorms. A small nuclear reactor has no such limitations.

Besides, if things began to go wrong with the reactor, we would have been getting readings. Water produced in the colony is used to control the temperature, so if the water supply is cut off, there is the possibility of a melt-down. But it is unlikely to produce an explosion. A nuclear reactor is not the same as a nuclear bomb."

"So, are you saying it wasn't a nuclear explosion?" asks Harper.

"We haven't eliminated any theory quite yet," says Farley. "If I may continue. The oxygen generator or, oxygenator, may have been the cause of the explosion."

Senator Bush is on feet and his face crimson red.

"I've heard enough of this scientific mumbo jumbo." Spit flies from Bush's mouth as he speaks. "Isn't it obvious that it was the damn Chinese?"

Harper bangs his gavel on the table. Farley looks over to Tuff who is trying to keep from laughing.

"They went ape-shit when we decided to go ahead and colonize Mars. I wouldn't put it past them to fire a missile at the colony."

The Chair slams the gavel, the sound echoes through the room.

"Come on, Sam," he snaps. "Our satellites would have picked up a missile." Harper turns his attention back to the witness. "Wouldn't we?"

"Absolutely, Mr. Chair," says Farley. "There's no way a missile could be fired without us knowing about it."

Harper leans forward with his arms crossed and elbows propped on the table, peering down at the witness. "Dr. Farley, regretfully your presentation this morning appears to be more speculative than factual. I suspect we are observing a lot of ass-covering on the part of NASA." Still leaning forward, Harper raises an arm and points a finger at Farley. "My goal is to make those responsible for this disaster also accountable."

"NASA has the same expectations," I say.

"Oh, good," says Harper, sneering. "Then the President can expect your resignation by the end of the day."

CHAPTER TEN

```
Mars
Earth calendar: 2039-10-17
Martian calendar: 45-12-626
```

I put the vacant land behind the house of my hosts to good use. For much of the past four weeks, I constructed a mini-farm using the seeds found in the salvaged lockers.

Gardening tools are not a problem as long as the 3D printer continues to function. I turned the soil with a shovel and planted rows of tomatoes, beans, potatoes, broccoli, spinach, green peas, and herbs. There's even a small section with coffee plants.

It turns out it's easier to grow plants beneath the surface than it had been in the colony. Plants need oxygen, hydrogen, carbon, and nutrients, which they get from air, water, and soil on Earth. The colony greenhouse was designed to provide these elements because they don't naturally occur on Mars. All those things missing on the surface are plentiful underground. Since it doesn't rain, Martians own extractors to remove water from the ground. Bleeker has the water collect in a tank behind his house. I connected a hose, provided by Bleeker, to the tank for watering my plants.

Even the lack of sunlight isn't an issue. The artificial lighting works the same as grow lights. The new farm turns out to be a piece of cake, and the plants are growing quicker than I expected. I'm especially thrilled with the marijuana plants.

While inspecting them, I spot a couple of weeds. I kneel and pull them out with a garden trowel. The idea of building colonies on the surface seems so dumb. I feel like I've made a Nobel prize-winning discovery. I just have no way to get the news back to Earth.

Part of my daily morning routine is to tend to my plants. While watering them, I become lost in my thoughts. At one point I look up, discovering a pair of large, black eyes watching me.

"Oh, I didn't see you there," I say.

Who is Mac? asks Bleeker.

Bleeker is reading my thoughts again. Annoyed, I put the hose down.

"He was my trainer back on Earth."

He educated you to design this?

"Yup."

This appears to be primitive. Bleeker says, bending to look more closely at the plants. *Why would anyone wish to grow nutrition in the ground? And what are these plant forms?*

"Those are the potatoes that I served you."

But these are green plants. Not anything like what you prepared.

"Potatoes are edible tubers that grow in the soil. You don't eat the leaves."

I hope you will provide us with more potato tuber plants, Bleeker say, patting his protruding belly. *They were exceptionally good uncooked.*

"Look, you don't eat potatoes raw," I say gruffly. "I've got a lot of different potato recipes."

Bleeker moved closer to another group of plants.

What other plant forms are you cultivating?

I put down my hose. "I'm limited by what was in the supply lockers," I say. "I have some herbs, over here are tomatoes and spinach. Right here are peas and beans." I don't mention the weed. "But my prize crop will be coffee."

Well, I look forward to sampling it all, says Bleeker. *Particularly, your prized plant form. When do you anticipate cooking your coffee plants?*

"You don't eat the plants," I say, shaking my head. "You grow coffee plants for the beans, which are made into an awesome, hot drink."

How long will it take?

"Normally, it takes about three to four years, but our scientist on Earth developed a hybrid plant for the mission. It should take no more than ninety days in these conditions to produce beans. I'm dying for a cup of coffee. Too bad Starbucks hasn't opened up on Mars."

What is Starbucks? ask Bleeker.

At that moment, Todd saunters out to join us.

"Starbucks is a popular chain on Earth where customers have their names misspelled on cups that contain overpriced coffee," says the bot.

I do not comprehend, says Bleeker.

"Never mind," I say. "Don't listen to him."

"I see you continue to indulge in your crude agricultural hobby," says the bot, turning up his nose. "It would seem more prudent to eat the indigenous cuisine."

"This isn't a hobby, Todd," I say. "I would like to have some Earth food."

"I don't understand why you make such a big deal about tomatoes and potatoes," says the bot. "And it's Sementric 3, not Todd."

Bleeker walks to a corner of the farm, pointing. *What are those immense plants in the corner?*

I block his path, hoping to direct him away from there. "Those plants...aren't nutrition," I say. "They're, um, for maintaining my state of mind."

How do they accomplish such an outcome?

I pretend to inhale on a joint. "One toke at a time."

I do not comprehend.

"You wouldn't understand."

"Good heavens," says the bot, shaking a finger. "Your persistent drug use is ridiculous. What a total waste of time."

"Unlike you, I have years to kill on this planet," I say. "I need this stuff."

"Thanks for reminding me that I only have two hundred and eighty-one days, four hours, and eleven minutes of battery power left, and I have to spend it rotting away on this Martian marijuana plantation."

Before I forget, the reason I came out here was to make a request, says Bleeker.

I pick up the hose and hang it on a hook next to the water tank. "Sure, what is it?"

If you recall, one of the reasons we took you in was to study you, says Bleeker. *You have had several weeks to adapt to your new surroundings. Seepa and I would now like to arrange an initial interview with you.*

"I'm okay with that," I say. "When do you have in mind?"

Later today?

"Hmm, I will need to check my schedule."

Schedule? says Bleeker.

"It's a joke, bro. Today is fine."

"I suppose I'm to be left alone?" asks the bot. "I might as well take up smoking marijuana. "Unfortunately, I wasn't designed to inhale. Just like former President Bill Clinton."

* * * * *

When the transporter reaches Bleeker's office, it stops inches above the roadway to allow us to step out. As always, I sense Martians gawking. I try my best to ignore it. This building has multiple levels with no stairs. I follow Bleeker and Seepa into a compartment on the main lobby.

The door of the cubicle is translucent, so I'm able make out images on the other side. Red and blue blinking lights run up and down the other walls. On a display next to the door are images of all the building's occupants. Bleeker waves his hand over the one of him. As the compartment moves, I watch figures flash by. We travel both vertically and horizontally until we stop directly in front of Bleeker's office door.

"Interesting device you have here," I say.

I bang my head when I exit the compartment.

I presume stairs are used in your primitive world, says Bleeker.

I'm about to respond, but the Martians have already darted into Bleeker's office. I follow them inside to a bright green reception area with several doors, each in a different color. In a corner of the room is a waiting area with a half-dozen of those mini-Martian chairs. An Arbiter receptionist sits at a workstation wearing multiple strands of necklaces and bracelets made up of polished stones.

Bleeker, is there anything I can assist you with? she asks as she waddles out from the workstation.

Hello, Jazza, says Bleeker. *We do not require any assistance. We are going to be occupied for several hours and do not wish to be interrupted.*

Jazza turns to Bleeker's partner. *Hello Seepa, nice to see you again.* She locks her big, black eyes on me. *Who might you be?*

Um, I'm the cousin from Nilosyrtis, I say, shuffling my feet. *Didn't Bleeker ever mention me?*

No, he did not, says Jazza, still eyeing me with suspicion.

Another time, Jazza, says Bleeker, leading us into an inner room. I can feel Jazza continue to stare as the door closes behind us.

We stand in a barren room with white walls and a black stone floor. Up against one wall sits a desk and two chairs. An examination table stands on the opposite side of the room. Several charts hang on the walls, and mounted to the ceiling, above the examination table, is a machine with a long arm that reminds me of a dental x-ray.

Dix, please lie on the table while I conduct a scan, says Bleeker.

I think we should initiate with a sociological review of his family, says Seepa.

The accepted protocol for a scientific research study is to commence with a physical examination, says Bleeker.

That is nonsense, says Seepa, flaring her nostrils. *You always try to take the lead. I think we should begin with an interview.*

Bleeker shakes his head. *Refer to any study and it begins with a physical examination. This is intended to be a collaboration, not a competition.*

"Look guys," I say. "I'm already on the table so let's just move on."

I say this but lying on the examination table is not a simple matter, as my legs hang over the end. I pull my knees up so that my feet rest on the edge. Bleeker shuffles over and grabs the device hanging from the ceiling, extending the arm so that it hovers over me.

I jerk my head up and scrutinize the apparatus. "Is that thing safe?"

It is a diagnostic scanner. I use it on all my patients. Please lie back.

"But is it safe for Earthlings?"

I cannot see how it would not be," says Bleeker, pushing down on my knees. *You will need to straighten out your legs.*

I stretch out, dangling at the knees. The machine hums as Bleeker guides it over my head, working his way down to my feet.

Hmm, this is remarkable, says Bleeker, staring at a screen on the back of the equipment. *I do not recognize these organs. Some of your bones are enormous. Seepa, come over and look at this.*

She moves closer and peers over his shoulder.

Incredible.

Yes, I just wish I understood how it all functioned, says Bleeker. *Dix, how well do you know Earth-being anatomy?*

"I sort of know the parts."

I can only detect one of your hearts, says Bleeker. *Where are the others?*

I sit up and snort. "You're pulling my leg."

I have not manipulated any of your limbs, says Bleeker.

"You're joking, right?"

No, says Bleeker. *I'm quite concerned that I cannot detect all your hearts.*

"I only have one." I say, tapping my chest. "Wait, how many do you have?"

Seepa's mouth drops.

Bleeker holds up three fingers. *Three. One for the upper torso, one for the lower torso and one for the cranium. You have a very inefficient system. I cannot envision you surviving long.*

"I expect to live eighty or ninety years. Unless your scanner does some internal damage."

Earth-beings can only survive that long? asks Bleeker.

"Yeah," I say. "How long do Martians normally live?"

At least 200 hundred years.

"That's incredible."

I shall endeavor to complete the scan, and afterwards you can enlighten us on what we observe. Like these. Bleeker pokes well below my abdomen.

I jerk upright. "Those are my balls!"

I am regretful, says Bleeker, *if I created some discomfort to your balls.*

Bleeker pushes me down. Several minutes pass as the scanning machine travels down my body and back.

Finally, Bleeker pushes the machine toward the ceiling. *You can sit upright now.*

The Martians pull up the two chairs and sit down. *We would like to interview you about your life on Earth,* says Seepa.

I swing my legs over the side of the table. "Sure, go ahead."

Tell us about your family unit, says Seepa.

I cross my legs with my hands on my lap. "We lived in Chatham, New Jersey. That's a small town outside New York, which is a freaking big city. My parents still live there. My dad works in finance on Wall Street, which is the financial district, and my mom spends her time decorating their enormous house, working out with her personal trainer, raising money for orphaned kids overseas, and hosting teas for the other ladies in the neighborhood."

Are you close with your parental-beings? asks Seepa.

"Not really," I say. "We didn't agree on a lot of things. For example, we always had hired help around the house. I never liked how they were treated."

What is hired help? asks Seepa.

"I guess something like your Arbiters." I look down at the floor, searching for the right words. "I've been a disappointment to them. My father accuses me of being irresponsible and has financially cut me off. They don't approve of my career and lifestyle choices."

Is this a common occurrence on Earth? asks Seepa, looking up from note-taking. *At a certain age, are offspring cut off?*

"Only if your dad is a hard ass."

What makes an ass hard? asks Bleeker.

"Chasing money."

Are there additional offspring in your family unit? asks Seepa.

"I have an older brother named Todd," I say. "He's a successful lawyer in New York. Obviously, he's my parents' favorite. They must all think I'm dead now," I mutter as my eyes well up. "I doubt they even miss me."

Were you not partnered on Earth? asks Seepa.

"You mean married?" I say. "No. I mean, don't get me wrong. I've been out with lots of women. But I'm not the type to settle down with one person."

What about this Tammy-being you have been thinking about? asks Bleeker.

"Yeah, I liked her a lot, but it was mostly about sex. She was hot."

Can you describe sex to us? asks Seepa.

I squirm in my seat. "Well . . . um," I stammer. "Well, how do you have babies?"

In birthing pods, says Seepa. *We both contribute genetic material and a Martian progeny incubates in the pod using an embryonic accelerator. But we are here to interview you. We want to get back to the subject of sex. Please explain.*

"Well...men and women on Earth have...um...different bits and pieces," I say. "Like where you poked me before. Women don't have that. The different bits and pieces work together until...um...until there is a climax, and everyone walks away happy."

The two Martians look perplexed. Bleeker feverishly makes notes.

And women's pieces? asks Bleeker, glancing up from his notes. *What are they like?*

My face flushes. "Like, um...flaps? Look, the two parts just fit into each other. Like a shovel into a hole."

Now how do these two parts work together? asks Seepa.

"Um... it's like digging? With the shovel?"

I see, says Seepa. *Is the idea to use the shovel to make the hole larger?*

Or deeper? asks Bleeker.

I wipe the perspiration building up on my forehead. "No, no, it's to—um—"

I have an observation to provide, says Bleeker. *When I conducted my examination, I found your shovel to be diminutive. Surely it could not properly deepen or widen a hole.*

I wave my hands in the air. "It's just an analogy! Look—"

And this climax. How does that transpire?

Yes, says Seepa. *Can you show us one?*

I realize the Martians are staring at my crotch. Bleeker has this creepy look. "Can we take a break?" I say as I slump back into my seat. That's it. No more talking about the birds and the bees with Martians.

CHAPTER ELEVEN

Mars
Earth calendar: 2039-10-24
Martian calendar: 45-12-633

An awful humming blares away in my head. As I open my eyes, it gets louder. There's someone at the door.

No one else is home, so I crawl out of bed and stumble to the front of the house. I open the door just enough to peek outside at three menacing Arbiters in uniforms. One of them hammers his shoulder into the door, before I have a chance to swing it open, and my back slams into the wall behind me.

Hey, what's going on? I ask.

The Martians step inside. These guys may not be as tall as me, but they are powerful, with thick necks and hands like oven mitts. The door slammer steps forward. He has a shiny monogram on his uniform.

We have been directed to detain you and bring you in for questioning, he says.

Bring me in where?

You will be afforded an explanation once you have been processed, says the Martian. *Either cooperate or we will employ force.*

I have rights, don't I? I say. *I didn't do anything wrong.*

He pulls out a device that looks like a TV remote and points it directly at me. The device emits a stream of lights and seconds later it feels like I'm wearing an invisible straitjacket.

You are deemed a security risk.

The other two Martians grab me by the arms and escort me out into a waiting transporter. Out of the corner of my eye, I notice Plinka peeking out her front door.

As the transporter pulls away, I ask my escorts where we're going.

No one responds.

Twenty minutes later, the transporter arrives at a nondescript, black building with no windows. Inside, a pair of guards waves us through. We march down a long, drab hallway, filled with Machers busy going somewhere. We finally stop in front of one door, and the Martian with the remote device pulls it out and points the thing at me, releasing my restraints.

This is where you will be lodging until we get several issues resolved, says the Martian.

What issues? I ask. *Can't we just sort them out now?*

The other two Martians shove me into the room, and I whack my skull on the top of the door frame for good measure. By the time the stars stop flashing around my head, the entourage has left and locked the door behind them.

Rubbing my scalp, I turn to look around. In front of me are nine Arbiters in a room that resembles a dormitory. Some are sitting at tables. A pair are fighting in a corner. One fellow is stretched out on a cot. They stop what they are doing to stare at me, the two fighters still holding each other by the throat.

I cautiously creep away from the door, keeping my back to the wall. This is a rough-looking group. Some are missing body parts, like fingers and eyes.

Hey fellas, I say. *Nice to meet you.*

They continue to stare. One Martian gets out of his seat and wobbles toward me. He is heavyset, with a scar on his forehead that would have made Frankenstein proud. He stops about a foot away.

What manner of being are you? asks the Martian.

I'm Dix, from Nilosyrtis, I say. *What is this place? A prison?*

The room breaks out into laughter. One Martian calls out, *Don't you know? You are a distinguished guest at one of Cheyhto's social re-education centers.*

My body tenses up. *Social re-education center?*

How could you not know? says the Martian with the scar. *This is a state-owned facility designed to rehabilitate wrongdoers so that they follow communal norms. Obviously, they have found you to be nonconforming.*

There must be some mistake, I say, as I hide my shaking hands. *I just look different.*

You do not look like you are from Nilosyrtis or anywhere else on Mars, says the Martian, his eyes locked on me.

I have a rare medical disorder. Glaberism. You've probably never heard of it.

Another Martian gets up from his seat and approaches me. *You are right,* says the second Martian. *Never heard of it. It sounds like a lot of twaddle.*

Yet another Martian gets up from his seat. He comes right up to me and touches my arm. *Your membrane is repulsive,* he says.

Talk about repulsive; these Arbiter would make zombies appealing.

He grabs me by the arm. *What are zombies?*

Zombies? Um, a sling team from Nilosyrtis, I say trying to pull my arm free. *Have you not heard of them?*

No.

I get the impression that I will not fit in well with my roommates. I'm sure one of these Martians would be happy to remove the knot in my stomach with a knife.

I have thoughts of horrible things happening when the door flies open, banging against the opposite wall. A pair of guards stomp into the room and point to me. I dash over to them like a scared chicken, more than happy to leave this glee club meeting.

They march me into another room with same drab, gray walls as the rest of the building, In the center of the room stands a black table with a heavily-scuffed top and two rickety chairs. The guards shove me into one of the chairs and leave.

My heart races, and my hands are cold and clammy. When Cheyhto strides in the room with three of his henchmen, a chill shudders through me, and beads of sweat form on my forehead. Maybe I would be better off back with my roommates.

Cheyhto sits down in the seat on the other side of the table. He leans forward and glowers at me. If I'm about to die, shouldn't I be having flashbacks of my life?

You are probably wondering why you are here? he asks.

Um, yes.

I hope he doesn't notice my knees knocking.

I had my subordinates examine the birthing pod records in Nilosyrtis and they have found nothing that pertains to you, says Cheyhto. *There is no documentation for a Dix in Nilosyrtis. Who are you?*

There must be a mistake, I say. *My parents even saved the pod as a memento.*

There is no record of your birthing pod, says Cheyhto, his cold, dark eyes locked on me.

This must be an administrative mix up, I say, trying to hide my panic. *You know what these bureaucracies are like.*

No, I do not, says Cheyhto, shifting his weight forward in his seat. *There is no conceivable administrative blunder.*

I choke back my fear, trying not to come unglued. This is the end of the line. I've been outed. I might as well come clean.

I'm...um...Dix...Dixon Jenner... I stammer.

Out with it, bellows Cheyhto, his fists slamming on the table.

Um . . . I'm visiting . . .

Just then another of Cheyhto's underlings rushes into the room. *Grand Leader, a new development has transpired.*

Cheyhto gets up from his seat and lumbers out of the room, returning moments later with Bleeker. I've never been happier to see someone in my life.

This is my cousin, Drageer. I had heard he was brought in and was concerned, because he didn't have his birthing pod record with him. So, I brought it here. I hope this resolves any outstanding issues.

Cheyhto shuffles toward Bleeker. *Have I met you before?*

Yes, Grand Leader, says Bleeker. *We met on the surface.*

Hm, yes, grumbles Cheyhto, staring at the token in Bleeker's hand. *And here you are again.*

Cheyhto grabs the record and reviews it.

My heart is still in my throat, but I try to pull myself together and go with the Drageer story. *You see,* I say. *I told you that there was a simple explanation. That's me, Drageer.*

Yes, this is a record for your cousin, Drageer, but this creature has identified himself as Dixon.

Dixon is a family nickname, says Bleeker, wagging a finger at me. *Drageer, how many times have I communicated to you that you confuse beings by informing them you are Dixon?*

Um...yeah, sorry, Bleeker, I say, forcing a smile. *But no one gave me a chance to explain.*

Cheyhto tosses the record onto the table and steps away, stumbling over one of his henchmen. He picks up the Arbiter by the neck and beats him in the head with his fists.

Sheesh, you don't want to get on this guy's bad side.

The battered Arbiter still dangling in the air, Cheyhto turns his attention back to me. *Why weren't you carrying this around with you?* he asks, dropping his subordinate. *That would have prevented all this confusion.*

I was at home when I was picked up, I say. *Why would I be carrying it around there?*

Remove them from my presence, demands Cheyhto, walking toward the door. *I have more important matters to deal with.*

An Arbiter guard grabs our arms to escort us out when Cheyhto stops and turns around.

There is still something not proper here, says Cheyhto. *Your glaberism tale is too peculiar. I will persist in reviewing this matter.*

The guard walks us down the long corridor, past the security desk, to the front entrance. We clamber into Bleeker's transporter. Once we're in the air, I lean back into my seat and laugh uncontrollably. I have no idea why.

"What the hell did you show him?" I ask after gaining my composure. "Whose birthing pod record was that?"

As I said, my cousin Drageer, says Bleeker. *Plinka alerted us that you had been detained. I contacted my cousin and he provided me a copy of his birthing-pod record.*

"What a relief," I say. "Hopefully we're done with this crap."

I am not persuaded, says Bleeker. *You heard Cheyhto. I am concerned that he will continue to have you investigated. We will need to be better prepared.*

CHAPTER TWELVE

Mars
Earth calendar: 2039-11-08
Martian calendar: 45-12-647

I tried scalloped potatoes, potatoes au gratin, potato casserole, herb roasted potatoes, and baked potatoes. They hated every dish.

What nutrition are you preparing today? asks Seepa, strolling into the kitchen while I peel another batch.

"They are called French fries," I say. "There isn't a person on Earth who doesn't worship these things. I'm positive you'll love them."

Dix, you do understand that it is not necessary for you to prepare Earth nutrition? asks Seepa. *We are content with our own.*

"I know," I say. "It's just that I'm a chef. That means I get enjoyment out of making food that people like. I'm gonna keep whipping up potato dishes until I hit the jackpot."

Then we look forward to your French-fried nutrition, she says, peering down at the bowl of peeled spuds. *The names of your nutrition amuse us. I am still bewildered by the missing mud potatoes we endeavored to consume last week. I did not detect any mud in the potatoes. Perhaps you did not include enough?*

"There was no mud in it," I say, shaking my head. "And it's Mississippi mud potatoes."

Maybe some mud would improve it?

"Let's forget about the mud potatoes. You're gonna love French fries."

Why are they named French fries? she asks.

I explain that "French" refers to stuff from a region on Earth.

So, the potatoes are grown in France?

I throw my arms in the air in frustration and accidently knock over my platter of potatoes. I drop down onto my hands and knees to pick them up. The dark stone floor is cold to the touch.

Are the potatoes always flung to the floor before frenching them? asks Seepa.

"No, you're killing me. They're fried."

"If they are not grown in France, then, does the recipe originate from France?"

"The dish originated from Belgium."

Belgium?

"That's another region."

Dix, are all Earth-beings as confusing as you? Mud dishes without mud. French-fried foods that have nothing to do with French. I do not comprehend how you can function as a chef.

"Probably because I've cooked for very few Martians," I mutter, picking up another potato to peel. "Let me finish here and I'll bring out the dish shortly."

We will wait with great eagerness, she says, forcing a smile as she shuffles out of the kitchen.

I look in the pot and notice that the fries are a golden reddish-brown. I'd discovered a reddish, oily substance in the Martians' kitchen and used it for frying. After draining the fries, I put them on a platter. I pop one in my mouth. It's perfect: crispy outside, fluffy inside, not greasy.

I scoop up the platter and carry it into the dining area where Bleeker and Seepa wait. I'm so focused on my creation I forget about the low doorways. The platter nearly flies out of my hands.

"I guarantee, you will love my latest creation," I say, putting down the platter to rub the welt on my head.

Dix describes them as French fries although they should be Belgium fries, says Seepa, winking at me.

What is the difference? asks Bleeker, wrinkling his flat nose.

I believe the only difference is where they are cooked, says Seepa.

Then they should be Martian fries, says Bleeker.

I believe you are correct, says Seepa, looking over at me.

"Let's just call them fries," I say with a heavy sigh. "Let's eat."

Bleeker picks one up with his long, leathery fingers. He examines the fry, turning it around.

Interesting, says Bleeker. *Does not resemble any of your other potato nutrition. I'm astonished at how you can alter your potatoes into something so different each time.*

He cautiously puts it in his mouth and slowly chews.

"Well, what do you think?"

His face contorts, and he spits the chewed French fry onto his plate.

Hideous, says Bleeker.

Maybe Martian fries turn out better on Earth? says Seepa.

I sigh and get out of my chair. "I'm takin' a walk."

Outside, I've rigged a basketball hoop and backboard next to my farm from building material provided by Bleeker. I get out my basketball and shoot hoops with a 3D-printed replica of my Bry'n DeMatwah autographed ball. Todd picks up the sounds of the ball hitting the backboard and joins me. I try a few free throws, some layups, and a slam dunk. I love how long I can hang in the air in the Martian atmosphere.

"You appear to get satisfaction from slamming the ball into the hoop," says Todd, standing at the edge of my makeshift court. "May I remind you that your athletic prowess is directly related to the low gravity on Mars."

"I'm not listening to you, Todd," I say.

"Well you should listen to this. If you're taking a left-handed layup shot, you need to take off using your right foot."

I stop and glare at him. "How are you such an expert?"

"Version 4 models of the Sementric robots possess an IQ of 135. A vast improvement over the 115 IQ of the previous model."

"I'm going back to not listening to you." I drive to the basket for a layup shot.

I spend the next half hour taking shots while being critiqued by the bot. Eventually, Bleeker comes out to join us.

I apologize for our reaction to your French fries nutrition, says Bleeker. *We appreciate that you want to create nutrition for us, but Earth-beings and Martians do not enjoy the same sustenance.*

I stop and give him a pat on the back. Then I make a perfect twenty-foot jump shot and pump my fist in the air.

"Nailed it!" I yell. "Yeah, I get it. Don't worry about it."

I also wish to inform you that I have a pair of tickets for next week's sling match, says Bleeker. *Are you interested?*

"I have real issues with the game," I say. "And the toll it takes on your Arbiter people."

I do not understand your concern. I will find another being to accompany me to the match.

"You know I've been thinking . . ."

You want to organize basketball matches?

Jeez, he's reading my thoughts again. "So, what do you think of my idea?"

"I think it's ridiculous," says Todd.

"I wasn't asking you."

"Nonetheless, the notion is ridiculous," says Todd, as he crosses his arms against his chest. "In addition, it would draw unwanted attention."

Dix, I would concur with Todd, says Bleeker. *Why would you want to incur the risk of being exposed?*

"I just think that there should be an alternative form of entertainment on Mars, that's less violent. A sport that all Martians can enjoy, and no one gets exploited," I say, cradling the ball in my arms. "Are you going to help me or not?"

Do you know how to organize and run a sports league?

"I can start small and learn. I've got plenty of time to kill. I could hold a basketball clinic and teach the game. Maybe some sling players might be interested. Is there any chance I can get into the locker room after next week's game?"

Let me attempt to make some arrangements on your behalf, says Bleeker. *One of my patients is the proprietor of another squad in the sling league. It is plausible he can arrange to provide you access."*

"Really? That would be great!" I say, spinning the ball on my right index finger.

"No good will come of this," says the bot, giving me a stern look.

I cannot promise anything, says Bleeker.

"Just get me in the door and I'll do the selling," I say.

Remember, you cannot divulge you are an Earth-being, says Bleeker.

"Yeah, yeah," I say. "I'll tell everyone I invented this new game."

I dribble the ball and then drive to the hoop for another slam dunk.

"Kaboom!"

"Oh, please," says the bot, waving his arms in the air. "I've experienced enough explosions in my lifetime. I'm heading inside."

I am in agreement with you, Todd, says Bleeker, following the bot into the house.

But I'm not alone for very long.

Dix, why have you been hiding from me? says Plinka.

I turn around to find Plinka grinning from her side of the yard. Martian women certainly know how to flirt.

I drop the ball and it bounces several times before it stops between the two houses. *Why would anyone want to hide from you?*

I think you have been, says Plinka, waddling into our yard. *You have been here for days but have had no time for poor Plinka.*

We've been kind of busy.

My basketball is on the ground right in front of her. She looks down at it and places her right foot on top.

You do not appear to be occupied now, she says. *You are just throwing that sphere in the air. I have some freshly-prepared bousou spread. Would you like to consume some with me?*

Sure, how can I turn down bousou spread?

I wish I could Google bousou spread.

Let me just freshen up and I'll be over shortly, I say.

How do you freshen up? asks Plinka, her eyes twinkling. *I hope it's something devoid of propriety.*

* * * * *

Plinka's place is elaborately decorated from what I've seen of Martian standards. There are colored crystalline objects, like icicles, that project from the ceilings and walls and radiate colored lights. I have to zig and zag to avoid impaling my scalp.

You have a very nice place, Plinka, I say from the middle of the maze of lights. I feel like I'm inside an arcade game.

It's more spacious than my apartment above the garage back in Jersey, despite the low ceilings. The interior floor, walls, and ceilings are made of stone, as smooth and blue as the outside of the house, like you're floating on the ocean.

I love how you've decorated this place. There are no closets; personal clothing and strange gadgets hang from hooks in the walls, giving the place a cluttered look. My ex-girlfriend Georgia would've had an anxiety attack in this place, which makes me feel right at home.

Thank you, Dix, says Plinka, guiding me through her house. *I created all the designs myself.*

Plinka has dressed up for my visit. Her arms and neck are heavily weighed down by bracelets, bangles, chains, and necklaces, made of red Martian rocks of various sizes and shapes. She squeezes my elbow, which is the Martian equivalent of a hug.

We move into a sitting room where two spiky lappa pets chase each other around the room. Now I need to avoid being stabbed in the head and in the legs. I plop myself down in one of her micro chairs.

I hope you haven't gone to too much trouble for me, I say.

It depends on what you refer to as trouble, says Plinka. *I will be right back with the nutrition. No one produces bousou spread as well as I do.* She wobbles out of the room.

I look forward to your spread, I say, forcing a smile; my experience with Martian food hasn't been great. *I can't remember the last time I had some.*

I don't know if she can pick up my thoughts from the other room. When she returns she carries a tray with some 'stuff.' I reserve judgement on whether it can be considered food.

She places the tray on the table and sits down opposite me.

Proceed to consume the nutrition, she says. *You do not have to be modest with me.*

I look down on the tray. Her spread is bone white and stiff, like spackling paste. She reaches across the table with her leathery, thin arm and drops a scoop in a bowl in front of me, then drops another scoop in her own bowl. She picks up some bousou spread in her fingers and puts it in her mouth. I might be imagining it, but the gesture seems sexual.

As she slowly withdraws her finger she looks at me.

Oh, that is so satisfying! she says.

I follow her lead and scoop some up with my finger. I hesitate, then slip my finger into my mouth.

This must be what battery fluid tastes like.

What do you mean it tastes like battery fluid? asks Plinka, pouting.

I didn't say anything, I respond, putting another scoop in my mouth.

I try to work the spread around in my mouth with my tongue, but it sticks. I take a big swallow and get it down without gagging. It hits my stomach like sand.

I've never had anything this good, I say, forcing another smile.

Thank you, says Plinka. *You should consume more.*

She scoops some up with her finger and brings it up to my mouth. I can't believe I'm sucking a Martian finger.

I wish I could eat more, but it's so filling, I say, patting my belly.

For a large Martian, you do not consume very much, she says as she pushes the tray aside and pulls her chair closer.

Dix, can I inquire about something?

Sure, go ahead and ask.

The evening we attended the sling match you stated that you didn't enjoy it. Why do you disapprove of sling?

I shift in my seat, not sure if I can be totally frank with her. *Well, I just feel it's unfair to exploit Arbiters for entertainment. From what I see, players get little in return other than getting crippled for life.*

I feel I'm being swallowed by her large, black eyes.

My feelings are identical, she says.

Amaze-balls! I declare. *I thought I was the only one who felt this way.*

No, there are many others, she says, *but you are the first citizen to express it so openly. Are you not concerned that agents of the Grand Leader will overhear you?*

I guess I wasn't being very careful.

Dix, there is another matter that I would like to discuss.

Okay.

Her eyes flutter and her mouth curls into a smile. *Would you like to ngono?*

I have no clue what she is talking about. Maybe it's some type of board game.

Sure, I say. *Why not?*

Wonderful, says Plinka. *I will return with it momentarily.*

She leaps out of her seat and totters out of the room, returning moments later with a yellow box the size of a toaster. She places it on the table, removes the lid, and pulls out a rubbery, oval object. It's translucent with grips on both ends. It reminds me of a ring I've seen the women at my gym use for Pilates. She hands me one end.

This is definitely not a board game.

I have thought about sharing my ngono with you since we first met, she whispers, leaning forward.

I have no clue what to do, so I fake it.

It's been some time since I last used one of these, I say.

I am certain you are popular with the feminine gender in Nilosyrtis. She teasingly waves the thing in front of my chest. *You have likely worn out several ngonos.*

I puff out my chest, grinning. *Maybe one or two.*

I rip it our of her hands and wave it in front of her. She reaches out and grabs one end of the ngono and a warm sensation floods through my body like stepping into a sauna. When it spreads to my crotch, the ngono warms up and red lights flash inside of it. Plinka pulls hard on her end. I jerk forward, crashing into her. We topple over, and I land on top.

Dix, you are so aggressive . . . she purrs.

The ngono is between us and we are both holding tight. The lights flash more rapidly. The warm sensation spreads and my arms and legs are burning up. My heart rate speeds up and my crotch pulsates. A pleasant tension builds in my chest, then my arms, legs, and the rest of me. Plinka's head tilts back, a faraway look in her eyes.

She repeats over and over, *I want you. I want you.*

The tension builds, and I feel an increased sensory awareness, almost like I'm stoned. I grip the ngono tighter, cheeks flushing, breathing hard. Droplets of sweat form on my bald head.

All the while Plinka chants, *I want you. I want you.*

I roll away, pulling the ngono toward me, forcing her closer. My body is on fire. I can't focus. Bright lights flash before my eyes. It's like tripping on LSD, only better.

In that moment, my mind *exhales*. Something like when a rollercoaster drops. I hear Plinka moaning next to me. I'm gasping for air like I just finished running a marathon. I'm really starting to like this planet.

I turn to look at Plinka and notice lights flashing from her bulbous eyes. It's obvious that she has experienced the same thing.

So, this is Martian sex. It was the best sex I've ever had. I could make millions selling ngonos back home.

Dix, why am I not surprised that you are so skilled at satisfying a Martian of the feminine gender, she says, relaxing her grip.

It's just like riding a bicycle. It becomes second nature.

I have no idea what that means, she says. *You have such unusual expressions.*

CHAPTER THIRTEEN

Mars
Earth calendar: 2039-11-16
Martian calendar: 45-12-655

It's November and back home we would have already had our first frost and the stores would be hauling out their holiday displays. I stare out the window at the view outside. The weather here never changes. I never thought I would say this, but I'm homesick for New Jersey.

It's just over five weeks until Christmas, and I'm determined to do something to celebrate. I walk over to the 3D printer and press the power button. The display panel comes alive, and I press the memory button to browse through the inventory of stored items. I stop at an image of a plastic nativity scene that looks identical to a ceramic one my mom used to put on the mantel over the fireplace. My eyes well up. It's been in her family for decades.

Christmas on Mars is never going to be like back home.

I continue to browse until I find everything I need, including an artificial Christmas tree and a range of ornaments: snowmen, angels, doves, reindeer. I even find candy canes and fake snow. I leave the room and head straight to the common room where Seepa is picking up the spikes that Poof has shed.

"You are probably not aware of this, but Christmas is just a few weeks away," I say.

What is Christmas?

"It's an important holiday on Earth."

I'm sorry, but I do not comprehend what a holiday is, says Seepa. *Please provide an explanation.*

"It's a special day when you don't work," I say.

How does an employment break determine that a day is special? she asks.

Poof scoots next to me. I pick up several pieces of lappa treats and toss them to the other side of the room. "What makes it special is that no one works on a holiday. Schools are closed. Families get together to celebrate. We have great big family dinners. We decorate our house or light fireworks."

It sounds appealing. What is your custom on Christmas holiday?

"My dad buys a live tree, always a fir. The smell is amazing."

What is the function of the tree?

"The tree is used to hold decorations," I say.

That seems to be a peculiar ritual, says Seepa. *Does the tree serve any other function?*

"Nothing else," I say. "Well, we keep the presents under the tree until Christmas day."

Does the tree also serve as nutrition on the festival day?

"Um, no," I say. "But the extended family would come over and we would have the most fabulous dinner. My mom cooked turkey with stuffing, mashed potatoes, gravy, cranberry sauce, squash. The best were the desserts, pumpkin pie and shortbread cookies."

That does sounds attractive, with the exception of the smashed potatoes. I assume you will miss Christmas this year.

Poof is back and rubbing up against my leg. "Unfortunately, yes," I say, trying to move away from the prickly pet. "The thought does make me sad."

Seepa jumps up and down, clapping her hands. *You can have Christmas here in our dwelling,* she says. *We do not know what rituals to adhere to, but you can communicate them to us.*

I grab my head with my hands. "Really? That's wonderful. I'll plan it all out. This will be awesome."

At that moment, Bleeker wobbles into the room. *I overheard your display of enthusiasm about this Christmas celebration. I am fully supportive,* he says. *Can you further enlighten us about this celebration?*

"Here's the background," I say. "Christmas celebrates the birth of Jesus. Over 2,000 years ago, his parents, Mary and Joseph, traveled to Bethlehem but couldn't find a motel room during the holiday season. So, they spent the night in a barn where baby Jesus made his appearance. Except Joseph wasn't his dad, God was."

Who is this God being? asks Seepa.

"God is the Supreme Being," I say. "God created everything, including us."

I was created by my parental-beings, says Bleeker.

"Sure, and your parental-beings were created by their parental-beings," I say. "But who created the first Martians?"

We cannot enlighten you, says Seepa. *We were not present when the first Martians were created.*

I look down and notice my leg is scratched and bleeding. "Of course, let's get back to Christmas."

I assume this Jesus being is no longer alive, says Bleeker.

"That is correct," I say. "He was killed by the Romans."

That is terrible, says Seepa. *Were the Romans from another planet or other Earth-beings?*

I wander back to my room and the 3D printer. Thank God it won't be Christmas for another five weeks.

* * * * *

That evening, we shuffle into a sea of Elysium red and yellow and scowl across Arsia Hall at a small contingent wearing Nazium black.

I'm pumped, because Bleeker has come through as promised and arranged for me to speak to some of the sling players after the game. My mind keeps wandering off as I picture which of the bouncing, deformed players might be best suited for basketball.

The first points are scored by an extremely round Nazium player, who bounces higher than the others. Not ideal for my purposes.

I scan both lineups for the tallest players and pick out the defenders most adept at jumping. When they leap into the air to block a launchee, they even remind me of basketball players blocking shots, but with much more violent outcomes. One reckless defender in particular makes me cringe. On one block attempt, he mistimes his jump and a foot of the airborne player catches him in the side of his head. The poor Martian goes down in a heap, an indentation visible where the foot struck his temple.

It only gets worse. A few plays later, two defenders jump simultaneously. Their arms tangle up and their heads collide, causing them to fall forward onto the court. Meanwhile, the launchee lands on them both, creating a mangled ball of arms and legs. A timeout is called, and a group of officials work for several minutes to untie the knot.

Bleeker is very much into the game, repeatedly elbowing me in the ribs as he flails his arms in the air like an inflatable balloon man, as if his efforts might somehow help the Elysium players to fly farther.

After one of his jabs and a cry of pain he says, *Sorry, Dix. You are subdued tonight.*

I rub my side. *I'm just concentrating on the–*

Watch your head! yells Bleeker as a Martian projectile hurtles in our direction, his little arms waving frantically in the air. He lands two rows in front of us, scattering patrons in every direction. The sling player bounces off a seat and lands in the lap of an Elysium fan who smacks the poor Nazium in the noggin, like the time my landlady beat off a mugger. When two Nazium fans jump in to shield the player, a full-scale rumble breaks out. When a couple of Nazium fans grab the sling player by the legs to pull him to safety, it soon turns into a tug-of-war. I decide this is a good time to get up and stand in the far aisle, away from the carnage. Bodies get stepped on, punched, and twisted. One tiny Martian pokes spectators in the eyes until several fans grab him and toss the little bugger onto the court.

It reminds me of a classic drunken NFL brawl. The match is delayed again while security staff restore order and the mangled player is carried down to the sideline. I return to my seat once everyone settles down.

The rest of the match is uneventful, and Elysium prevails by a score of 48-41, which means much of the crowd leaves happy. About ten minutes after the conclusion of the match, we make our way to the Nazium change room. Two Arbiter custodian types stand outside the door. As we approach, one of them steps forward and glowers at us.

There is no access to the change room for members of the public, says the guard.

I'm a colleague of Cubano, the squad proprietor, says Bleeker.

What is your name? asks the guard.

Bleeker.

Do you have a pass for a Bleeker? the guard asks his colleague.

The second guard checks a list on the wall. *Yes,* he says. *We can let them in.*

Bleeker pushes the door open, and I follow him in time for something to hit me on the side of my head. I turn to see a shoe. Players' gear is now flying in every direction. About half the players are crowded around a table of nutrition in the corner, climbing over each other to get a handful to shove in their mouths. A heap of fallen food forms a slippery layer of slime on the floor, and a few players lose their footing and fall. Other players step on them to get to the food.

In another corner of the room, two injured players are stretched out on tables, being treated by what I presume to be staff, if you can call it being treated. The staff look like bakers kneading dough.

I wonder how we will get their attention, when I pick up a shrill whistling in my head. I assume it came from Bleeker, because he is waving his arms in the air. Everyone's head turns to look at us. Bleeker stands on a bench.

Friends, we come here to discuss with you a new opportunity, says Bleeker.

What about? someone calls out.

I hop on the bench to join Bleeker. The players look shocked to see me.

What class of Martian are you? asks a player in front me.

He cannot be from here, responds a player in the back of the room.

Greeting friends, I say. *I know I look unusual, but I have a rare medical condition. One morning, I arose from restoration mode with this unusual white rash. Then my facial features became deformed. It's been horrible. My physician, Bleeker, has been working on finding a cure.*

Over time, I find I embellish.

But the reason I'm here is that I'm recruiting players for a new sports league. The game is called basketball and those who decide to join will be pioneers.

One scruffy Arbiter steps forward.

We are sling participants, he says. *We know nothing about this basketball. Why would any of us be interested in your league? Unless you plan to compensate us better.*

No, I can't, I say. But *I've seen how banged up you get from being flung all over the sling court. None of that will happen playing basketball. You are on your feet at all times and there is no physical contact. Anyone who signs up will be taught how to play the game. I can't make promises as far as wages, but I don't intend on profiting from this venture. Everything earned will be used to pay players after expenses. I will keep nothing for myself. But the big attraction for you will be player safety.*

What about nutrition? asks a rather stout Martian over to my left. *We are provided with a feast following each match. Why would I consider playing if there is no nutrition?*

There are a lot of nodding heads in the room. Who knew you could bribe players with food?

At that moment, my mind shoots back to the potatoes sitting in my storage locker.

Oh, there'll be nutrition, I say.

CHAPTER FOURTEEN

Sixteen Weeks Earlier
Inside the Cupernicus:
Orbiting Mars

For the fifth time in the past two hours, the ship's public-address system replayed David Bowie's *Space Oddity*. I'd made it the mission's theme song in honor of our Commander, Tom Jonas, who at that moment barged into the galley.

"Jenner, we need to talk," said Tom as he pushed away a bag of freeze-dried squash soup that floats into his face.

I drifted over to greet him. "Major Tom, nice of you to drop in."

"Look, just Tom will do," said the Commander. "I appreciate your attempts to introduce some spirit onboard the ship. But you can't commandeer the PA system."

"Major Tom, the usual music sucks," I said. "It's like being in an intergalactic elevator."

"We try to accommodate a broad spectrum of music preferences—"

"Then who asked for Taylor Swift?"

"Never mind who asked for it," said Tom, his face flushed. "Just keep your mitts off the PA system. We are a few hours away from landing. Can you at least try not to annoy anyone until we've landed? Like popping out of a floating cargo bag?"

With that, he pushed off an outer wall and propelled himself out of the galley. I turned back to organizing the nutrition pantry. That's what the NASA trainers called food - nutrition. I would have given anything for a burger and fries.

"Whatcha doin', Dix?"

I turned around as Tammy floated through the galley entrance.

"I'm perfecting my juggling skills in zero-gravity," I said. "It's kinda easy since nothing ever falls down."

I grabbed a few items out of the pantry and imitated a juggler trying to keep all the objects in the air, but I ended up frantically snatching objects that didn't drop back down.

Tammy reached out and snagged a bag of dehydrated potatoes. "So, your two mission specialties are cooking and juggling? I'm sure they will both be useful on Mars."

"I have many more skills and talents."

"I look forward to checking them out," said Tammy, her baby blue eyes mocking.

"When I'm done here," I said, "I wonder whether Mission Engineer and Geologist Spanner would like to join me for some star gazing before we officially leave deep space?"

"Sorry, but I need to run some of our landing systems through tests before we touch down," said Tammy. "I suspect you would prefer everything is in working order."

"Ah yes," I said. "Speaking for all the crew, we would like a gentle landing over a hard one."

Tammy slowly unzipped her jumpsuit down to her waist to reveal her bra. She pulled me close and kissed me. "You never know, you might be the first man to get laid on Mars," she said. "Catch you later, Jenner."

* * * * *

Commander Tom announced we were nine minutes from landing. From where I was strapped in, I couldn't see out a porthole, so I had to take his word for it.

The spaceship vibrated violently as the retrorockets and parachutes kicked in, trying to slow our descent through the thin atmosphere of Mars. What brainless scientist came up with the parachute idea?

My organs felt like they were in a cocktail shaker.

I glanced over at the five other crew members in our compartment. No one showed any reaction. Closing my eyes, I tried to think of something other than the ship crashing onto the surface of Mars in a spectacular fireball.

"Touchdown in three minutes, thirty-five seconds," announced the Commander.

There was so much crackling that came through my headset that I could barely make out the words over the roar from the retrorockets. I broke into a sweat. I wasn't sure if it was nerves or if the ship was burning up.

A huge thud made my body jerk forward, straining my seat harness. No more movement. Then a cheer spread through the ship. We had landed.

An hour later, twenty-four residents stood assembled on the surface of a huge empty planet. I was hyperventilating. *I'm on Mars. This is crazy!* I tried to control my breathing and calm down.

I stepped away from the group to look around. Red sand and rocks coated the surface, barren but also seductive. It could be a typical dusty summer day on the South Jersey shore, with the wind picking up sand and forming small reddish clouds. In the distance I could make out the walls of the Valles Marineris canyon, towering over the valley floor.

Beyond the cliffs, the sun was smaller in the smog-brown sky. About a quarter-mile away, containers like railroad cars lay scattered around the site where Futurum would eventually be assembled. Dropped off by unmanned missions, they contained life support units, living quarters, rovers, and communications equipment.

The Commander's voice through my headset interrupted my train of thought. "Gather round, crew. We have a busy day ahead of us. Our first priority is to hike over to the colony site, unload the cargo, and assemble everything. I want the robots activated right away. There will be a congratulatory call from the President at twenty-hundred hours today. Everyone be back in the ship for that. Let's move."

Although we'd all trained in our suits, it took some time to get used to moving around in them in Mars' lower gravity. We were told our suits had much more maneuverability than those used in previous space missions, but you wouldn't know it. In low gravity, I felt like I was walking at half-speed. It took close to ten minutes to trek 400 yards.

Once we arrived, I teamed up with Tammy, our physician Greg Markowski, and our exobiologist Okuma Nikko. Our job was to open the crates that contained our living units and activate the robots, which would unload the crates and construct the units. After that we would supervise and drink coffee.

I banged on the side of one of the containers. The walls were thick, judging by the sounds they made. We had two sets of robots for the mission – three large Canadian-made Probotic and six smaller Sementric robots with full artificial intelligence. The Probotic robot looked a little like a Bobcat compact excavator with large wheels and two robotic arms. I couldn't wait to get them running.

Okuma's voice buzzed in my headset. "Let's start with cargo bin number twenty-two," he said.

The rest of us responded with 'Roger' as we plodded among the bins, until Okuma located our container. The bins were still attached to their original parachutes, which were partially buried in sand. Okuma and Tammy unhitched the parachute and unbolted the doors before swinging them open. The walls and floor of the container were made of a dull metal, making it look like a giant tin can. Inside, bolted to the floor sat three vehicular Probotic robots. Okuma unfastened one with one of our three-thousand-dollar NASA wrenches and climbed into the cab to power up the robot. I jumped into the cab next to him.

"Let me handle this one," I said.

Okuma got out and I slid over to the driver's seat. I drove the robot out of the container and headed over to one of the bins holding the components for our living quarters. Tammy had already opened the doors, so I rode over to a collapsed pod, meant to inflate into a living unit. Using the robotic arms, I picked up the pod and carried it to the site of our future home, a flat stretch of land close to where the containers were dropped. Greg had already put down markers to indicate where the living modules would be situated.

The trip was slow and tedious as I avoided large rocks. When I arrived at the site, I placed the living unit on one of the markers.

Okuma's voice blared through my headset, "Dix, you're driving the Probotic too fast with a load. You're at risk of tipping over."

I had a good view of the activity around me from the robot's cab. The Sementric bots were fun to watch, scurrying around securing all the living modules together. When one bumped into another, it would apologize. It was great to have them around.

I got out of the cab and stopped one of the bots.

"Hey buddy," I said. "I could use a coffee."

"My name is not buddy," said the bot. "I'm Sementric 5. I'm also not programmed as a server bot. I'm a construction bot. You will need to speak to my programmer."

"I'm just joking around with you, Sementric 5," I said.

"Thank you for the moment of levity," said the bot. "I need to resume my work."

"What are you doing messing with the bot, Dix?" asked Okuma. "We have a lot of work to get done."

"Roger," I said as I climbed back into the cab. "I was just asking for directions."

As I dropped off my next load, I heard Okuma's voice again. "Dix buddy, drop your load gently. Our equipment survived the trip to Mars. Let's not destroy it while setting up."

"Rogerrrrrrrr!" I said.

What a dickhead he turned about to be. It would be easier to get along with extraterrestrials.

When I got back to the cargo bins, Tammy hopped into the cab with me. Her piercing eyes radiated through the plastic visor of her helmet.

"I'm coming along for the ride," said Tammy. "I want to see those big, strong, robotic arms in action."

"Ah, yes. Want to see me flex my biceps?"

That grating voice came through my headset. "Dix, are you are putting the units on the correct markers?" asked Okuma. "Please concentrate on what you're doing."

"Tammy, do you think I can teach this robot to juggle?"

"Dix, you are too much," said Tammy.

I laugh. "Spoken like a true Southern belle."

"Dixon Jenner, are you listening to me?" said Okuma.

Oh my God, he reminded me of Miss Dawson from the third grade!

"ROGER!" I replied, swerving to drop off another unit.

I looked out the cab to see where I was supposed to leave this one. The living units were a series of pods that interconnected. Each with an airlock used by the crew whenever we left the habitable settlement. Except that I forgot which unit I carried and may have put it down on the wrong spot. That means they might not connect properly. I stopped the robot, so that Tammy and I could get out of the cab to scrutinize the situation.

"You're the engineer," I said. "Does this look right to you?"

"Um, no," said Tammy. "Look, at the top of the pod, it's labeled seven but marker seven is over here."

"It looked like the right spot from inside the cab," I said.

A Sementric bot approaches us and looks at the units.

"Your placement is incorrect," said the bot. "I will not be able to connect them."

"Thanks for pointing out the obvious," I said.

"You're welcome," said the bot.

I got back in the cab and instructed the Probotic robot to lift all the units to check that they were on the correct markers. When all the units were properly placed, we headed back to the cargo bins. I noticed Greg waiting for us.

"Dix, Okuma told me to take over for you," said Greg. "Why don't you take a break, buddy?"

"Good idea. My arms are tired from carrying these heavy pods." I hopped out of the cab leaving Tammy with Greg. I looked around. This place was as welcoming as a frigid Sahara. NASA forgot to set up picnic tables and lounge chairs for staff breaks, so I climbed up on one of the cargo bins and brushed off the dust. Sand clouds blocked out the sun. Everything was a drab brown.

I stretched out on my back and closed my eyes.

CHAPTER FIFTEEN

```
Mars
Earth calendar: 2039-12-01
Martian calendar: 46-01-001
```

I look over at the ngono still glowing where we dropped it. I roll over on the bed and notice Plinka staring at me with a big grin on her face. I get up on my elbows and stretch my legs.

I hope you are not planning to leave immediately after our ngono session? she asks.

Um, no, no. I was, um . . .

Dix, I read your thoughts.

I wince. *Oh, right.*

You should know you can't block thoughts when using the ngono, she says. *Everything is open for your partner to see.*

Oh, crap. I wonder what else she picked up. Maybe the ngono stuff is not a good idea. Even if it's amazing.

Well, if you've read my thoughts then you know I have a big day, I say as I get up off the bed. *It's the first day of basketball practice and I can't be late.*

She puts her thin, leathery arms around me. *You better be back later,* she says, faking a stern look for my benefit.

I assure her I will and wave goodbye as I head out. I stop back at my place to pick up Bleeker for the tryout and find him, Seepa, and Todd sitting in front of the Christmas tree.

I'd spent several days producing the thing and its ornaments, and the final results look pretty good. The kiwi green, artificial spruce tree is six feet tall and thin as a Ralph Lauren model, reaching just a few inches short of the low-ceilinged Martian home. I pick out the glowing green and red lighted icicles I snagged from Plinka, and an astronaut wearing a white extravehicular mobility unit suit sits on top like a star. It even has a NASA patch.

"What are you guys up to?" I ask.

We were thinking that we should start opening the presents, says Bleeker.

We see no purpose in delaying the festivities, says Seepa.

I jump between them and the tree.

"Hold it right there," I say. "We don't open presents today because it's not Christmas."

Well, it turns out today is Martian Christmas. Is that not the case, Bleeker? says Seepa.

"Christmas doesn't begin until twenty-three days, eleven hours, and thirty-nine minutes from now," says the bot. "And today is the first day of the Martian calendar. I believe on Earth it's referred to as New Year's Day."

"Thank you, Todd," I say. "You are a wealth of information. Now, knock it off, guys. I need to get ready for my basketball tryouts. Bleeker, are you still coming?"

* * * * *

Bleeker and I take his transporter to a small, dingy gym facility in a part of the city I have not been to before. It is in a grimy Arbiter neighborhood that's not exactly a slum, but it's not exactly attractive either. The houses are smaller, the stone exteriors are pitted and cracked. Household waste litters the roadway. I guess Arbiters don't own those fancy Garbatrons that Seepa uses to vaporize our garbage.

I drag two large bags full of basketballs from the transporter. The 3D printer has been busy copying my souvenir ball. Arbiter pedestrians pass us by on their way to work, glaring at me but saying nothing. My stomach quivers as we head into Fraleco Hall.

Bleeker, is it safe to walk in this neighborhood? I ask.

Certainly. It may not look as aesthetically attractive as my community, says Bleeker. *But you are not exposed to any risks being here.*

It's depressing to see how the Arbiters live. Such a contrast in living standards.

As I struggle to carry the bags through the front entrance, an awful stench engulfs me. My eyes water, and I gag on the bitter taste in the back of my throat.

Damn! What is that smell?

That would be your Arbiter basketball participants, says Bleeker.

I never noticed the smell when we were in the change room after the sling match, I say.

The sling change rooms contain crystals to absorb the odor, says Bleeker. *I presume they don't provide the crystals in this facility.*

I think we need to get hold of some of those crystals, I say.

I scan the gym, trying to determine what adaptations might be needed since it is not designed for basketball. The facility is nothing as elaborate as Arsia Hall. There are no hardwood floors on Mars, but rather a spongy flooring similar to what exists at Arsia. Here, the flooring is in bad shape and rutted with age. There are stains in some spots, the color is faded, and the lighting is poor, which makes the place look that much dingier. I estimate there is enough seating for several hundred spectators.

I raise my gaze to the hoops. Bleeker had arranged for a craftsman (or I should say craftsMartian) to design two backboards. They have been mounted at each end of the court so that the rims are ten feet above the floor. However, the backboards are mounted onto the walls. Not ideal if momentum drives you past the hoop. There are also no free throw lanes and circles, and no three-point arcs painted onto the court surface. I guess this will have to do.

Bleeker, nice job getting the basketball court ready, I say. *We will have to make a few adjustments, but I can live with this.*

Do we have to situate the hoops so far up from the surface? asks Bleeker. It seems so high to toss the sphere into it without the assistance of a sling.

Yes, they have to be that height, I say. *We will follow official NBA rules. Now where are the change rooms? I would like to say a few words to players.*

Just down this corridor, says Bleeker. *I will accompany you.*

He waddles through a doorway. I duck and follow him, slipping into the first change room. I instantly choke.

Pinching my nose with my hand, I look around the room and at the seven Arbiter misfits, each bearing the scars from their sling battles: misshapen heads, flat noses, twisted arms and legs.

Thank you for coming out today, I gag, trying to breathe through my mouth. *My name is Dix, and I'm going to serve as the Lead Coach and Commissioner of the future Martian Basketball Association. This is Bleeker who will serve as the league's Deputy Commissioner and Director of Player Development. Today we start training.*

Out of the corner of my eye, I see Bleeker grinning.

Why don't we begin by having each one of you tell us your name and something interesting about yourself, I say, and point at the player sitting closest to me. *We'll start with you.*

The player shifts his weight on the bench and looks around the room. I can't help but notice that the top of his head is concave and his arms are different lengths.

My name is Nebbish, says the player. *There is nothing interesting about me.*

There was some snickering around the room.

Hello Nebbish, I say. *Tell me something you enjoy doing.*

I like to poke friends in the eye, says Nebbish.

He reaches across to the player next to him and pokes him in the eye. The injured player takes a swing at him but misses, probably because his vision is impaired. He ends up punching himself in the head. That elicits some additional snickering.

Thanks Nebbish, I say, and point to the player with the blurred vision. *You're next.*

His face is a darker shade of blue than the others in the room. As I look more closely I realize he has hundreds of scars on his face and scalp, which gives his skin a darker complexion. He is missing part of his nose and one finger on his left hand.

Shlepper, says the scarred player. *When not participating in sling, I enjoy restoration mode.*

We move on to the next player. His head is rotated about forty-five degrees from its original position, which means he is permanently looking over his shoulder.

Kvetch, says the player. *Me and my partner like to ngono.*

Everyone in the room grins.

Thanks for sharing that, I say and point to the player next to him. He is the tallest player in the room, about four feet, six inches.

I am Shlemiel, he says. *I enjoy watching Nebbish poke friends in the eye.*

The icebreaker isn't going as expected. I remind myself I'm on Mars. I move on to the next player whose face is faded like an old leather sofa.

Shmendrik, says the player. *I enjoy sneaking onto the surface to stare at the sun.*

Thank you for coming out, Shmendrik, I say.

The next player shows no obvious deformities until I notice his feet. They are different sizes and shapes. I can only imagine how they got that way.

Klutz, he says. *I want to be as tall as you, friend.*

I glance at the last player on the bench. He has a rotund shape, like my Uncle Ned, a big fan of the Chinese buffets in North Jersey.

I am Fresser, says the portly Martian. *I love to consume nutrition. Lots of it.*

So does my Uncle Ned. I gaze around the room at this dismal group of Arbiters. I feel like I'm in some bizarre recreation of Snow White and the Seven Dwarfs.

Thank you, I say. *That wasn't quite what I had in mind but it's a good start. Why don't we head out onto the court and start training camp? Bleeker, lead the way.*

When Bleeker jogs out of the room, the other Martians shuffle to their feet. But instead of following in single file, they try to exit at the same time. Klutz trips and falls and is stepped on by the others. They won't be taking on the Harlem Globetrotters any time soon.

When we get out on the court, I get things organized. *Let's start with some drills. Pick a partner and we'll practice passing,* I tell them. *I want you to form two lines. Bleeker, you can join in, so we have an even number.*

The players form something that resembles two lines and I demonstrate a bounce pass. My expectations are already low, but the drill is a disaster. Balls bounce off heads and other body parts. Shmendrik throws the ball so hard, he knocks over his partner. They have no concept of where a bounce pass should be fired so that it arrives at their partner's chest. Some balls bounce over heads and others need several bounces to reach the receiving player.

But after about fifteen excruciating minutes, some of the Martians get it. I call for a break.

Bring it in guys, I say. *I want to start working on dribbling.*

I grab a ball and dribble between the two imaginary foul lines. Then I line them up at one side and have them dribble back and forth.

I should have expected what happens next. Some slam the ball onto the spongy surface only to have it bounce back into their face. Shmendrik has a ball rebound off his chin, which deflects into the side of Fresser's head. He falls to his side and slides into Kvetch. It creates a chain reaction as balls and players are knocked around. Shlepper improvises and carries his ball between foul lines. After another fifteen minutes of watching this, I need another break.

Bleeker, let's bring out the refreshments, I say.

Etiquette is not a concept that exists in this culture. The Martians rush the table, and Fresser is the first to reach the food, scooping some up and pushing it into his mouth with both hands. When the others arrive, they shove him onto the table to get at the food. Pigs feeding at a trough eat like the royal family compared to these guys. In less than two minutes, all that remains of the food are traces of slime on their hands and faces.

After that, we work on shooting. The second half of the day goes a little better as the players get a feel for the ball. It turns out that Bleeker's concern regarding the height of the basketball hoops is unfounded. Low gravity on Mars allows them to jump much higher than what would be possible on Earth. The Martians soar through the air, trying lay up shots. Not very many balls find the basket, but quite a few players sail right into the wall.

On the ride home, I don't say much. My little Arbiters are enthusiastic, but perhaps I expect too much. It's like trying to teach ballet to football players.

Dix, I don't know much about basketball, says Bleeker, *but you appear to be an exceptional coach. I consider that to have been an exceedingly successful practice.*

I burst out laughing.

CHAPTER SIXTEEN

Mars
Earth calendar: 2039-12-25
Martian calendar: 46-01-024

It's Christmas Day on the Earth calendar and I'm peeling potatoes for dinner. Back home it would have been a dull day. I would have driven to Chatham for a family dinner, my warm and charming Dad would have spent the day comparing me to my incredibly successful brother, and I would have hated every second.

I miss it.

By four o'clock in the afternoon, Uncle James would be on his fifth vodka martini and Aunt Ginny would admonish him, but always in a whisper, as if we can't hear her. Mom would be on her second meltdown in the kitchen and I would have jumped in to lend a hand. I imagine the celebration would be even more subdued this year, since my family probably thinks I'm a mound of ashes blowing across a distant planet.

I miss the food. Turkey so tender that it almost melts in your mouth. The smell of savory, rich dressing, permeating through the house with the aroma of sage and rosemary. Roasted sweet potatoes with a maple syrup glaze.

I reach over to pick up another potato. Today's dish won't be like back home. The creamiest mashed potatoes made with mascarpone cheese, the roasted Brussels sprouts and apples, garnished with walnuts and cranberries, and my homemade cranberry sauce. The meal is always topped off by my own a decadent pumpkin custard pie.

My feast today isn't going to be as elaborate, but it'll be a feast nonetheless. I'm good at improvising.

And for this, I have to improvise.

I put down the potatoes to stir a pot, which contains my version of bousou spread. The spoon stands up on its own without falling over. If it thickens anymore the spoon might get stuck.

I need to pull something out of my locker and dash out to my bedroom. When I pass through the common room, both Bleeker and Seepa wait for me. Their eyes are locked on the gifts under the tree. They are having an argument, as per usual.

Seepa spots me first. *Dix, I am very relieved that you are here,* she says. *Bleeker wanted to unwrap the gifts, but I told him it was inappropriate to do so.*

I just wanted to examine the packaging with a possibility of glancing inside the ones intended for me, says Bleeker.

I am certain that is not what Dix has devised, says Seepa.

I break out laughing at the grown-up Martians as excited as kids.

"I've planned out the day," I say. "Let's not get at the gifts quite yet."

Please excuse my impatience and share with us your timetable, says Bleeker, his shoulders drooping.

Todd enters the room and heads straight for the tree.

"Is it time yet?" asks the bot. "Let's dispense with the drama."

"Merry Christmas to you too, Todd," I say. "What is it with you? Always popping into conversations."

"Dix, someone has to talk some sense into you. And I don't believe in your anachronistic religious practices," says the bot. "My only salvation would be a Sementric battery pack under that faux shrub."

"You know I can't get hold of a battery for you," I say. "I would if I could."

"So, am I to just count down the minutes for the next two hundred and twelve days, two hours, and forty minutes?" asks the bot. "Merry Christmas indeed, Scrooge."

Todd turns around and scoots out of the room.

"I'll tell you what," I say. "We will open the gifts shortly. But first I would like to recite a remake of a famous Christmas poem."

Please proceed, says Bleeker. *We are eager for you to communicate your poem.*

Bleeker sits in a chair next to the Christmas tree, and Seepa sits next to him, holding Poof in her lap. The flashing lights from the tree makes their eyes sparkle like large, onyx gemstones. I stand and pick up a Martian inscribing tablet borrowed from Bleeker.

Twas the restoration period before Christmas, when under the roof,
Not a creature was stirring, not even a Poof.
Hosiery was meticulously suspended by hooks on the wall,
In anticipation that visitation from St Nicholas would befall.

The offspring were nestled all snug in their beds,
While visions of bousou spread danced in their heads.
And Seepa with her dangly bracelets, Bleeker in his cap,
Had just settled their cerebrums for a long Martian nap.

When out in the laneway there arose such a dissonance,
I tripped over the bed to see what was outside the residence.
I stumbled to the entrance though I intended to march,
Threw open the latches and stooped under the arch.

The glow from the lighting on fallen red dust,
Gave lustre to objects corroded by rust.
When to my optical sensory organs should appear an apparition,
A miniature transporter, and eight tiny Blue Martians.

With a little Red operator, so lively and thick,
I knew in a moment it must be St. Nick.
Rapid as sling competitors his diminutive helpers came,

And he relied on telepathy as he addressed them by name!

"Now, Steeto! Now, Prinko! Now, Deela and Prakin!
On, Cooma! On, Breema! On, Gonomo and Ranen!
To the top of the dwelling! To the top of the wall!
Now scurry away! Scurry away! Scurry away all!"

As crystalline particles that before wild dust storms fly,
When they meet with an impediment, ascending to the sky,
So up to the structure-top the miniature aides flew,
Transporter glowing like a ngono, and St. Nicholas, too.

And then I heard them above us, so full of glee,
The waddling, stomping and shuffling of each little tootsie.
As I retracted my cranium, and spun around to see,
Through the rear passage, St. Nicholas leaping to me.

He was dressed in shimmering garments, including his feet,
And he accessorized with flashy stones, his outfit complete.
A bundle of gifts was carried by his Blue assistants,
And he looked like an important being, at least from a
distance.

His eyes-how they twinkled! His ears non-existent!
His cheeks were like roses, his nose quite insistent!
His coppery skin had so many wrinkles,
And the top of his cranium was hairless, without even
sprinkles.

He clenched between his incisors a medical device,
From the look on his face, he bought it at bargain price.
His visage was wider than it was high for a reason,
His abdominal region made me think it was basketball
season!

He was plump for a Martian, a multigenerational gnome,

And I laughed when I saw him, nothing like St. Nick back home!
A wink of his eye and a twist of his head,
Soon led me to know I had nothing to dread.

He transferred no thoughts, but went straight to his work,
And filled all the hosiery, then looked at me with a smirk.
And laying his finger in front of his face,
And giving a nod, disappeared with no trace!

He boarded his transporter, to his squad gave a sign,
And away they all flew toward the next shrine.
But my mind picked up a thought, 'ere he drove out of sight,
Happy Christmas to all, and to all a good night!

When I finish, I notice the two Martians have not moved a muscle; their eyes fixated on me and their mouths open. Coming from people who spit out French fries on impact, I'm don't know how to take this reaction.

Seepa has her hand on her cheeks, beaming. *That was beautiful, Dix, she says. It was very good of you to incorporate us into your poem.*

I am not clear on who this St. Nicholas is, says Bleeker. *Is he intended to be a Martian or an Earth-being?*

Naturally, Bleeker wants to critique the poem.

"He would be from Earth, but in my poem, I made him a Martian."

How does this Nicholas or Claus-being relate to Jesus? asks Bleeker. *Is the Jesus being you had mentioned to us his offspring?*

"No," I say.

Where did Nicholas locate his Blue assistants?

"Come on, Bleeker," I say. "It's a poem, not a true story."

I am just attempting to determine what is factual in your poem, says Bleeker.

"That's enough on the poem," I say. "Thank you for listening. Why don't we open the presents now?"

I am extremely eager to unwrap the gifts, says Seepa. *It was quite considerate of you to provide us with these objects.*

"Why don't you start off by opening this one," I say.

I hand Seepa a small, wrapped package. I made Christmas wrapping with my handy 3D printer. She grasps it with her long, thin fingers and unwraps the package, breaking out in a smile as she pulls out four bracelets. Each has red, blue, orange, and black irregular-shaped stones the size of lima beans. She slides them onto her wrists with her dozen others.

Thank you, Dix, says Seepa. *I adore them. Where did you find them?*

"I'm a very resourceful guy," I say with a wink and a nudge. However, there's no reaction from Seepa, just a bewildered look.

"Bleeker took me to a shop," I admit. And he paid for it as well. Part of my arrangement to cooperate with their study. "Alright, Bleeker, it's your turn."

I hand the next package to Bleeker. Instead of opening it, he gives it a shake, then holds it to his nose.

"Go ahead, open it," I say.

That is my intention, but first I would like to conjecture on the content of the package, says Bleeker. *What are these interesting creatures on the wrapping material?*

"They're reindeer," I say. "You've been dying to open the gifts. Now you're trying to dramatize the process. Christmas will be over, and you'll still be playing with the package."

He finally rips open the package and carefully pulls out a jersey. He holds it up to show Seepa and then slips it over his head.

Could this conceivably be a basketball jersey? asks Bleeker.

"Indeed, it is."

I am overwhelmed by this gift, says Bleeker. *Where did you locate this?*

"I arranged for one of our basketball players to alter a sling jersey," I say. Fortunately, Nebbish is capable of more than just poking people in the eye. "I provided him with the specifications. You know Arbiters are much more capable than you give them credit for. I found some excellent coaching candidates."

That has not been determined yet, says Bleeker.

But do you like the jersey?"

I do categorically.

"Well, you are the first person on Mars to own one," I say. "I plan to make more of these when the league starts up."

An excellent initiative, says Bleeker. *What other gift items do you have for us?*

Bleeker, you are being discourteous, says Seepa.

I was just inquisitive, says Bleeker. *After all, we are in the process of exchanging gifts.*

"It is presumptuous of you," says Seepa.

"Don't get your knickers in knots, folks."

You are mistaken, says Bleeker with a frown. *We are not wearing any knickers.*

I let out a sigh as I shake my head. I reach down under the tree and pick up another package and hand it to him. "This gift is for both of you."

It has an interesting aroma, say Bleeker, holding the package up to his nose. *Heavy and pungent. What is it?*

"Open it and see."

They pull it apart and examine a bag of roasted coffee beans. Bleeker picks up a handful of beans and studies them.

Are these your coffee beans? asks Bleeker.

"Yeah," I say.

Interesting, says Bleeker. *They do not look like the beans I observed in the farm.*

"That's because they've been roasted," I say. "I recently picked my first crop and roasted the beans when you weren't home. Next, I'll grind them to make a hot drink called espresso. I have all the necessary equipment thanks to my 3D printer. I plan to serve some after dinner."

I do not anticipate that I shall enjoy espresso, says Seepa with a frown.

"Hey, give it a chance."

I'm thankful for small blessings.

Dix, we have a gift for you, says Seepa as she grabs another package and hands it to me. I was surprised to see it wrapped in actual Christmas paper.

"Thank you," I say, "But where did you get this paper from?"

I crept into your room and created it using your 3D printer, says Bleeker.

"I can't wait to see what it is."

I open the package and remove a smooth, brown sphere that fits into the palm of my hand. It has a glowing spot about the size of a quarter on its surface.

"What is it?" I ask.

It's a sling alarm indicator, says Bleeker as he takes it out of my hands. *You place a finger on the activator and it signals a stoppage in play. I thought you would need it for your basketball league.*

His index finger touches the glowing spot and I pick up a screeching sound in my head.

"This is perfect," I say, as I continue to examine the ball.

I'm impressed that the Martians put so much thought into a gift. The last Christmas gift from my parental-beings in Jersey was a sweater and a couple of shirts. "Now, let's get to the best part of the holiday."

What would that be? asks Seepa.

"The food. I've been preparing for days."

I was fearful you would say that, says Bleeker, pouting.

Bleeker, don't be discourteous, says Seepa, wagging her finger at her partner.

I put down my gift and run into the kitchen to check on dinner. When I return, I usher them to the table and bring out platters of food with the help of Todd. I planned a mix of Martian favorites and foods, originating from my farm. We pass the dishes around the table, but I notice that the Martians stick to the Martian grub and just pick at the rest.

When Todd brings out my potato dish, Bleeker forces a smile. *What do you call this nutrition?*

"They are called mashed potato pancakes," responds Todd. "They originated in the eastern European countries of Germany, Austria, Russia, and Poland as a peasant food."

"Thank you, Mr. Google," I say.

"Dix, you have previously prepared smashed potatoes," says Bleeker.

"These are different than those smashed, um, mashed potatoes," I say.

Is this another customary Christmas nutrition? asks Seepa.

"They are also known as latkes," says Todd, "Which are potato pancakes that Ashkenazi Jews have prepared as part of the Hanukkah festival since the mid-nineteenth century."

You will have to enlighten us on the Hanukkah story, says Seepa.

Given how painful it was explaining Christmas, I can't imagine how they'll handle the eight-day oil miracle. "Maybe another time. What do you think?"

Seepa's reddish complexion turns green as she forces them down. *Oh, these are utterly appetizing.*

"I can see how you're enjoying them." I grab the platter and carry it into the kitchen, where I drop the potato pancakes into Garbatron to be vaporized.

When we finish eating, I brew the espresso, using a low-tech stovetop machine created by the 3D printer. Whether my hosts are or not, I'm excited. It's been almost four months since I've had any coffee.

I return with three cups and set them down. The steam rising from the cups clouds the shiny, stone finish of the table. I grab mine and drain it. The acidity of the warm, thick liquid awakens my taste buds. I can't wait for the caffeine to rush into my blood stream.

I look over to the two Martians, staring at the cups on the table. "Go ahead, try it," I urge them.

They pick up their cups and look at each other, as if waiting for the other to drink first. Seepa slowly throws back her shot like a pro and Bleeker follows her lead.

I give them the thumbs up, but as they place their cups back on the table, they have a weird look on their faces.

"Are you guys okay?" I ask.

Their copper complexion turns cherry red and their eyes bulge out of their sockets like near-sighted toads.

Bleeker leaps from his chair, turns, and runs head first into the wall. Moments later, Seepa does the same.

Their house shakes from the impact, and both Martians drop to the floor, knocked out cold.

This is not the reaction I expected. My heart pounds out of my chest. I kneel and shake them, but their arms and legs only twitch. At least this means they can't be dead.

Several minutes later they regain consciousness. I get off the floor and drop back onto my seat. "For Christ's sake, I thought I'd killed you."

I know they're going to go on and on about how horrible coffee is, how I tried to poison them, and how I will have to stay out of their kitchen.

Bleeker stares at me with a blank look. *Do you possess more?*

CHAPTER SEVENTEEN

White House: Washington, D.C.
Earth calendar: 2040-01-20
Martian calendar: 46-01-050

It took him a moment to realize someone was talking to him. "Dr. Farley, can I get you a coffee?"

It's one of the President's assistants.

"No, thank you," he says. "I'm fine with water."

The Roosevelt Room is warm this morning, and the cold water wets his dry mouth.

It's hard to believe this was once Theodore Roosevelt's West Wing office. The east wall is a half circle, with a centered fireplace and doors on either side. Cast bronze bas-relief plaques with profile portraits of Theodore Roosevelt and of Franklin Roosevelt hang on the south wall. The room is done in a buff color with white trim. It has no windows and is lit by a false skylight.

The seat opposite Farley, where the President always sits, remains empty. Senators Ted Harper and Sam Bush sit on the other end of the table. They look pissed. This makes him want to smile. He assumes they argued through the entire drive to the White House.

Farley picks up his smartphone and scrolls through emails to avoid having to make conversation. He doesn't care for this room. Windowless, it doesn't overlook the Rose Garden. He peers through the doorway, which is kitty-corner to one of the entrances to the Oval Office. Ed Bronstein, the President's Chief of Staff, walks through.

"Sorry to keep you folks waiting. The President will be here momentarily," says Bronstein, then turns around and marches out again.

Farley looks up from his phone and glances over to Senator Bush, who alternates between fidgeting with his tie and tapping his fingers on the table. The Senator finally looks over at him.

"Dr. Farley, I read your report on the colony disaster with great interest," says the Senator, an annoying smirk on his sweaty face. "Frankly, I found it to be a mighty big pile of manure. I'm from Texas, so I know manure when I smell it."

Farley doesn't respond and instead returns his attention to his phone.

President Harriet Bondar enters the room, followed by her Chief of Staff. She is the second female president ever elected but parts of the country still haven't accepted that women can be capable leaders. Senator Bush falls into that category.

"Sorry to keep you all waiting," says the President as she sits in her usual spot. "Let's get rolling. I read both reports and I'm just a little puzzled how the two bodies came to such different conclusions. Chuck, we'll start with the NASA Board of Inquiry."

"Thank you, Madame President," he says. "The evidence from satellite photos clearly indicates that the colony experienced a violent end, no doubt an explosion from within. We listed all the possible sources of an explosion to determine which were the most likely. The list is quite short. There was an oxygenator."

"Yes, I recall the discussion on the oxygenator," says the President.

"As you may recall, it requires high heat for the chemical reaction to take place," Farley continues. "The heat source is an electrical current. There is a small chance that the oxygenator shorted out and triggered a small outburst, which might have created a chain reaction leading to a major explosion. We believe that such an explosion would have done a lot of damage, but not destroyed the colony."

"I see you are also not convinced it was the nuclear reactor."

"We would have been getting readings. It was operating fine right up to the moment the colony blew up."

"Your report points to the kitchen as the source of the explosion," says the President as she leans across the table. "Why are you so sure?"

"The kitchen, which used energy from the nuclear reactor to generate a flame, may not have been shut down properly. This would have created a chain reaction," says Farley. "Although the equipment had several safety features to prevent something like this from happening, we believe the crew member responsible for the kitchen, Mr. Jenner, was negligent in handling the equipment."

At this point it looks like Senator Bush is ready to burst.

"I can't listen to this crap anymore," says Bush. "I'm telling you it was sabotage, but not by one of our American boys and girls. It was the Chinese. They took out our colony with a missile."

"Come on, Sam," says the President. "Your China shtick is getting old. I'm sure you don't even believe it yourself."

"I do, indeed," says Bush. "The Chinese are ruthless and envious of our Mars missions. But I've also received information that it could conceivably have been the North Koreans."

"Well, let's move on from the conspiracy theories," says the President, trying hard not to smirk. "Ted, do you want to quickly walk us through the rationale for your Commission's conclusions?"

"Thank you, Madame President," says Harper. "As Dr. Farley has indicated, the systems in the colony were safe and stable. There were no signals received that any equipment failed so, we can't rule out sabotage. But it's unlikely that it was caused by something as simple as forgetting to shut off the stove. It's deplorable that NASA is trying to blame one of the…"

Farley slams his hand down on table. "Just hang on there, Ted."

"Come on, Chuck," pleads the President. "Let him finish. You will get a chance to respond."

"Thank you, Madame President," says Harper. "The Commission believes the most likely source for the disaster was an external source. Most meteors that enter the Earth's atmosphere burn up. But Mars's atmosphere is thinner, so meteors are more likely to survive and hit the surface. We support the theory that a meteor made a direct hit on the colony."

"Chuck, why doesn't NASA consider this option as a possible cause?" asks the President.

Farley sips at his water. "It would have to have been a massive meteor, which our satellites would have picked up," he says. "The crater would have been much larger and deeper. This explosion would have occurred from within the colony to spread debris as far as it did."

"Well it's obvious no one has the answer," says the President as she leans back in her chair.

Farley bends down to pick up his briefcase from under the table. He pulls out a folder and opens it up. "There is one new development I need to share with everyone," he says in almost a whisper. Nothing like a little drama to get people's attention.

"Um, well…just this morning I was handed a new set of satellite photos that I ordered for this meeting. I had intended to use them to point out how the site might be deteriorating over time by weather, but. . ."

He passes out copies of the photos. The room goes silent.

"Chuck, what are we looking at?" asks the President.

"The first set doesn't show anything different than we've seen previously. But one of my people blew up the photos." He holds up a photo and points a finger to the top corner. "You will notice in photo eleven, in the left quadrant, there appears to be an SOS."

"Holy sweet Jesus," utters Bush.

"When was this done?" asks the President.

"We don't know for sure," says Farley. "But it wasn't there the first time we surveyed the site shortly after the colony was destroyed."

"What does it all mean?" she asks. "Does this mean we have a survivor?"

"As our report points out, we believed Jenner survived the explosion only to expire shortly after," he explains. "Based on these photos, he might still be around."

"Everything about this mission is a series of contradictions," says the President, pursing her lips and exhaling. "The American public needs some clear answers. Damn it, *I* need some answers."

"I wish I had those answers for you," he responds.

"Well, get them or I'll find someone who can," she snaps. "Twenty-four…or maybe twenty-three Americans died up there, and no one knows how. We can't conduct new missions until we have answers."

"Yes, Madame President."

"I want you to develop plans to send a team of forensic scientists to examine the site and find out what happened, including who sent us that SOS," says the President. "I need this to happen sooner rather than later. I'm up for re-election in just over a year. I don't need this 200-billion-dollar disaster hanging around my neck."

Farley's emotionless face hides his growing frustration. He knows Jenner had to have caused the accident and somehow managed to survive it. Jenner must have left that SOS. Deep down, Farley knows that fucking chef might still be alive. If they manage to bring him home, he would be happy to wring his neck.

CHAPTER EIGHTEEN

```
Mars
Earth calendar: 2040-02-09
Martian calendar: 46-02-069
```

I poke my head into the common room where Bleeker is reviewing medical files.

You need to circumvent battering your cranium, says Bleeker, looking up from his work. *You can develop a permanent impairment.*

"Yeah, I'll try to keep that in mind once I recover from the latest concussion," I say, rubbing my scalp. "Do you mind if I borrow your transporter again?"

That is acceptable, says Bleeker. *You have been excessively occupied over the preceding week. Do you have additional preparations for tonight's basketball match?"*

I pull out some notes from my pocket. "I plan to get together with the two referees and give a pep talk to the coaches."

I am still not persuaded that Arbiters have the intellect and the leadership qualities essential to instructing to a team.

"I know my views on this are not shared with Machers, but I think given a chance, the Arbiters I've chosen will be great. They are former star sling players who understand competition, sports psychology, and training methods. They picked up fast on the technical parts of the game."

This has been creating anxiety for me. I do not want to witness your league develop into a disastrous failure.

"Thanks for the vote of confidence."

I merely want to warn you of the potential perils that may transpire, says Bleeker. *Inviting Arbiters to attend the matches poses an even greater risk. Machers and Arbiters sitting adjacent to each other will generate complications. At the very least, situate the Arbiters in their own sector in the stands.*

"I don't like the idea of segregation. I'm sure nothing will happen."

I commend you on your confidence, but I remain skeptical.

"You're overthinking this," I say. "I'm off. I'll see you at Fraleco Hall."

As I head out the door, Todd shouts at me. "I don't understand your obsession with a game played by oversized Sasquatches stuffed into spandex shorts like sausages."

"You don't know everything, Todd," I say.

"I do know that you placed us both at risk by foolishly putting yourself in the spotlight," says the bot.

"Thanks for the tip, C-3PO."

* * * * *

The gym has undergone a remarkable transformation since the day I first walked into the facility. The place has been freshened up with upgraded lighting, and the noxious odors are gone. Odor-absorbing crystals have been placed in wall-mounted receptacles throughout the building. The new MBA logo painted onto center court gives the playing surface a professional look. None of this would be possible if Bleeker hadn't donated the funds.

I amble over to Shmeker and Kranker, the two coaches for tonight's game, who are standing in a corner of the court.

Hey Coaches, how's it going? I ask. *Are you ready for your big night?*

Kranker played professional sling for thirteen years and Shmeker for eleven. Both were forced to retire due to injuries. Kranker's left foot is turned around, which makes running impossible. When he walks, he sways backward and forward, in contrast to the typical Martian waddle of side-to-side. Poor Shmeker is hunched over, the result of a bent torso, which means he is always looking at his feet. He resembles a blue Quasimodo.

Hello Commissioner Dix, says Shmeker as he wobbles in my direction. *We have a query for you.*

We have been having a discussion, says Kranker. *We believe we should be dressed in basketball jerseys similar to the participants.*

Yes, says Shmeker. *After all, we will be on the bench alongside them.*

I pick up a rule book, which happens to be sitting on the officials' table. *League rules are quite specific with regards to dress code,* I say, stabbing the book with my finger. *Coaching staff are to be properly dressed in street attire. The court officials are going to be confused and think you are players. Let's keep it by the book.*

Kranker frowns. As for Shmeker, I can only see the top of his head.

Look, it's a tough transition from being a player to coaching, I say. *You are both trailblazers. Not just because you are the first basketball coaches on Mars, but because you are the first Arbiter coaches ever on Mars. You want to look as professional as possible.*

Thank you, Commissioner, for enabling us to have this opportunity, says Kranker. *We will not disappoint you.*

I know you won't, I say. *Have a great game tonight. And enjoy the moment. Remember, you're making history.*

I go behind the stand to where the dressing rooms are located, seeking out my refs. I only recruited two. It's a four-team league this season, and we haven't scheduled more than one game per day. I need these guys to hang in there for the season.

I find Boychik and Khaver in the referees' dressing room, sitting quietly on a bench and staring at the ground. They are also former sling players, but a bit less maimed the coaches.

Hello refs, I say. *Are we ready?*

Hello Commissioner Dix, says Khaver, looking up at me. *I am not confident we are suitably prepared. This is unfamiliar to us.*

We have been engaging in discussions and believe we would benefit from further preparation before officiating games, says Boychik.

Guys, we don't have more time, I say. *The season starts in a few hours.*

We have all the regulatory provisions confused, says Boychik. *Such as traveling and double dribbling. It is bewildering for us.*

I know, I say, *but you are both doing great. Do the best you can. It's not like the spectators will know the rules.*

The two refs look scared. I pull a flask out of my back pocket.

I have something to perk you two up and bolster your confidence, I say.

What is it? asks Khaver.

It's called espresso, I say, pulling out the stopper. *It's a unique creation I've come up with. I brought it along because I figured you guys might need a boost. Take a sip of this, but not too much, it has quite the kick.*

I know I'm taking a chance here, but these two look like a mess. Maybe a small sip will give them a boost. I pass the flask to Khaver who raises it to his lips and pours in a mouth full.

Hey, I said just a sip.

I reach for the flask, but Khaver has already passed it to Boychik.

They both stand up with that same weird look on their faces. Their blue skin tone turns dark purple and their eyes look about to burst.

One Martian turns to his right and runs around the room while the other turns to his left and takes off in the other direction. About half way, they meet and collide head first.

Oh man, Martians don't seem to be able to handle their caffeine.

* * * * *

Bending over, Bleeker examines the referees. Seepa and Plinka stand behind him. I pace the length of the dressing room. If I've killed them, I might be arrested and charged with homicide, or whatever it's called on Mars.

Are they alive? I ask.

I am confident there is no basis for concern, says Seepa.

Look at them, I say. *It looks like rigor mortis has set in, or whatever happens to Martian corpses. We need to hide these bodies somewhere.*

Compose yourself, says Bleeker. *Your basketball officials are, in fact, not deceased.*

What the hell is wrong them?

They are unconscious, says Bleeker. *They may awaken restored and alert in approximately one hour. Or recovery could also be prolonged for as much as twelve hours. It is not feasible to be precise with these circumstances.*

You're pulling my leg, I say, as I kneel to give the refs a shake. *You and Seepa woke up in minutes.*

It appears they consumed an excessive amount of espresso, says Bleeker. *How much did you provide to them?*

They just gulped it down before I could pour a shot into something, I say. *I need them conscious now. Can't you give them something to wake them up? You're a doctor!*

Regrettably, I have nothing that will bring them out of this state, says Bleeker. *You will have to be patient.*

What am I supposed to do about the game?

Can you not reschedule the match?

It's too late to reschedule. We have a full house out there, I say. *Okay, let me think.*

You can officiate the game, says Bleeker.

That's not possible. I need to supervise the game, deal with the security staff and . . . I step toward Bleeker, putting my hands on his shoulders. *You will have to ref the game.*

Me? That is nonsense, says Bleeker. *I have neither the knowledge nor the skill set to fill the role.*

I'm begging you, I say, close to tears. *I'm desperate. We are going to have a gym full of spectators and no officials for the game.*

I am not educated on the regulatory provisions, says Bleeker. *How could I officiate the match without some basic knowledge?*

I know what you're saying, I say. *But you have nothing to worry about. No one knows the rules. The game is new to the fans, the players, coaches, everyone. No one will be focused on you. Just go out there, look confident, and fake it.*

Truthfully? Do you think I can succeed?

I've been faking it my entire life.

Dix, you have a remarkable philosophy on life, says Bleeker. *Do all Earth-beings share it?*

Hell no, I say. *Now get ready. I've got to get out there and work the crowd.*

I rush out of the dressing room and into the corridor. If I didn't know better, I would guess that the building is near empty from the silence. It is something I'm still not accustomed to.

On the way to the court, I stop at the two dressing rooms assigned to the players and give the signal to head out. The players shuffle out in two rows. Their spindly arms and legs look odd in the generous jerseys and shorts. One Martian stops to greet me.

Greetings, Commissioner Dix, says Fresser. *What happened to our nutrition?*

I haven't forgotten, I say. *That's for after the game.*

Some of the participants will become hungry prior to the match.

After the game.

He nods and waddles out onto the court. I follow him and stroll to center court. The players are lined up on the two foul lines, ready to be introduced. The stands are a sea of red and blue faces, with barely an empty seat to be found. Neither Machers nor Arbiters dominate, suggesting that it is close to an even split. I raise my right arm and wave to the crowd.

I hold in my left hand a telepathy amplifier, which I've learned is how you can be "heard" in a large venue. *Friends, I'm*

Dix, Commissioner of the new Martian Basketball Association, I say. *I welcome you all to this historic event. You will be part of the first league game between the Brootus Celtics and the Niandus Knickerbockers. They, along with the Landos Lakers and the Celius Bulls, are the teams you will be able to follow in this inaugural season.*

Okay, I stole the team names. NBA licensing doesn't extend to Mars.

This league has been a dream of mine for many years, I continue. *And in a few moments, my dream will come true.*

Sure, it's a bit of a stretch, but I like the way it sounds.

I've recruited the players, the coaches and the officials, I say. *I created the rules, the uniforms, and the court.*

Well, maybe I've borrowed some of them.

I hope that you enjoy what you see, and decide to come out again, I say.

I stop to wave at the crowd one more time. They respond with some light cheering. This crowd is more subdued than sling fans. I hope that changes once the game starts.

Let me introduce the two starting lineups, I say. As I call out each player's name, they step forward.

The players look nervous and a little confused. But that is nothing compared to Bleeker. He stands at the sidelines trembling, as if he is about to bolt.

It's time for the opening tip off, and I signal Bleeker to come to center court. He doesn't move, so I rush over and grab him by the arm. He takes the ball and waits for the two centers to line up before tossing it in the air. Except that he throws it over his shoulder rather than straight up and the ball lands out of bounds. While he retrieves the ball, I get his attention and motion to throw it straight up.

The second time he is semi-successful. The two centers jump, swinging at the ball, which veers off to the left. The Knicks player slaps the opposing player in the side of the head. His foot catches the Knicks player in the stomach. They land on their butts with the ball rolling around on the floor. My neck muscles tighten. I have to remind myself this is not the NBA.

Bleeker doesn't call a stoppage, so Nebbish, who plays for the Celtics, picks up the ball and attempts to dribble with it. After a few steps, he trips over his own feet and the ball bounces into the hands of Klutz of the Knicks. As he dribbles the ball, Nebbish sticks out a leg and trips him. Bleeker stops the play and calls a foul. Unfortunately, he calls Klutz for travelling.

When Klutz gets back on his feet, he argues the call with Bleeker. Soon there is a scrum of players surrounding him. I try to get Bleeker's attention by shaking my head. He finally notices me and reverses his call, awarding Klutz a free throw, which he sinks into the basket. The Celtics take a 1-0 lead.

Halfway through the first quarter, it is still 1-0 because there has only been one shot taken, and that sailed over the net and backboard, off the backwall. Shlepper tries a layup shot, but another player cruises through the air like a missile and intercepts him. Bleeker calls a foul on the play, but he is confused and can't figure out who has been fouled. The players stand around waiting for the call, and Bleeker finally waives off the call, which sets off another argument. Shlepper trips over someone's feet and falls forward into Bleeker, who calls a foul on the bewildered player.

At the end of the quarter, it's still 1-0. The two coaches go over strategy with their team. Hopefully, they're going over some practiced plays that will lead to a few baskets. Off the opening tip, Nebbish grabs the ball, takes it down the court and scores a basket with a perfect jump shot. It's the first field goal in league play; however, he shoots the ball into his own basket, so it's 2-1 for the Knicks. At least someone finally makes a field goal.

On the next play, Fresser brings the ball up the court and passes it to Kvetch who finds Nebbish under the basket. Nebbish takes the pass and attempts a layup. To stop him, Shlemiel drives his shoulder into Nebbish's back as he releases the ball. The ball drops into the basket while Nebbish sails into the stands and lands headfirst in a seat.

This game definitely has a 'sling' feel to it. This is not what I had in mind.

However, Bleeker seems to have found his rhythm, because he immediately calls a foul. Nebbish makes the free throw, and it's a 4-2 game for the Celtics.

By half time, the Celtics lead 16-7. There is a bit of a tempo to the game, with the ball moving up and down the court without too many stoppages. One player leaves with an injury after falling during a scrum and getting stepped on, remaining on the bench with the impression of a foot on his hand.

During the halftime break, I join Bleeker in the referees' dressing room. He's having a drink of water from one of the bottles left in the room.

How is my performance thus far? asks Bleeker.

"You're looking good," I say. "Though I think you can assume when someone is knocked off their feet by an opponent that a foul can be called."

Thank you, says Bleeker. *I will consider that in the ensuing half of the match.*

I pick up a bottle of water and open it. "Don't you think it's been going great?" I ask. "The crowd has been terrific. I have a feeling this is going to be an overwhelming success."

Bleeker stands up and uses his hand to smooth out the wrinkles in his clothes. *Dix, we haven't even survived the first match. I would reserve such judgement until we have completed a few more matches.*

I spray him with water from my bottle. "Such a pessimist."

We should return to the court, says Bleeker, toweling off his head. He tosses the towel onto a bench and waddles out to the corridor.

For the second half, I join Seepa and Plinka, who are sitting several rows behind the Niandus bench.

This is all so bewildering, says Plinka, her eyes fluttering for my benefit. *How are the participants expected to get the sphere into such a small receptacle? It does not seem reasonable.*

If it was simple, I say, *it wouldn't be as exciting.*

I suppose, says Plinka. *But I feel distressed for the unfortunate participants who are unsuccessful at their sphere tossing.*

I reach over and tap Seepa on the shoulder. *How are you enjoying it so far?*

You know I am not enthusiastic about athletic endeavors, she says. *What about you? Do you have a favorite team?*

Hey, you know I'm a Knicks fan.

When the second half starts, it has a different feel. The Knicks come out swinging, literally. On the tip off, someone takes out the feet of the Celtics center, which allows a Knicks player to take possession of the ball and pass it to Klutz, who waits under the basket for an easy layup.

After the fifth or sixth tackle by a Knicks player and no reaction from Bleeker, I climb down from the stands. Before I get to the sideline, the Celtics players retaliate. Kvetch dribbles the ball down the court with two Celtics teammates acting as blockers. A Knicks player comes from behind, grabs Kvetch by the neck and pulls him down. The Knicks player grabs hold of the ball and tries to wrench it out of Kvetch's grasp. The ball comes loose, and the Knicks player uses it to repeatedly bang Kvetch over the head. I wave at Bleeker, trying to get his attention.

That's when all hell breaks loose.

Players wildly throw punches at each other. A Celtics player stomps on a teammate's head. Klutz has the ball and uses it to batter an opponent. Someone jumps Klutz and tries to pull the ball from his hands. His teammate dives in to assist and soon they are having a tug-of-war with Klutz, who's still holding the ball. Bleeker tries to separate the brawling mass of players, but is knocked over and buried by the tumbling bodies.

Seepa has now joined me on the sideline. *I do not want to see Bleeker injured by these blue ruffians,* she says, biting her lip. *This is why I despise these sporting endeavors.*

Don't worry, I assure her. *We have security staff.*

Six security personnel are now on the court, but it is difficult to tell if they are diffusing the situation or contributing to it. Bleeker crawls to the sideline on his hands and knees. Meanwhile, Shlemiel's head is being stomped on. His nose has been flattened, and he lies on his back with his arms and legs thrashing around in the air. After several minutes, the security staff drag each player to their respective bench.

I look over to the section next to ours, where two Arbiter fans are pummelling a Macher. A female Macher grabs an Arbiter by the neck and attempts to pull off his head. Two Arbiters grab for his legs and try to pull him free. I swear his neck stretches in the process. Martian anatomy does freaky things.

A Macher fan dives from an upper row into a section of Arbiters and takes down six of them. Soon the stands are a sea of thrashing blue and red bodies. I wave my arms in the direction of the security staff, hoping that they can calm the situation.

I grab one of the security staff and direct him to the stands.

I sigh heavily and put my head in my hands.

But when security appears, it's clear they have learned from the rumble on the court, because they immediately separate Macher and Arbiter fans by dragging them to different sections. It takes about a half hour to resume play.

The game ends with the Brootus Celtics squeaking out a 29-26 victory.

After the court clears and the stands begin to empty, I wander down to the dressing rooms to thank the players, but they are already distracted by the buffet. I know never to get between an Arbiter and his food. Watching them eat reminds me of vultures picking entrails apart. I can't stomach it, so I make my way back to the referees' room. Bleeker is there along with Seepa and Plinka.

Hey, that went well, I say. *Aside from a few dented heads.*

I thought basketball was a less violent sporting endeavor, say Bleeker with a scowl. *It is not dissimilar to sling.*

It isn't supposed to be like that, I say. *I guess that's what happens when you recruit sling players. I hope over time we can create a change in the culture.*

I found it to be a pleasurable and entertaining experience, says Plinka. *I would come again. Dix, how did you ever come up with the concept?*

I break out into a big grin. *I guess I have a vivid imagination . . .*

The two referees stagger into the room, holding their heads.

Sorry, we were overcome by a need for restoration mode, says Khaver. *But we are prepared for the match. How much additional time before tip off commences?*

News flash, guys, I say. *Your refereeing debut will have to wait.*

Oh, that is disappointing, says Boychik. *Dix, would you happen to be in possession of more of that exceptional espresso beverage you provided to us? It was most pleasurable.*

You guys are cut off. Especially on game day.

We are gathering our things to leave for home when the door bursts open. Cheyhto stomps in the room, followed by several of his miniature Martian cronies. All eyes follow him as he struts across the dressing room toward me. It's as if my dad just got home from work.

Congratulations on the launch of your new sporting enterprise, says Cheyhto with a sneer on his face. *However, you appear to have borrowed a quantity of sling participants with neither my consent or knowledge. A most discourteous deed.*

I throw my arms in the air. *Well, um…I consider it to be an open market for players,* I say. *Plenty to go around.*

I don't like the notion of someone disturbing the harmony I have established in my league, says Cheyhto, glaring. *Your basketball enterprise has produced some discontent within the participant establishment. Owners are not pleased. I am irritated.*

I need to diffuse this situation. I don't need this guy upset at me. *Perhaps we can work out something that satisfies both of us?*

Cheyhto steps forward until we are almost eyeball to eyeball. *There is something about you that does not seem right,* he says. *I understand you have a disorder but there is more here than an ailment. Where are you from, again?*

I am his cousin and physician, so I am well situated to authenticate his condition and origin, says Bleeker, trying to hide his knocking knees. *He is from Nilosyrtis.*

I know people in Nilosyrtis and no one recollects seeing a large Martian covered with a white membrane, says Cheyhto. *I am planning to conduct further inquiries regarding you. Something is not logical.*

With that, he and his entourage barrel out of the room.

CHAPTER NINETEEN

Mars
Earth calendar: 2040-03-30
Martian calendar: 46-02-118

I awake to a sensation of needles in my head. At first, I believe I'm dreaming about acupuncture, because Poof has curled up on my scalp.

I jump to my feet and the little pest leaps off and scurries behind my locker. I throw one of my space boots but miss.

I have no idea what time it is, but I must be late for my appointment with Bleeker and Seepa. I'm late for everything. They continue to insist on interviewing me for their study. I wish they'd put as much energy and thought into finding a way to get me back on Earth, but then again, without interplanetary transportation and communications, there's not much they can do.

The only way to make this session tolerable is to smoke weed first. I pull out a joint and light up.

I shave, wash up and try to make myself look presentable. I step outside to grab the transporter and bump into Plinka. She is wearing so many of those wild bracelets that I wonder how she can lift her arms.

Morning greetings to you, Dix, says Plinka.

Don't you look lovely today, I say.

You have an abundance of attraction, Dix, she replies. *Are you urgently going anywhere?*

What do you mean?

Do you have time to visit me at my dwelling?

She has a lustful look that is probably universal, if not interplanetary. *Sure, I would love to drop by.*

By the time I close her door behind me, she is already thrusting the ngono into my hands. Warmth spreads through my body and the red lights inside of it flash rapidly. My back hits the wall as she presses against me. I feel like one of those ancient pinball machines about to declare a TILT.

Plinka, you naughty girl.

Destroy me, my Nilosyrtis beast, she shouts.

You mesmerizing Elysium seductress, I shout back.

Let yourself go, Dix, she says again and again. *Let yourself go.*

My head spins, and the pressure builds. Then before I know it, we reach the release point and it's over. Talk about wham bam.

There is something about you that is different, says Plinka as she releases her grip on the ngono. *It is not merely your appearance. I feel there is something you are concealing from me.*

What are you talking about? I ask her, as a flush spreads across my cheeks.

Dix, I am aware you are blocking your thoughts, says Plinka. *I want you to know that whatever it is, you can trust me.*

I'm not blocking anything, I insist.

She stands in front of the door, saying nothing, still holding the ngono.

Look, I say, *I can't tell you.*

Tears form in her eyes. *Why not?*

I pace to the wall and back, my hands in my pockets. *If I tell you, you must promise not to tell anyone.*

I know Bleeker and Seepa will be pissed to know that I revealed my identity, but I know I can trust Plinka. I have few friends here and don't want to jeopardize this relationship.

I assure you, she says. *Your secret will be safe with me.*

I stop in front of her and take a deep breath. *I'm not from Nilosyrtis or anywhere on Mars.*

Plinka stares at me with her arms crossed in front of her. *I do not comprehend. What are you insinuating?*

I come from the planet Earth.

Her body goes rigid and her eyes narrow. *Is this one of your pranks?*

No.

The color drains from her face.

Now things appear to be logical, she says, as she plops onto a chair. Plinka studies me, trying to make sense of what I've told her. *Your identity will be protected.*

I don't like the idea that we have secrets from each other, I say.

Plinka stands up and walks toward me. A smile appears as she wraps her arms around my waist. *Maybe I will use this information to extract further visits from you,* she says, picking up the ngono and tracing her fingers along its outside edge. *I anticipate significantly more gratification from your secret.*

I can't tell if she is teasing me or not.

This is serious, I say, pointing my finger at her. *You need to keep quiet about this.*

She grabs my finger and pulls it down. *Dix, I have not seen you so distressed since your arrival on Mars,* says Plinka. *You have nothing to fear. I would never betray you.*

I pull away from her. *Thank you. I'm an alien here. Who knows what crap might happen to me if word gets out.*

Plinka grabs my hand and directs me to a seat. *I want to know about Earth. What is it like?*

I nod. *What would you like to know?*

Tell me about how you got here, she says.

I lean back in my chair, sitting on my hands. *Well, I came here in a spaceship with twenty-three other people. We built a colony on the surface and I was the chef.*

Your job was to prepare nutrition?

Yes, it was pretty boring. I was up before everyone else prepping for the day's meals. The first thing I would do was... Then it came rushing back. The last day of the colony. I was having problems starting the stove. I remember now that instead of powering down the heating element, I put it in the hold position.

Where are the other Earth-beings? she asked.

My eyes well up and tears trickle down my cheeks. *They died in an explosion... I was the only survivor then... Bleeker and... Seepa found me.*

Her mouth drops. *That is so tragic.*

I think it was my fault, I whisper. *I killed them.*

What are you referring to?

The colony explosion was my fault, I sob.

Are you certain? she asks. *How do you know?*

My head slumps down and I grip my knees. *Because I didn't power down the stove. It must have overheated and exploded,* I say, wiping my face with my sleeve.

And that would make it explode?

I think so, I say, sniffling. *I was warned so many times during training to power it down properly.*

You are not obliged to discuss this any further, she says. *You can tell me about Earth another time.*

Thank you, I say. *I just remembered I'm late for an appointment.*

* * * * *

When I arrive at Bleeker's office twenty minutes later, that bitch, Jazza, is outside the office glowering at me as usual.

I am not familiar with your bitch expression, say Jazza, *but I am sure it is not positive.*

I've given her another reason to hate me.

They are waiting for you inside, says Jazza.

As I rush into Bleeker's office, I forget to bend down. I'm probably one bang short of brain damage.

You are so tardy that we became alarmed, says Seepa.

"Sorry, I'm fine," I explain. "I ran into Plinka and lost track of time."

You have been expending significant time with Plinka, says Seepa, waving a hand in the air in a dismissive fashion.

"Not that much. I need to tell you something," I say. "I told her that I'm from Earth."

Bleeker bangs his fist on a table. *We told you to be careful with her*, he blurts out.

"Don't worry," I say. "She can be trusted."

I hope you are correct, says Seepa shaking her head.

Now that you are present, says Bleeker, *we would like to carry out a neurological scan.*

"Didn't you already do a scan?"

Affirmative, responds Bleeker. *This scan is dissimilar. I want to probe the content of your cranium and your central nervous system.*

"Huh? No one is poking around in my brain," I say.

There is no basis for distress, says Bleeker. *The probe is non-invasive. It will be analogous to any other scan, but the apparatus will trigger responses as a result of stimulus to the brain.*

I want to get this over with before the buzz from the weed wears off. "I'm already here," I say. "Let's do it, so I can leave."

Bleeker directs me to his examination table.

Please lay on your back, says Bleeker.

I reluctantly climb on the table. "Well, you haven't screwed me yet."

How does one screw? asks Bleeker.

"Never mind, it's just an expression."

Seepa drags a piece of equipment over to where I'm stretched out. It has a long, flexible tube that Bleeker grabs in his wrinkly hands. When he turns it on, it emits a thin, green ray of light.

Let me outline the procedure I shall execute, explains Bleeker. *I will project an image of your brain from a previous scan onto the wall. Then I will utilize my exploratory scope to probe each sector of your brain and document the response. Are you prepared to proceed?*

I stretch out on my back with my hands behind my head. "As ready as I'll ever be."

Do not move your cranium, says Bleeker as he points the end of the tube at the top of my scalp.

I feel nothing as an image of my brain appears on the wall next to where I lay. Out of the corner of my eye, I can make out a color image that could easily pass for a photo of my gray matter. Bleeker studies it for several minutes.

This is astounding, says Bleeker. *It is markedly dissimilar to anything I have ever observed.*

Bleeker positions the probe-thingy at my forehead. For no reason at all, I have this irresistible urge to cry. Tears are streaming down my face and I'm unable to stop. The two Martians watch me but say nothing.

Bleeker moves it slightly, and my left arm reaches straight up. It startles Seepa, who jumps back a step. He moves it again, which causes me to jolt up into a sitting position. I bang my head on the tube.

We need you to resume a prone position, says Bleeker as he pushes me back down onto the table.

Again, he moves the probe, this time to the back of my head. I lose my ability to see color.

"Hey, you guys are no longer red," I say. "What's going on?"

Unperturbed, Bleeker continues to stare at the image on the wall.

What color are we? he asks.

"Gray," I reply. "I don't see colors anymore."

Bleeker, what if you move the probe to this region? asks Seepa, pointing to a darker area of the image.

Bleeker swings the probe to the other side of my head. The room becomes frigid. My skin is cold and clammy, and I shiver.

What do you feel now? asks Bleeker.

"Darn cold," I say as I sit up and climb off the table. "Turn this thing off before you have me wetting my pants."

I think we should remove that organ and examine it more closely, suggests Bleeker.

I don't think we would ascertain much without it connected to the host, says Seepa, shaking her head. *And do you realistically believe you could appropriately reattach it?*

Are these two serious? They're talking about removing my head like it was a Lego piece. I'm about to throw up.

"Hold on Dr. Frankenstein," I say. "You people have enough material to write your dumb papers. I'm out of here."

* * * * *

I fall asleep on the ride to Nebbish's house. I dream about Tammy. She is running ahead of me, her flaming red hair trailing behind. A large crater opens and swallows her. I awake with a start. I have no idea how long the transporter has been hovering in front of Nebbish's front door.

His place is small with a pale green stone exterior that looks grimy compared to Bleeker's house. The stone doesn't have much shine to it.

I slowly climb out of the vehicle and let out a big yawn. As I approach the door, it flies open and Nebbish's head pops out.

Mid-day greetings, Dix, he calls out.

How's it going?

How is what going, Dix? asks Nebbish.

Just an expression, I say.

You asked me to come by?

Yes. I would like to speak to you regarding a matter of importance. Please come in.

I duck as I step into his doorway. The place looks drab and tired - the furniture, the floors, the decorating. This must be the equivalent of Martian trailer trash. I follow Nebbish into a small room to an even smaller table and chairs.

Please sit, Dix, says Nebbish.

He motions to one of his chairs. I delicately try to balance my butt on the teeny seat.

You have a lovely place, I say, forcing a smile.

Then I notice three more Arbiters in the corner of the room. Two are miniatures with bulging, black eyes.

Dix, this is my partner, Tzuris, and my offspring, Gornisht and Bupkes, says Nebbish as he waves them over.

Greetings, I say.

Mid-day greetings, Dix, says Tzuris. *I have heard many superior things concerning you. I apologize for our offspring.* The kids are hiding behind their mom. *They can be exceedingly timid.*

I bend over and pat the little Arbiters on the head. *You have a lovely family.*

We will depart to permit you to have a conversation, says Tzuris.

She leaves the room with the two alien rug rats close behind.

I turn back to Nebbish. *Now what's on your mind?*

Nebbish hesitates, looking down at his feet. *I regret to have to tell you, but I must withdraw from the basketball league,* he says.

You're kidding, I say. *You're one of the stars of the league. Why would you want to leave?*

It's not just me, says Nebbish. *All of the sling participants are being coerced into withdrawing. There have been threats.*

It's Cheyhto, isn't it? I ask. I feel my face turning red.

Nebbish stares at the floor. *He has informed all participants that those who do not cease association with basketball will be expelled from the sling league.*

What the hell, I say. *He is such a dink.*

I prefer basketball to sling, says Nebbish. *But I need to provide nourishment and shelter to my family. That is not achievable playing basketball alone.*

I can't believe this is happening, I say, my shoulders slumping. *I've worked so hard to get this going. We all have.*

Commissioner Dix, we would prefer to remain playing basketball, says Nebbish. *But no one will oppose Cheyhto. Citizens find themselves in his social re-education centers over the slightest provocation.*

I get up to leave. *Well, thank you for letting me know. I need to think things over.*

As I walk out the door, Nebbish calls out, *My regrets for disappointing you. You have been so supportive to Arbiters.*

Back in the transporter, I slam my fist on the side window. Cheyhto's nothing but a bully with a big ego. His exploitation of Arbiters is disgusting. Someone needs to speak up. I should give this ugly Martian a piece of my mind.

CHAPTER TWENTY

Mars
Earth calendar: 2040-04-01
Martian calendar: 46-02-120

I don't tell Bleeker and Seepa where I'm going. I've done some crazy things in my life, but this may top them all.

The transporter stops in front of the Assembly building that houses his office. The brilliant orange structure is one of the largest ones I've seen on Mars, with a team of Arbiters on scaffolds polishing the stone exterior. I jump out of the vehicle and join the stream of Martians entering through the front doors. Butterflies are taking over my inner rage. I need to do this before I lose my nerve.

As soon as I step into the building, a security detail of three guards, set up at a table just inside the front door, stands in my way.

One of the guards looks up at me, clearly unsurprised by my looks. *You are Dix, the misshapen being. What business do you have here?*

How does he know who I am? I take a deep breath. *I would like to see Cheyhto.*

A second guard stands up, frowning. *Is that so? What makes you think the Grand Leader would like to see you?*

I have a proposition for him, I say.

The three guards look at each other, perplexed. Then one waves his hand over the table top, which pops up to display a screen. His thoughts are blocked, so I'm not clear what is happening. My face is flushed, and I keep an eye on the front entrance in case I need to make a quick exit. He looks up at me.

Today is your lucky day. I am to escort you to the Grand Leader's office.

One of the guards gets up from behind the desk and motions for me to follow. He takes me down a corridor filled with still and video images of Cheyhto on monitors imbedded in the walls. I guess he likes to look at himself.

My instincts tell me I should turn around and bolt. Emptiness gnaws at my gut and my mouth feels like a big ball of cotton.

One of those Martian elevator devices takes us to the front of the Grand Leader's office on the top floor, where massive, orange double doors block our path. The guard steps on a mat and the doors slide open. He drops me off inside.

From there, one of Cheyhto's burley henchmen leads me into a meeting room. I look out the window. Elysium sparkles: miles of shiny stone roof tops, transporters zipping through the air, and Martians lumbering around on the roadways beneath me. I notice a Macher, loaded down with bags of food, stop to hand items out of the bags to Arbiter children playing on the roadway. It's not the first time I've seen such an act of kindness toward Arbiters. Funny, I used to see people in New York and think of them as animals. Maybe I just didn't look close enough to notice what they were about.

I sit down at a table with about a dozen chairs around it. The table is polished orange stone. In fact, everything in the office is orange. Everywhere there are Cheyhto images. Monitors on the walls show videos of Cheyhto in the Assembly, at sling matches, making speeches and attending various ceremonies. A life-sized statue stands in one corner, holding an ornamental sceptre. Above the door is the official coat of arms for the Martian government, an image of the planet with two moons revolving around it.

I'm about to get up and look around when the door flies open and Cheyhto shuffles in without his usual entourage. He plops down in an oversized chair at the head of the table. *I should detain you,* he says. *You must be guilty of something—larceny, sedition, fraud.*

I shift around in my seat. *I know you are unhappy with my basketball league.* The butterflies in my stomach are the size of pigeons. *My proposal is to offer you part ownership in the new league. A second sports league to add to your empire.*

Cheyhto leans back in his chair, his head cocked to one side. *Are you one of those Arbiter sympathizers that we sometimes come across?*

Um, no. I don't like where this is going.

Good, because I treat such sentiments as seditious, Cheyhto says, sneering.

Maybe it's not a good idea raising how Arbiters are being treated. I don't fancy returning to a social re-education center. *My interests are only in my sports league,* I say. I don't feel as brave as I did earlier, placing my hands in my lap so he doesn't notice they are shaking.

I have no interest in this basket thing you attempted to form. You only came here because your attempt to pilfer sling players has failed miserably.

I really think you should consider my proposal, I say. *We could come up with clever cross-promotional events to push both sling and basketball. There's a huge potential basketball market out there.*

Why would I want to collaborate with you? I become nauseous looking at you. Now, get your disgusting face out of my office.

Short, but not sweet. I get up to leave.

Once outside the meeting room, a Cheyhto underling escorts me to the front door. This was probably a stupid thing to do, hardly what I would call flying under the radar. All things considered, that could have gone worse. Like being escorted to a cell instead of the front door.

Back inside, a scowling Cheyhto points to one of his underlings. *Enlighten me about what has been uncovered regarding this being,* he demands.

Our surveillance has uncovered a few details, reports the Martian. *He continues to dwell with his cousin, Bleeker. We have observed that he has spent considerable time intervals with a neighbor, Plinka; we speculate that the relationship may be amorous. It also appears he is forming a commercial enterprise. The name on the license application is Bean Me Up Café. He will be marketing nourishment, but we do not know what type.*

A particularly unusual name, says Cheyhto as he leans back in his seat and scratches his chin. *But what would one expect from such a malformed being? If he is marketing nourishment, then he would be purchasing it from one of my enterprises.*

Yes, but there have been no acquisitions by Bean Me Up or Dix from any of your enterprises, says the underling.

I want surveillance intensified, says Cheyhto. *I want to be apprised of everything this being undertakes. I also want his establishment inspected the moment it commences operating. If there are any contraventions, have it shut down.*

* * * * *

You spoke to Cheyhto? says Nebbish, leading me into his common room.

I did, but he wouldn't listen to me. The basketball league is dead.

That was perilous.

I grab a chair, balancing my butt on the narrow seat. *I know.*

You don't want to be sent to one of his social re-education centers, says Nebbish. *You might never come out.*

I neglect to mention that I've already seen one.

What are you going to do without basketball? asks Nebbish.

I have other plans, just in case the basketball league didn't work out.

That was very prudent, says Nebbish. *What are your plans?*

To open a café.

What is a café?

A place to buy coffee.

Are you referring to your warm, black liquid? asks Nebbish, his eyes brighten up at the mention of coffee. *It is exceedingly popular with the basketball participants.*

Yeah, I say, stretching out my cramped legs. *I've been going through a lot of it lately.*

It is my judgment that you have a viable commodity if you are interested in retail.

I nod. *I've already applied for a license.*

Splendid. I am confident it will be a success, he declares, reaching over to give me a high five. *Can I ask how you acquire the beans that you convert into the coffee beverage?*

Well, um...I grow them.

They are a remarkable commodity, says Nebbish. *I am confident that many Martians would line up to purchase this liquid.*

I lean back on the chair, grasping my hands behind my head. *I've always wanted to run my own place.*

CHAPTER TWENTY-ONE

Johnson Space Center: Houston, TX
Earth calendar: 2040-04-03
Martian calendar: 46-02-122

"Dr. Farley, I need to set you up with an earbud and lapel microphone now," says the CNN production assistant.

"Yes, go ahead," he says. "What did you say your name was again?"

"Beverley," she says, clipping the microphone to his jacket. She hands him the earbud, and he puts it in his right ear.

"Video feed is up and running," announces the camera guy, sitting opposite Farley's desk. Farley can't stop staring at the guy's tattooed head, in particular, a snake that winds its way across his face. A voice comes through the ear bud asking him for a test.

"This is Charles Farley from my office in the Johnson Space Center," he says.

"Audio feed is working," says the camera guy.

"Dr. Farley, the interview will be similar to a telephone conversation," says Beverley. "Look straight at the camera. Imagine the camera lens is a small window through which you and Dennis Poile in New York can see each other."

"Two minutes until we go live," announces the camera guy.

Farley catches himself studying the man's tattoos again. He grabs a glass of water on his desk and takes a long sip. Beverley leans over the desk and dabs some makeup on his nose and forehead.

The camera guy counts down, "Five, four, three, two..." and points at the camera lens.

Through the ear bud, the voice of CNN news anchor Dennis Poile come through. "I'm joined from Houston by Dr. Charles Farley, Administrator at the National Aeronautics and Space Administration. Thank you for joining us, Dr. Farley."

"Thank you for having me, Dennis."

"Just yesterday, NASA announced plans to send another mission to Mars," says Poile. "Can you tell our viewers what's behind this new mission?"

He clears his throat and focuses on the camera lens. "Following the loss of NASA's Mars colony last fall, two inquiries were established to determine the cause. Neither report was able to come up with any firm conclusions. The President feels it's important to learn more about what went wrong on Valles Marineris in order for the American space program to move forward. As a result, she has directed NASA to send another mission to the Futurum site."

"Just like that?" asks Poile. "NASA has a rocket and astronauts available for a mission on such short notice?"

"A spare Hermes rocket is being prepared for the mission," he says. "As for the team, we're predominantly using former astronauts."

"When will this all happen, Dr. Farley?"

"We expect to touch down on the Mars surface during the first week of September."

"Doesn't it take years to prepare for a space mission?"

He smiles. The questions are so predictable. NASA communications staff like to refer to them as lob questions. "Astronaut training normally takes eighteen months, but we've been asked to shorten the time frame considerably. Training has been reduced to just eighteen weeks. But most of the team members have been on previous NASA missions and will be able to handle the accelerated time frame. Ellen Sanchez, the mission commander, has been in space on three previous occasions. The payload commander, Walter Chui, has been up twice now."

"I'm surprised by your timeline. What's the urgency?"

Staring at the camera is a distraction, but he resists the urge to look away and maintains his smile. "The families of the dead crew members and the American public want to know what happened to their loved ones. We owe it to them to provide answers sooner rather than later."

"Dr. Farley, I have to ask this question," says Poile. "With an election this fall, I sense this is building toward an October surprise. Care to comment?"

He hates these political questions, but he knows the President is watching. "I'm aware of the election timeframe," he says, pausing for effect. "NASA is eager to conclude its review. We have put all other missions on hold until we have answers. The election has no impact on our decision process. I won't be giving the okay for the crew to get strapped onto that rocket until I'm damn sure they are ready for this mission."

"Is it possible that you won't be able to make conclusions after your team examines the colony site?" asks Poile. "If so, what's next for NASA?"

"We hope that's not the case," Farley says. "All I can say is that at the end of this process, we will examine all the evidence we have and try to reach some conclusions. Then we will make whatever changes need to be made to prevent another tragedy like this one."

Farley wishes he could see interviewer's face. He assumes Poile didn't like that answer, but it's what the American public needs to hear.

"Since you may not find the answers you are looking for in that pile of rubble," says Poile, "how do you justify the cost of this mission?"

Farley takes a deep breath. The cost question always comes up.

"Every time we send rockets, drones, or people into space, we learn new things," he says, leaning forward into the camera. "Regardless of our conclusions, our team will return with information that will further our space program."

"This must be taking quite a toll on you personally," says Poile. "I have heard rumors for months now that you are to be fired. Any comments?"

Damn it. Farley has been hearing the same rumors and getting sick of them. More and more, he's becoming convinced that the entire project was sabotaged by that fucking chef. Maybe NASA should have screened the mission personnel better. Farley doesn't care about the job, but he cares about his legacy at NASA.

"I'm here to serve the President," he responds calmly. "When she no longer has confidence in me, I will happily step down."

"I just have one more question," says Poile. "Will this mission only be studying the disaster site? Or will there be a secondary goal, to search for possible survivors and bring them home?"

He struggles to remain expressionless, although he has the urge to roll his eyes. "As much as we would love to bring people home, there is no conceivable way that anyone can survive outside the colony for this period of time. We will attempt to recover any remains. If they exist, they would be relatively well-preserved."

"Thank you for you time, Dr. Farley," says Poile. "Good luck on your mission."

"My pleasure, Dennis."

CHAPTER TWENTY-TWO

Mars
Earth calendar: 2040-05-09
Martian calendar: 46-03-157

I step out the back of Bleeker and Seepa's house to check on the coffee plants. As I tramp between the dark, leafy rows, I marvel at how this cavernous underground world is so different from the surface. I'm convinced the quality of the beans would match those from Ethiopia or Columbia.

The plants remind me of Christmas trees, but with waxy, green leaves and clusters of red berries. I yank one of the riper berries off its stem and peel it open, pulling out the pit. Inside are two halves of a green coffee bean. I bring the bean to my nose and inhale, picking up a faint, sweet scent like jasmine. It's roasting that brings out the coffee.

I turn back to where my watering hose is stored. I remove the hose from its hanger and unravel it before turning on the water. To accommodate a café, I'll need to produce a lot of coffee. That's why I expanded the number of coffee plants from two to twenty-five.

I recruited Nebbish to help me look after the farm, which has gobbled up all available land at our property and Plinka's. She's now involved in this budding enterprise as an extension of our growing relationship. It's been nice that we have something in common.

Your coffee plants have grown higher than your stature, says a voice in my head.

I turn around and find Bleeker examining the berries.

"Oh, hello, Bleeker," I say. "Don't get any ideas about eating the raw beans."

I most certainly would not, says Bleeker. *I enjoy drinking the liquid form immensely.*

"I hope you aren't here to tell me about how concerned you are about my planned café," I say.

You are an exceedingly persistent Earth-being, Dix Jenner, declares Bleeker.

"That's because you refuse to appreciate how important this is to me," I say. "To run your own restaurant is what every chef dreams about. Maybe not on Mars, but life takes you on some strange journeys, man."

I accommodated your basketball enterprise, and it is fortuitous we are not residing in a social re-education center, responds Bleeker.

"Come on Bleeker, you're being dramatic."

You have gotten the attention of Cheyhto and have already been detained by government authorities, Bleeker reminds me. *These are very serious matters.*

"Everything has been straightened out," I say, handing Bleeker a hose to hold while I turn on the water. "Remember? I'm your cousin, Drageer."

I insist that you be less conspicuous, demands Bleeker. *You are putting our study in jeopardy.*

I take the hose from him. "Oh, that's what this is all about."

Yes, of course, replies Bleeker. *We have an agreement. I consider it to be a social contract. We provide you with shelter and even funding for your enterprises in exchange for the right to release our study. You should be more appreciative.*

"Go right ahead and publish your study," I say. "In the meantime, I've got a meeting to attend."

With that, I stomp out of the back yard to the front of the house. I know I'm indebted to Bleeker and Seepa for saving my life, but they can act so paranoid sometimes. I'm not even sure if they're worried about me or the study.

I plod down the roadway and locate a secluded spot between a couple of taller buildings. I pull a joint out of my pocket.

Ten minutes later, the tension in my body has drifted away.

I start back in the direction I came from, this time heading for Plinka's. When I arrive at her front door, I reach for the hummer. That's what I call it. It sure isn't a knocker. The door springs open and Plinka grabs my elbow.

Dix, you arrived so much in advance of our meeting, says Plinka. *Nebbish isn't here yet, but I am delighted to see you.*

"Yeah, I had an argument with Bleeker and needed to chill out," I explain.

You need to get cold?

"It's an expression," I say. "It means to relax."

I am fond of your many expressions, says Plinka. *It makes you appear so alien. Come in and sit. We can chill out together.*

"Yeah, great idea," I say as I follow her into her common room, avoiding her overhead hazards.

Dix, what is that odor that I detect?

"What odor? Oh wait, it must be the weed."

What is weed?"

"It's a plant that I smoke," I say as I pull out a joint from my pocket. "It helps me chill out."

Dix, I would like to chill out, too, says Plinka. *Demonstrate the process.*

"Okay, but just a little bit," I say.

I put the joint in my mouth to wet it with my saliva. Next, I pull out my lighter and get the end of the joint burning.

"Watch what I do," I say. "Hold it up to your mouth, inhale, and hold it in as long as you can."

I demonstrate by drawing in a lung full of vapors, exhaling after a good hold, and releasing a small cloud of smoke that dissipates within seconds. I pass the joint over to Plinka. She brings it to her mouth and takes in a big breath. About thirty seconds go by and she is still holding in the vapors.

"Okay, let it out now," I say.

She blows out a large cloud of smoke. *Am I meant to feel something?* she asks.

"You should feel a little euphoric," I say. "It may take a couple of minutes."

She puts the joint to her mouth and takes in another large toke and holds it. After she exhales, she repeats the process again.

"Plinka, I think you've had enough," I say.

But I am not experiencing anything, she says, frowning.

"Maybe this stuff has no affect on Martians," I suggest.

That is a regrettable. I was looking forward to chilling out with you, she says as she gets up from her seat. *I am going to bring some nutrition before Nebbish arrives.*

When she returns, she carries two platters loaded with food. She puts down bousou spread, prankas, tradsik, and other exotic Martian snacks.

I get a sudden case of the giggles. "Plinka, you brought enough food to feed all of Elysium," I say.

She looks down at the platters. *It is not that much nutrition.*

As soon as she sits down, Plinka reaches for the bousou spread, scoops some up with a finger, and slips it into her open mouth. Then she grabs a pranka from a platter and takes a bite from it.

I don't know why I am so ravenous today, says Plinka as she shoves the rest of the pranka in her mouth.

I pick up an unusual looking item that resembles a blue dumpling. After sniffing it and not detecting an offensive smell, I take a bite out of it. It's not that bad, just a little chewy. I eat the rest of it and reach over to pick up another one, but Plinka grabs it first.

"Slow down there," I suggest. "Leave some for someone else."

There is no reason to protest. There is sufficient nutrition.

"Not for long."

She breaks off a piece of tradsik with her hand. Food bits fall to the floor where the lappas are waiting to pounce on them.

They thrash about fighting over the scraps. I move my legs to avoid their spikes.

Dix, are you not going to consume any nutrition?

"I'm fine watching you suck up all that food."

Just a little more nutrition, she says. *Then I am sure I will feel improved.*

"I think you have a major case of the munchies."

What are you implying?

"It is well known on Earth that weed can increase your appetite," I explain.

I realize she isn't listening to me. Instead, she hurries into the kitchen for more food, the lappa scampering after her. The door hummer goes off and I get up to let Nebbish in.

Morning Greetings, Dix, says Nebbish.

Hey Nebbish, are you hungry? I ask.

I could consume some nutrition.

Well, you better grab some before it's all gone.

Plinka returns with the lappas still following her.

Greetings, Nebbish, says Plinka, returning the platter to the table and sitting down again. *I have produced some tradsik. There is a small quantity remaining.*

Plinka holds out a plate with a few small pieces on it. Nebbish reaches across the table to pick one up.

Careful, I warn. *Plinka may confuse your fingers for food and chew on them.*

I grab the platter of blue dumplings and pass it to Nebbish. He takes two and is about to put the platter down, when Plinka yanks it out of his hand.

I will just finish these, if no one else wants them, she says, as she shoves another one into her mouth.

"You're going to explode if you keep this up."

The lappas have lost patience and finally hop onto the table. A fight erupts over something that resembles a cantaloupe rind. Plinka leans forward and scoops it up, popping it into her mouth while the lappas sulk.

I am still exceedingly ravenous, she blurts out.

When does our meeting commence? asks Nebbish, still chewing on his tradsik.

I guess when Plinka runs out of food.

CHAPTER TWENTY-THREE

Mars
Earth calendar: 2040-07-04
Martian calendar: 46-04-211

I leap out of bed like it's my birthday.

"Aren't you the busy one today," says the bot, as I run past him through the door.

"I don't have time for you," I tell him. "It's opening day."

The bot follows me as I gather up my things and get ready to leave. "First it was the nonsense with the absurd sporting endeavor, involving those Martian cretins," says the bot. "Now you want to over-caffeinate them to the point that they will obliterate their own planet."

"Oh, God, another lecture," I say, rolling my eyes. "Why do you even bother?"

"You know I'm right," says the bot. "No good will come of this."

"Everything is fine," I say, searching for shoes.

"And you look ridiculous carousing with the Martian tart next door," says the bot.

"I'm getting tired of your act," I respond, dashing past him.

"I predict you'll be residing in a social re-education center in no time," he shouts. "I'll be left here alone to fend for myself."

Outside, Plinka waits for me behind her house. We get into her transporter and head to the café, which is off a main shopping area in the center of the city.

Dix, I am full of anticipation, says Plinka.

"I know what you mean," I say. "I've got butterflies in my stomach."

What type of nutrition are butterflies? she asks with a smirk. *Why have you not disclosed them to me previously?*

"You Martians take everything so literally. It just means I'm excited."

Then you should have just said that, she replies.

It is still early and there is little traffic around us. Today is American Independence Day. A year ago, I was in deep space on the flight to Mars. There was a small celebration onboard, and then Tammy and I snuck off while most of the crew were asleep. We looked at the stars. We talked about how much our lives would change over the next five years. Who could have imagined how much change would take place? So much time has passed since then.

Dix, what is Independence Day? asks Plinka.

"Are you peeking into my mind again?" I reply. "I hate that."

I was just being inquisitive.

"It's an important national holiday for my country on Earth," I explain. "Every Fourth of July, we celebrate the signing of the Declaration of Independence. We were a small struggling new nation back in 1776. Today, we are the most powerful country on Earth."

That sounds impressive, says Plinka.

We whiz across the city toward a busy commercial district. Below us, I spot two Arbiter kids playing with a basketball. Earlier in the week, I had seen something similar. At first, I thought I was imagining it. Despite shutting down the basketball league, the game seems to have caught on with Arbiters. I lean back in my seat and smile.

Plinka points out the Bean Me Up Café in the distance. *Look at that.*

A line has already formed. We aren't even open for two more hours.

Plinka breaks out laughing. *I think this enterprise is going to be a substantial success. I am looking forward to my new barista career.*

The transporter lands next to the café. A scrum of Martians forms in front of the vehicle.

"It's going to be a lot of fun," I say, as I reach over to the dashboard display to activate the transporter's door.

The café is a narrow, black stone building. Above the door is a three-foot-high sign with our logo – a stream of coffee beans pouring into a coffee cup. We work our way through the crowd to the front of the café and let ourselves in. My store manager, Nebbish, is already there. The place smells heavenly. We've been roasting beans for the past few days and the coffee scent hangs in the air.

Nebbish darts over to greet us wearing a huge grin. *Happy Opening Day!*

I hop onto a chair to get everyone's attention. *Alright folks, let's hustle and get everything set up. There's a huge crowd out there so we need to be ready.*

We have five staff working behind the counter this morning and they scurry about getting things set up. Two people are working the roaster, someone is grinding beans, and another staff member is stacking cups. I have made it a point to hire both Machers and Arbiters, but my plan is to always have an Arbiter as manager. It's not that I'm interested in reengineering Martian society. Well, maybe I am a little bit.

I peek out the door. The lineup continues to grow. There's some jostling and elbowing, but no punches thrown. We don't know quite what will happen when the first customers walk through and down their espresso, but I'm ready for anything. Staff are on hand for crowd control and security. When the time arrives, I nod to Nebbish who unlocks the door.

The first customer is an Arbiter. She approaches the counter where Plinka is stationed and uses our catch phrase: *Bean me up.* Plinka scans her payment chip, then prepares a shot of espresso and places it on the counter. The customer picks it up and drains it in seconds. As she puts down her cup, her eyes immediately protrude, and her face turns that familiar purplish color. The little Martian turns and runs head first into the wall. The store fixtures shake from the impact. She knocks herself out cold.

The next customer, a Macher, approaches Plinka and repeats the same line. He hesitates when handed his drink and looks around the café, then at his cup before throwing the contents down his throat. His face turns fiery red and his forehead slams against the counter. The caffeine-charged Martian turns to his right and takes off full speed into the wall. The impact causes fine dust particles to float around the store as he falls. I signal to two of my security staff.

I am surprised about how durable the Martians are. I can't see humans recovering from hard blows to the head.

You know what the drill is. We can't have unconscious customers piling up everywhere in the café.

Where would you like us to pile them up? asks one of the guards as he looks down at the prostrate patrons.

Pick them up and drop them anywhere outside until they regain consciousness?

Yes, boss.

He nudges his co-worker and they lift the first of the two customers and make their way to the door. There's another crash, and a blue Martian drops at my feet.

About an hour later, I step outside and discover a considerable number of Martians scattered around the entrance. A few have regained consciousness and have stumbled to their feet. The line that snakes down the roadway continues to grow. I'm about to return inside when I notice Bleeker and Seepa in line. I wave them over.

You guys don't need to stand in line for coffee, I say. *You can get all you want at home.*

We came here to support your coffee enterprise, replies Seepa. *But Bleeker is unenthusiastic.*

Seepa, I merely expressed the opinion that Dix would be preoccupied today, says Bleeker.

We weren't coming here to be entertained, but to wish him well, says Seepa.

Alright you two, I say. *You can debate this when you get home.*

We are astonished by the sizeable turnout you have attracted, says Bleeker.

I'm overwhelmed, I say, shaking my head in disbelief. *This is going to be a huge success. And you were so worried.*

There is one issue I have meant to discuss with you, says Bleeker.

What's that?

Seepa and I are preparing to publish our study on Earth-being anatomy and social structure, he says.

Yeah, great to hear, I say as I point to a prostrate customer in the corner for security to take care of. *Sorry, it's the first day and we're a little disorganized.*

Just thought you should know, says Bleeker.

The building shudders as another wired customer slams into a wall. Bleeker looks at the mound of customers laying in front of the café.

You are not concerned that incapacitated and battered clients will become an issue? asks Bleeker.

Before I can answer, a serious-looking Macher approaches us.

I request to meet with the proprietor of this enterprise, says the Martian.

I eyeball him. He is dressed in an official-looking outfit. I would guess he was either here in some formal capacity, or he's just a bureaucrat trying to jump the queue.

I'm the guy you are looking for, I say. *How can I help you?*

My name is Nudnik and I am a representative from the Sound Structures Sector of the government, and I'm here to examine the structure of your enterprise, he says, looking me straight in the eyes.

I don't understand, I say as beads of sweat form on my head. *I've done all the paperwork and have a license. No one mentioned an inspection.*

This is a special investigation requested by the Office of the Grand Leader, says Nudnik.

Cheyhto requested this investigation? asks Bleeker, the tendons standing out in his neck.

I have nothing to hide, I say, taking a deep breath. *Go right ahead and look around.*

Thank you for your cooperation, he says and heads for the front door.

Once Nudnik is inside, Bleeker pounces on me.

I warned you that this enterprise would generate too much attention, says Bleeker. *You need to be less conspicuous.*

Let him look around, I say with a shrug. *What is he going to find? We did this by the book.*

Bleeker, I concur with Dix, says Seepa. *We should wait for the official to conduct his examination and not overdramatize.*

Bleeker paces in front of the café. Several minutes later, Nebbish pokes his head out the door.

Dix, that Nudnik being would like to speak to you, says Nebbish.

I wander inside as security carries out another satisfied customer.

Is everything all right? I ask the inspector.

Regretfully, no, says Nudnik. *I have concerns about the soundness of this structure because of the stress put on by your customers colliding with the walls. I am concerned that the structure might collapse one day.*

You can't seriously believe a few Martians bouncing off the walls will bring the place down? I say.

That is precisely what I am communicating to you, says Nudnik. *You have three days to resolve the problem, or we will have to close this enterprise.*

CHAPTER TWENTY-FOUR

Mars
Earth calendar: 2040-07-05
Martian calendar: 46-04-212

Our first day of operation is an overwhelming success, minus the visit by Cheyhto's inspector. That is the priority for day two. First thing in the morning, the entire management team assembles in a tiny meeting room. There's a lot of energy in the room based on the conversations bouncing around. I get up on my feet at the head of the table and wave my arms over my head to get everyone's attention.

We had a great day yesterday, I say. *Thank you for your hard work and dedication.*

We've been open for over an hour this morning. Another crash causes me to fall back into my chair. Both the chair and I skid backwards and slam into the wall like one of our Martian customers. Dazed and embarrassed, I get up and move back to the front of the table.

Rubbing my head, I say, *I'm extremely excited to be involved in this ground-breaking enterprise. Before going over first day sales numbers, I want to discuss our public safety issue. The inspector from the Sound Structures Sector has informed us that the facility can't withstand the ongoing stress created by our caffeinated customers.*

There was another loud crash and the building shuddered.

Does anyone have any ideas? I ask.

I gaze around the room and there is no immediate reaction from the group. Nebbish is always the keenest, so I look directly at him, hoping he can suggest something.

Dix, you have acknowledged that caffeine causes the customers to crash into the building, says Nebbish.

Yes, that's my theory, I say.

Cannot the caffeine be separated from the espresso to make it harmless? asks Nebbish. *Customers would then be able to enjoy our coffee without causing any harm.*

I have no clue how to do it.

An eager Plinka pops out of her seat. *If we cannot modify the behavior of the customers,* she says, *I would like to suggest that we remove things off the shelves or at least move them back. That will prevent items falling off and striking a customer.*

That's a great suggestion, I say. *But I don't think this will satisfy the inspector.*

I look down the table. *Does anyone else have any ideas?*

A soft female voice drifts into my head from a staff member in the back of the room. She is one of our baristas.

Why not serve the espresso outside the café? she says. *That way, after drinking their espresso, customers can harmlessly run down the roadway.*

A brilliant idea, I say. *We could build a takeout window. I'll draw up some plans right away.*

After wrapping up the meeting, I send everyone back to work except for Nebbish. I step to the front of the café and point to a location on the wall beside the entrance, which shudders as another Martian hurtles into it.

I want an opening right here with a sliding window, I say. *The baristas can take orders from this location and pass them through the opening.*

Dix, that is very creative, Nebbish says. *I will begin installing it immediately, but it will take several days to complete.*

We don't have the luxury of several days, I say, shaking my head. *This must be in place for tomorrow morning.*

I have no experience with construction, says Nebbish, scratching his head. *It will take considerable time to determine how to properly build this.*

Okay, I say. *I have someone who should be able to get this job done today.*

Less than an hour later, I come back with Todd.

Nebbish, this is Todd, a construction bot, I say. *He will have no problem installing the window by the end of the day. Isn't that right, Todd?*

How do you do? And the name is Sementric 3, says the bot, eyeing the marked-up wall. *Let me see what you have here.*

Where does he come from? asks Nebbish, looking puzzled.

He's not a live being, I say. *I designed him.*

Oh really? says the bot. *What a load of nonsense. Rest assured, I will have this window installed in no time. I can't believe I'm getting involved in this absurd venture. It's fortunate you asked me now, because my battery will die in nineteen days, eighteen hours, and thirty-nine minutes. It's like a death sentence hanging over my head. I'm a mess from the stress.*

Just build the window, I say.

"To think, after all we've been through together . . . I hope you will be happy all alone on this wretched planet."

* * * * *

I'm back at the Bean Me Up Café first thing the next morning. It is just minutes before the regular opening and there is already a long lineup of Martians at the window. I turn to eyeball the lineup when I spot Nudnik, standing off to the side, waiting for the opening. He is the grimmest Martian I've ever encountered. I mosey over.

Good morning, Nudnik, I say.

Greetings, he mutters without even looking at me.

The take-out window opens as he speaks, and Plinka signals for the first customer to step forward. The first Martian in line scampers to the window and purchases an espresso. Less than one minute later, he gulps down the shot. The coffee rage strikes moments later as he bursts into a run and races down the road.

I look over to Nudnik, but he shows no expression. The next customer is already at the window. She is a tall Arbiter with unusually large feet. Plinka hands her a cup with a shot of espresso, from which she gingerly sips. As she drains the cup, she undergoes the same transformation and launches herself forward in an awkward sprint. Unlike the first customer, she runs in the opposite direction, directly into the side of the building. She bounces off the wall and drops.

The inspector from the Sound Structures Sector marches over to me, his face dour.

Your modifications appear to be deficient, says Nudnik. *It will be necessary to close your enterprise until you are able to demonstrate that you are complying with the Sound Structures conventions.*

Damn Cheyhto and his inspector. I need to come up with something fast before another of my business ventures is shut down.

Why don't you come inside so that we can sit down and discuss this? I say. *I'm sure we can work this out.*

There is nothing that you and I need to work out, says Nudnik, frowning. *I have completed my evaluation.*

Come inside, I insist. *You can have an espresso. Have you tried one yet?*

No, I have not, he says. *But an espresso will not change my report.*

That's fine, I say. *But at least hear what I have to say.*

I'm relieved when the bureaucratic curmudgeon follows me inside. All the tables are empty, so we sit down at the one closest to the coffee roaster. Nudnik lifts his nose into the air and inhales.

What is that peculiar odor?

That is the smell of freshly roasted coffee beans, I say. *We make the espresso drink from the beans. You should try some.*

It does smell appealing, he says. *Let me try this beverage. One cannot cause any harm.*

Marvellous, I say, holding up two fingers for Nebbish. He prepares two shots of espresso and sets them down on the table. There's a small shudder as another customer crashes into the exterior wall. Some of the coffee spills over the sides.

You can sip it slowly or drink it all at once, I say while raising my cup to my mouth. *I recommend all at once.*

I drain my cup and slam it down on the table. Nudnik hesitates for a moment and then does the same thing. I sit back and wait.

By the time he gets up out of his chair, his entire face is bright red. He takes two steps and then charges forward until he crashes into the wall, spinning off and collapsing as usual.

Nebbish waddles over and looks down at the unconscious Martian.

Dix, did you intend on achieving this outcome? asks Nebbish.

I did, I said, smiling. *Can you get a hold of Bleeker? We need to properly look after our guest from Sound Structures.*

When Bleeker arrives, Nudnik is still lying motionless on the floor. Bleeker kneels to examine the inspector while I look over his shoulder.

How much longer until he recovers? I ask.

I do not believe he will be in this condition for too much longer, says Bleeker as he looks up at us. *I detect signs that he will regain awareness momentarily.*

Excellent, I say.

Dix, I do not comprehend why you would deliberately create a situation where he would lose consciousness, says Bleeker.

You'll see soon enough.

While it's siesta time for my comatose guest, I arrange for some adjustments to our take-out window. I have staff set up rope barriers, so that customers will file away from the building after picking up their drink.

When Nudnik stirs, Bleeker taps him several times in the head.

Nudnik, can you hear me? asks Bleeker.

Nudnik slowly rolls to one side and, with some effort, sits up. I wave my hand in front of his face.

You need to take it easy drinking this stuff, I say.

As he gets to his feet, I can barely make out his response. *Need to consume more espresso,* he mumbles.

I think you've had enough for today, I say, as I help him to the door. *Come back tomorrow.*

Nebbish, who has been watching from behind the counter hurries over.

Are you not troubled that Nudnik will file an order to close the café? he asks.

And lose his only source of espresso? Nah.

CHAPTER TWENTY-FIVE

White House: Washington, D.C.
Earth calendar: 2040-07-22
Martian calendar: 46-04-229

Farley arrives in a town car at the White House approximately an hour before the official launch of the Mars mission. He's dropped off at the intersection of 17th Street and Pennsylvania Avenue, the closest the robot-driven car can get to the White House. From there, he hikes down Pennsylvania Avenue, past the Eisenhower Executive Office Building to the Northwest Gate of the White House. The Executive Mansion lawn is a lush green, despite the drought-like conditions. Farley loosens his tie to reduce the amount of sweat building up under his collar.

After standing in line at the gate to be screened, he finally reaches the front of the line where he's greeted by a guard in the booth. "Your name, sir?" he asks.

"Charles Farley."

He peers down at a computer monitor sitting on the desk in front of him. "Dr. Farley, I need to see your government ID."

"Certainly." Farley hands him his card.

After he examines the card, the guard hands it back. "Please empty your pockets and walk through the metal detector."

Once he gets past the Secret Service, he heads up the walkway toward the West Wing entrance and shows his identification again, until he's finally allowed inside the building. Inside the West Wing Lobby, the receptionist points to the elevator, which takes him to the ground level, where the Situation Room is located. When the elevator doors open, he encounters more security, who confiscate his phone and computer.

He finally enters the Situation Room. There are computer terminals in front of each seat and six television monitors throughout the room.

Farley is uncomfortable watching the launch under the gaze of the President. It's not a good time to be questioned by nervous politicians, but you don't turn down an invitation from the President.

This launch has him more nervous than usual.

Ed Bronstein, the President's Chief of Staff, gets up to shake his hand. He strolls around the room to say hello and introduce himself to the spattering of officials sitting around the table. The television monitors display a network feed of the Mars launch. No one pays attention. Another reason why he wishes this was Houston.

When the countdown to liftoff reaches thirty minutes, President Bondar appears and sits at the head of the table.

"Good morning, everyone," says the President.

"Dr. Farley, it's good of you to join us for the launch. Are we still running on schedule?"

"So far," replies Farley. "The crew are strapped in and going through their prelaunch routine. I want to call the Mission Operations Manager for an update."

"Let me get the White House switchboard to patch him in," says Bronstein, pressing a button in the console in front of him.

"White House operator," says a voice over the sound system.

"I'm calling from the Situation Room. Can you connect us to Mission Control in Houston?"

The room goes quiet. A minute later a burst of crackling noise comes through the speakers.

"John Fleck, here," says a voice.

There are microphones built into the table in front of each seat. The one directly in front of Farley glows red. "Hi, John, it's Chuck. I'm at the White House now. Are we still on schedule?"

"Hi Chuck," says Fleck. "There's going to be a small delay. A series of warning lights went off when we ran the launch system through some tests. We are reviewing the cause right now."

"A malfunction?" asks Farley.

"Yeah, one of the thrusters isn't responding," says Fleck. "We are looking into replacing it. But our window of favorable weather is small today."

"Oh, dear," says the President. "Does this mean the launch might be canceled?"

"Hello, Madame President," says Fleck. "We hope to quickly fix the problem, so we can go ahead with the launch. Keep your fingers crossed."

"John, call me with an update once you know what's going on," says Farley.

"Will do," says Fleck as he disconnects the call.

"There's a lot of media covering the launch," says Bronstein. "We don't need any more bad press."

"I want to remind you that launch delays are a common occurrence," says Farley. "Very often it is due to weather conditions, but mechanical issues also happen."

This is exactly why he didn't want to come here. Now he has to face these nervous stares. While the President obsessively scrolls through emails on her phone, Bronstein dashes in and out of the room like a hyperactive kid. Farley has no phone, as it was confiscated by the security staff, so he kills time, watching the launch coverage on the television monitors.

If the launch gets scrubbed, these people will not be happy. Forty agonizing minutes later, the phone system chirps, and Bronstein presses a button on a console.

"This is the White House operator. I have the Johnson Space Center looking for Charles Farley," says the operator.

"Put them through," says Bronstein as he nods to Farley.

"Farley, here. What's the latest on the launch system?"

"The problem has been cleared up," says Fleck. "Everything is a go. We're about to recommence the countdown."

The President reveals a faint smile. "Tell them at Mission Control that the White House is behind them for this mission," she says.

"Thank you, Madame President," says Fleck.

"Bye, John," says Farley. "We'll talk later."

Bronstein disconnects the call and the room turns to the television monitors, which displays the countdown. Occasionally, someone gets up for more coffee. At T-minus thirty seconds, the room goes silent, every set of eyes fixated on the monitors, as the countdown is transferred from Mission Control to the spaceship computers. A voice on the television audio feed from Houston announces the mission is a 'go'.

At T-minus zero seconds, the solid rocket boosters ignite, and the bolts that have secured the shuttle to the ground release, allowing the spacecraft to hurtle into the sky. As the rocket lifts off the launch pad, Ed Bronstein remarks, "There goes six billion dollars."

CHAPTER TWENTY-SIX

Mars
Earth calendar: 2040-07-25
Martian calendar: 46-04-232

I empty bags of green coffee beans into a large container. I plan to take the beans to the store for roasting. As I seal the container, Todd stumbles into the room. His gait is awkward and jerky.

"I've come to say farewell," says the bot.

I lift the container and carry it toward the back of the house. "Are you going somewhere?"

"Good heavens, aren't you self-absorbed," says the bot.

"You are in full snark-mode today," I remark, putting down the container. "What's up? I have a busy day."

"Well I don't . . . want to be . . . taking up . . . too much of your . . . valuable time," says the bot. "I justtt . . . have . . . threeee minutes . . . annnd . . . sixteen seconnnds . . . of batterrry . . . life lefffft."

"Crap," I say. "I've forgotten all about your battery."

"Ovvv . . . courrrrse . . . youuuu . . . havvvvve," says the bot. "Iyyyy . . . neeed . . . toooo . . . warrrnn . . . youuuu . . . thaaaat . . . youuuu . . . arrrrrre . . . flirrrrting . . . withhh . . . dannngerrr... byyyy . . . angggerrringg . . . Cheyyytttho. Ggggivvve . . . upppp . . . . theee . . . caaaaffffffe . . . beeefffforrrre . . ."

The bot freezes mid-sentence, his eyes flutter and shut, and his arms drop to his side. The sudden silence is nice. Maybe too nice. Damn, I'm really going to miss him.

* * * * *

I'm loading another pound of green beans into the roaster when someone taps me on my shoulder.

You are late for the meeting that you scheduled, says Nebbish.

I instinctively look down at my Mars watch. Everyone in Futurum was assigned a watch that operated on Mars time – where a day is thirty-seven minutes longer than on Earth.

So I am.

You seem pensive, says Nebbish. *Is something distressing you?*

No. I mean, yes, I say. *Sorry, sort of lost a friend. I'll be right there.*

That is regrettable, says Nebbish.

I start the roaster and follow Nebbish to the back of the café. Everyone is there waiting. I take my place at the front of the table.

Good morning everyone, I say. *I just want to give all of you an update. Today marks three weeks since we've opened, and the café has exceeded my expectations. Sales have increased each week. We do no promotions and rely on word of mouth, but everything is going great. We had that issue with the people from the Sound Structures Sector, but that's resolved now.*

Are you not concerned that the inspector will return and fabricate another issue as justification to close the café? asks someone from the middle of the table.

That inspector is here first thing every morning, I say. *He orders a double shot and then scoots down the road.*

Nebbish raises his hand. I give him a nod.

Dix, with superior-than-anticipated retail transactions, will we have sufficient coffee to meet demand? asks Nebbish.

I've been stockpiling beans and expanding plant production, I reply. *I don't think we have anything to worry about.*

The on-duty barista pops his head in the room.

Dix, you must appear out here, says the barista. *We have a situation.*

I'll be right back, I say to the room full of Martians.

I march out of the room and run into three familiar Arbiters in uniforms.

Not you guys again, I say. *What is it now?*

You are to come with us for questioning, says the largest goon with a menacing grin.

What about? I ask. *I have a business to run here. Why don't you guys make an appointment with my secretary.*

He pulls out that device that looks like a TV remote and points it at me. A stream of light hits me, and my arms drop to my sides, immobilized. The café staff and customers go about their business as if this is normal.

When they drag me out to their transporter and shove me into it, my head bangs against the doorframe.

Careful, fellas, I say. *My brain is one of my favorite organs.*

My escorts say nothing; they're as charming as the vehicle we're traveling in. I sit in silence as we travel the now-familiar route, pondering what triggered this particular arrest. I've got all this stuff to do in the café and instead, I have to deal with some Martian bureaucracy.

We eventually arrive at a familiar, black building. I know the drill. As I'm pulled out of the vehicle, I duck to avoid hitting my head. But I mistime it. I mistime it again going in the front door, then going up the stairs, and then being shoved into a room with other detainees. By this time, my head throbs and stars sparkle before my eyes. As the flashing lights die out, I realize there are fourteen big, black, Martian bug eyes staring at me.

Hey fellas, I say. *It's great to be back.*

One Martian waddles in my direction. I recognize him by the gruesome scar on his forehead.

You are the being with the repulsive membrane from Nilosyrtis, he says.

Yup, Dix. I say. *Hey, Scarface. How's the wife and kids?*

I am Ganef, he says, then points to the other Arbiters in the room and introduces them. *That is Ligner, Dreykop, Yold, Kapore, Prostak and Khitrak.*

These dull-witted Martians make me feel like I've stepped onto the set of an intergalactic zombie movie.

Nice to meet you all, I say. *So why are you here? Stealing transporters? Counterfeiting sling tickets?*

I bit off two of my boss' digits, says Ganef, sneering.

Um, I bet they were yummy, I say. *I hope you aren't insulted if we don't shake hands.*

The room breaks out into laughter.

The Martians return to their normal activities, throwing insults and an occasional punch. They seem mostly bored. I really can't blame them. There's nothing to do here. I sit down on a cot and put my head in my hands.

Hey, Ganef, I call out. *Do you guys do anything besides sitting around?*

We receive nutrition and some exercise, he responds. *We also have much time for restoration mode.*

Doesn't sound like much social re-education takes place here, I say. *Maybe I can come up with some ideas.*

That would be good, says Ganef, flopping onto his bed.

I'm not sure how much time passes, when several custodians at this lovely facility bring in some food. They place it on a small table in the center of the room and step back. I look away from the carnage. Within minutes, there is nothing left of food but the occasional belch.

I drift off to sleep only to be awakened by a fist pounding on my chest. I open my eyes and find two Martian gendarmes standing over me.

I sit up and yawn. *What seems to be the problem, fellas? Were my dreams disturbing the others?*

The chest pounder responds, *Arise and follow us.*

I push myself off the cot and march in step with the guards to my interview.

Five minutes later, Cheyhto plops down in the chair on the other side of his orange table and faces me, flanked by three henchmen. It's like having dinner with a mobster.

Cheyhto glares at me for a moment and then leans forward.

I am grateful that you agreed to have this encounter with me today, says Cheyhto.

Next time make an appointment. I tell him.

I have several queries regarding your new enterprise, says Cheyhto. *What is coffee?*

It's a caffeinated, hot beverage. Why don't you drop by and try some?

I am intrigued. How is this coffee beverage created? asks Cheyhto. *I distribute most nutrition on the planet and your enterprise has not purchased any nutrition from me.*

I bite my lip. Where is this going? *The . . . eh . . . coffee is made from coffee beans,* I explain. *I grow the beans myself. Then they are roasted and ground into fine pieces.*

But from where do these coffee beans originate? asks Cheyhto, pointing a big fat index finger at me. *I've never heard of such a bean, nor has any other being.*

I wipe my sweaty palms on my lap. *Cheyhto, you know very well I can't tell you,* I say, giving him my best innocent look. *It's a trade secret.*

That doesn't go over well. Cheyhto's nostrils flare.

You are an abomination and distrustful, says Cheyhto. *Your story about originating from Nilosyrtis is dubious. Your appearance is grotesque. Now you are peddling a beverage produced from a bean of secret origin. Perhaps you can persuade Arbiters of your bizarre narratives, but I am not accepting them.*

Wait, what parts aren't believable?

I have also become aware that your enterprise is being managed by an Arbiter, says Cheyhto, glowering. *Are you some form of subversive?*

No, just an equal opportunity employer.

Cheyhto gets out of his seat and waves his arms at his underlings.

I have had enough of this being's nonsense. Escort him back to the lockup unit until his narrative is adequately altered.

Two of the Martian goons pull me out of my seat and escort me back to my roommates down the hall.

Make yourself comfortable, says Ganef.

CHAPTER TWENTY-SEVEN

```
Mars
Earth calendar: 2040-07-28
Martian calendar: 46-04-235
```

I had this impression that the Martian social re-education centers were brainwashing facilities where they strapped you to chairs or injected you with drugs, like in *A Clockwork Orange*. As it turns out, this is an ordinary prison whose main mode of punishment is boredom.

Therefore, I've no choice but to organize a euchre tournament.

It's simple to produce several decks of cards. A little more frustrating is trying to teach euchre to Martians. Prostak enjoys waving his cards in the air, showing the others what a great hand he has.

I spend day one going over the fundamentals. On day two, the tournament begins. There are eight of us in the cell and everyone plays. I split us into four pairs and develop a schedule.

My partner is Yold. He is slow picking up the game. He can't ever remember the card ranking, so he carved the order into his arm. A little extreme, but it seems to be working.

Yold deals the cards. Our opponents are Ganef and Khitrak. I put my hand on top of the hand that is holding the deck.

Yold, you're dealing in the wrong direction again, I remind him.

Sorry, Dix.

He collects the cards back up and re-deals them. After each of us have five cards, he places the remaining four cards face down in front of him, forming the kitty. He flips over the top card to reveal the ace of spades. I pick up my cards and study them. No spades in my hand.

Pass, declares Khitrak.

Pass, I say.

Pick it up, says Ganef.

Yold waves his hands to get my attention, *"But I wanted to—"*

Shh. We'll get our turn, I say.

I'm going loner hand. Is that how you say it, Dix? asks Ganef.

What the...yeah that's right, I say.

Khitrak puts his cards on the table face down and looks around the room.

When do they bring in some nutrition? asks Khitrak.

Khitrak, we are playing cards here, says Yold, his fingers tapping.

I lead with the ace of diamonds, which Ganef trumps with the jack of clubs.

Oh, crap. I slump back in my chair.

Ganef goes on to win all five tricks. He smirks as he plays the last one.

That is four points for this hand, which means we claim victory in the game, says Ganef.

Yold bolts out of his chair and turns over the table.

You cheated, shouts Yold. *Hearts was supposed to be trump.*

A chair flies to the table next to ours and slams into the back of Ligner's head. He gets up and punches Yold in the face, who stumbles back and knocks over Kapore. I watch this chain reaction impassively. These social re-education centers are so effective at eliminating anti-social behavior.

I'm on my hands and knees collecting the cards when the door clangs open. My two escorts are back. I get up.

Welcome, I say. *Let me guess. You want to enter the euchre tournament?*

They look at each other and one of them grabs my arm.

You must come with us.

Sure. I know the drill, I say.

Back in the orange room, I wonder if spending time with Cheyhto has been engineered to be torture. Moments later my host saunters in with Bleeker.

Bleeker grabs a chair next to mine and Cheyhto sits down opposite us. He leans forward, his chubby arms resting on the table.

You have been uncooperative with us. Fortunately, your cousin Bleeker has been most accommodating, says Cheyhto.

What have you told them? I ask, glancing over to Bleeker.

I know that you and your cousin went to the surface, says Cheyhto. *That you found beans left by aliens.*

I kick the table, causing the others to jump. *Oh man, why did you tell him?*

Dix, be reasonable, says Bleeker. *Do you want to stay here indefinitely?*

The startled guards finger the restraint devices clipped to their waists. I fall back into my chair.

You should be more appreciative, says Cheyhto. *Bleeker has paid a substantial levy on your behalf. You should be mindful that salvaged articles left by aliens are the property of the government. Technically, your beans belong to me.*

Dude, can he really do this? I ask.

Bleeker only nods.

They're my beans, I say, waving my hand dismissively. *I found them, grew them myself, roasted and ground them. Besides, possession is nine-tenths of the law.*

I do not know what law you speak of. I am the law here, says Cheyhto, his expression tightening.

I straighten up with a determined look, my hands folded in front of me.

You strong-armed me out of my basketball league. But it's not going to happen again, Grand Leader, I say, dripping with sarcasm as I recite his name. *You own the beans. That's fine. Do you know how to grow coffee plants? Or when to pick the beans?*

How about roasting? Do you own a coffee roaster? You may own the beans, but they are useless to you.

I wait for the Martian ogre to explode. Instead, a smile appears.

You are an astute being, says Cheyhto. *I see that we require each other. I will allow you thirty percent of the proceeds for your collaboration.*

Bleeker's jaw drops and his body stiffens.

Thirty percent doesn't buy you very much cooperation, I say.

For a being sitting in a social re-education center, you are very self-assured, says Cheyhto. *We can apportion the proceeds in half. Each of us will take fifty percent.*

Just as I thought, he has no real bargaining power. He's all bluster. I look him directly in the eyes.

This is what would be acceptable to me, I tell him. *You will take thirty percent. In exchange for your share, you will be a silent partner. And you will ensure that any new cafés that we open don't run into any regulatory tangles. Also, I decide who manages the cafés. Do we have a deal?*

You are an impudent being, declares Cheyhto, jumping to his feet. He turns to his subordinates. *Take him and his cousin back to the lockup.*

Okay, boys, I say. *I have a euchre tournament to get back to.*

Dix, accept the proposal, pleads Bleeker. *Do not act so reckless.*

Cheyhto steps from behind his desk and approaches. *Wait,* he says, as the guards are about to drag me out of the room. *You are a crafty being, Dix. It is true that I do not possess the knowledge to operate a coffee enterprise. I could have my security staff extract the information from you using force. But you will be more valuable to me if you are cooperative. You have yourself an agreement.*

CHAPTER TWENTY-EIGHT

```
Mars
Earth calendar: 2040-08-29
Martian calendar: 46-05-266
```

Sanchez studies the monitor in front of her. She looks over to her second-in-command, Walter Chui, who gives her a thumbs-up.

"Houston, T-minus ninety seconds until touch-down," Sanchez says into her headset. "The parachutes and retrorockets have slowed us to eighteen kilometers per hour. We're on target. Over."

"Roger, Commander," a crackling voice responds. "Looks good from our end. Over."

"T-minus sixty seconds . . . speed down to fifteen kilometers per hour. We have disengaged the parachutes. Over."

"This is Houston," says Mission Control. "Remember, you still need to get down to below seven if you plan on reusing Archimedes. Over."

"T-minus twenty seconds . . . speed is now ten kilometers per hour . . . nine . . . eight . . . seven . . . six," says Sanchez, her face flushed and palms sweaty.

There is a loud thud and the spaceship rocks back and forth.

"Houston, Archimedes has touched down," says Sanchez as she finally exhales. "We are sitting pretty in Valles Marineris. Over."

"Commander, they're applauding in Mission Control," is the response from Houston. "Great job. Over."

She leans over and gives Chui a high five.

About twenty minutes later, the crew is assembled outside the spaceship.

"This is our home base for the next week," says Sanchez. She points to the left. "About 800 meters at nine o'clock is the colony site, and about 400 meters at eleven o'clock is where Galileo is situated. Unfortunately, NASA didn't have enough time to send over some rovers, so we will be hiking to the colony site and back. We know about five hundred meters at four o'clock, there is a rover parked that survived the explosion. Walter, take Sean with you and see if it's functional. We could use it."

Chui gives her the okay sign with his right hand.

"Everyone else follow me," says Sanchez.

The remaining six crew members hike across the Martian surface toward the Futurum site. Sanchez tries to walk at a brisk pace, but the Martian gravity is harder to get used to than she had expected. She feels like she's walking in water.

About one hundred and fifty yards from the colony, Chui shows up driving the rover. Sanchez climbs in as it pulls up beside her.

"I see the rover started up alright," says Sanchez. "What luck."

"Yeah, it started without any problems," says Chui. "Has anyone come up with a theory on how the rover got all the way over there? It was parked next to a canyon wall. And I didn't see a body anywhere nearby."

"We are guessing that Jenner survived the explosion and drove it over there. We have no idea why," says Sanchez.

"He couldn't have just disappeared," says Chui.

"I know. It's what has been driving NASA crazy for the past twelve months."

* * * * *

I tap my fingers on the door panel of the transporter.

"Can't these things fly any faster?"

The transporter regulates its own speed. I am not going to operate it in manual mode, says Bleeker.

"But this is urgent," I say as I graduate from finger-tapping to hand-wringing.

Dix, you need to be chilling out, says Bleeker. *We will be at the opening of the new café at the appropriate time.*

I can make out the new Bean Me Up Café in the distance. A healthy line snakes down the road. We push our way through the crowd to the front door. I've appointed Nebbish as the manager of the new café and promoted another Arbiter to manage the original one.

Inside, Nebbish goes over the production and serving processes with the staff one last time. When he sees us, he rushes over.

Dix, I am very glad you have arrived, says Nebbish. *Our guest celebrity has not appeared. I am concerned.*

Relax, I say. *Cheyhto isn't going to appear until the last minute. You don't expect him to be mingling with the minions out front?*

My emotional state will be much improved when this event has concluded, says Nebbish as his eyes dart around the café.

I'm about to respond when one of the staff opens the door, and three of Cheyhto's underlings bound into the café. Why do his people always travel in threesomes?

The Grand Leader is ready to make his statement, one of the Martians informs us.

"And where is...?"

Before I can finish, Cheyhto waddles into the café. He grabs my arm as he wanders around, looking at the coffee equipment.

He stops in front of the service window. *This is the renowned espresso enterprise?*

This is it. Thanks for agreeing to take part in the opening, I say as I lead him back to the front.

Well, thirty percent of the café belongs to me. It is going to be tremendous with me involved, he says as he puffs out his chest. *Look at all these beings who are lined up to see me.*

That may be what he believes, but I know the real reason the other Martians are here.

Remember, you make your speech and then you go back to being a silent partner, I say.

But first, where is my espresso? asks Cheyhto. *I have been full of anticipation regarding your remarkable beverage.*

I don't think it's a good idea to be drinking espresso before you speak. We need you to be focused on the opening, I say. *You can have a celebratory drink after.*

Yes, of course, says Cheyhto, nodding in agreement. *Are we prepared to proceed? I have a demanding schedule today.*

I escort Cheyhto outside, where a small podium has been set up. His henchmen stand in front of the podium to ensure onlookers don't get too close. Others are handing out pins displaying a hologram of Cheyhto. He steps up to the podium.

Greetings fellow beings, he says. He pauses, raising his arms in the air, and is greeted with a muted cheer. *"I am so proud to be standing in front of the newest Bean Me Up Café. If you have not tried coffee, it is terrific. You are going to love it. Believe me when I say this; this chain of cafés is going to be huge. Anything associated with me does amazing because I am a winner.*

A narcissist never runs out of superlatives. He turns to me.

My business associate, Dix, has done a tremendous job. So, buy lots of espresso, so we can make lots of income and open many more locations.

With that he steps down from the podium and waddles toward me. His eyes glow like hot coal when he sees I hold a cup of espresso for him. He takes the cup from my hand and admires the steaming, black liquid.

He lifts his cup. *To my new collaborator and his extraordinary enterprise.* And then he gulps down the espresso.

I take a step back, I don't wait long. Cheyhto drops his cup and turns toward the crowd in front of the café. His bulging cheeks turn wine red and his mouth falls open. He awkwardly jogs down the road, which soon turns into a gallop. His henchmen look on, confused.

Wait? one of them says.

Wait, another one adds.

WAIT! cries the third, and then they're all running like linebackers.

I smile. This will be a good day.

* * * * *

At the end of the day, I'm exhausted. I can't remember ever being as busy as I've been the past few months. The transporter drops me off in front of Plinka's. I drag myself to the front door and press the hummer.

The door pops open, and Plinka grabs my arm to pull me inside, ringing my head off the doorframe. She wears a crimson tunic top that highlights her complexion, and a large necklace with a considerable number of dangling beads and colored stones.

Oh, I hope that injury does not create excessive pain for you, says Plinka as she examines the welt on my forehead.

"I'm fine," I say, rubbing my head.

I had anticipated you would be here significantly earlier, says Plinka, pouting.

"It was hectic today," I say as I flop down on a seat. "It felt like three days in one."

But was it a success?

"A great day," I say. "Or in the words of Cheyhto, *it was terrific, we are going to be huge.*"

Plinka claps her hands in mock applause.

How was our Grand Leader?

"He was giddy because of the size of the crowd, thinking they had come to hear him," I say. "They couldn't wait for him to leave so they could get their espresso."

I cannot believe that you provided him with thirty percent of your enterprise, says Plinka.

"I really had no choice. He could cause a lot of problems for me," I say with a shrug. "It's totally worth it."

Plinka sits down in the seat opposite me, looking very serious. *There is something I desire to converse with you.*

"About what?"

I want to understand what is to transpire between us, she says.

"What do you mean?"

Dix, I would like to establish a relationship with another being, and you would make an ideal partner.

I sit back and rub my chin with my hand, trying to come up with the right answer.

"Plinka, it's not that I don't enjoy your company," I say. "I would have gone insane if it wasn't for you. One day, another mission from Earth will land on Mars, and I'll return home. So, our relationship may end up being temporary."

I can accept that, says Plinka, forcing a smile. *Nothing lasts an eternity.*

"It's only a matter of time before people realize I'm not a Martian. Will Martian society accept an interplanetary couple, or, for that matter, will Earth?" I ask.

She wraps her thin arms around my waist. *They will have to learn.*

CHAPTER
TWENTY-NINE

```
Mars
Earth calendar: 2040-08-31
Martian calendar: 46-05-268
```

With Cheyhto's assistance, I acquired another plot of land for my expanding farm. It's a short trip from home.

Today, I follow Nebbish as he wanders between the rows of news plants. Some are flowering, producing a heavy jasmine scent.

I'm hoping these will help us keep up with the growing demand for coffee. Nebbish completes his plant count.

Dix, we have four hundred and sixty-four plants that are producing beans.

That should be enough for now, I say. *Bur we need to keep expanding if we're going to open more locations.*

How are you going to find more staff for the new locations?

Why are you concerned about staffing? I ask. *These are good jobs for Arbiters.*

We are having difficulty maintaining staffing levels, he says.

We walk towards a shed, so I can check the irrigation system. *Why? Our compensation packages are very good.*

We have had several staff taken to social re-education centers.

I haven't heard anything about this, I say, *frowning. Is there a crackdown of some sort taking place?*

No, say Nebbish. *There is a game that has spread through the facilities. It has become so popular that some Arbiters are intentionally getting themselves detained.*

That's nuts. What game is this?

It's called euchre.

As we reach the shed, I notice someone tearing up the path toward us. Martians never rush to get anywhere. It's Plinka, her face flushed. A few steps away from us, she collapses, gasping for air.

Dix... something terrible... has happened, she says, trying to catch her breath.

What happened? I ask, kneeling to check on her. *Are you okay?*

The news is on every media.

What news? What are you talking about?

Plinka gets up, still breathing hard.

Bleeker and Seepa . . . just released an academic dissertation . . . about you . . . everyone knows you are an Earth-being, she says.

That can't be true, I say. *We had an agreement.*

All I know is that you are the lead news item.

Jesus, I can't believe they did that! I say, waving my arms in the air.

How can you be an Earth-being? asks Nebbish, looking very confused. *You are from Nilosyrtis.*

I start pacing up and down the pathway. *I'm not from Nilosyrtis.*

Everything was going so well. The cafés were thriving. And how will my business partner react to the news? I'm screwed.

Since Bleeker is your cousin, is he also an Earth-being? asks Nebbish, following me as I pace.

For God's sake, he's not my cousin.

I am very confused, says Nebbish.

What shall we do? asks Plinka.

My pacing picks up speed.

I don't know. I need to think. But first things first. I rush to my transporter, with Nebbish right behind me. *I need to have a conversation with my hosts.*

* * * * *

We arrive at their house just as Bleeker leaves, waddling out the front door with a spring in his step. I catch up to him as he hops into his transporter. The moment he sees me, his expression changes.

Morning greetings, Dix, Bleeker says, forcing a smile. *I am late for an interview . . .*

I grab him by the neck and yank him out of the transporter.

"We need to talk, good buddy," I say.

No need to turn to violence, Bleeker says as he tries to pull free.

Plinka steps forward, poking Bleeker in the chest with her index finger.

How could you do this to Dix? she says.

"Without any warning," I say. "Talk about an ambush."

Dix, I discussed this with you on the day of your café opening, says Bleeker. *I recall you responding with approval.*

"That's bullshit," I say. "I don't remember having any conversation about this."

Perhaps it was a bad idea to have discussed this on that day, responds Bleeker.

I lose it and push him against the side of his transporter. He tumbles over as I stand over him.

Bleeker looks up at me, wincing. *We took you in. Sheltered you. Saved your life,* he says. *Are you now going to repay us with beatings?*

"So, you saved my life, and now you just toss me aside?"

Dix, we had an arrangement, explains Bleeker. *Seepa and I would furnish you with refuge in exchange for the opportunity to conduct a study on the anatomy and habitat of Earth-beings. We kept you alive, and now we have made our study findings public.*

"You could have warned me ahead of time," I say, unable to contain my anger. "All this time you used me."

Bleeker gets back on his feet, brushing himself off. *But we did advise you. You were aware from the beginning what would occur at the conclusion of our study. Besides, you can now return home, now that Earth-beings have returned to Mars.* He shrugs. *Is that not what you wanted all along?*

My jaw drops. "What are you talking about?"

We detected that one of your spacecrafts landed two days ago, says Bleeker.

"Why didn't you tell me this?" I ask. "Or did it just slip your mind while you were busy chasing fame and fortune?"

Nebbish tugs at my sleeve.

Dix, I believe there are three of Cheyhto's security subordinates coming for you, says Nebbish.

I look up and recognize the three Martians. I push Bleeker out of the way and hop into his transporter. Nebbish follows me into the vehicle while I direct the robotic driver to take us across town.

The transporter rises about fifty-feet in the air and picks up speed. I glance down and see the three Martian agents get into their transporter.

"Do you know how to manually operate this thing?" I ask.

No, I do not. I would probably crash it, says Nebbish.

"I drove a car a couple of times as a teen," I say with a shrug. "It can't be much different."

I press the manual drive button and two levers pop out of a compartment in the floor. What the hell. I grab one and push it forward. The transporter goes in a dive.

"Whoa!" I yank it back until we are flying level again. I play with the lever and determine it also turns the vehicle to the right and left.

I reach down and push the other lever forward, causing the transporter to speed up. When I pull it back, we slow down. Now that I've figured out the controls, I'm in business. I look over to Nebbish who has a tight grip on his seat.

"Don't worry," I say. "I've got this under control."

Where are we going?

"No clue," I say. "I'm just trying to get away from those goons."

I look over my shoulder to try to locate our pursuers.

Look out for that building! shrieks Nebbish.

I turn around to find a green stone structure directly in front of us.

"Oh shit!" I yell, pulling hard on the first lever. The front of the transporter jerks up and we're thrown back into our seats. We climb higher in the air and clear the top of the building by no more than two feet, only to find ourselves facing another transporter. I immediately pull to the left, throwing Nebbish against the right side of the vehicle. We miss colliding with the other transporter by less than a foot.

Can you please put us back on autopilot? pleads Nebbish. *I would rather be captured than splattered against the side of a building.*

I accelerate. So do the Martians.

You do not seem capable of getting away from them, says Nebbish. *Pull over, so we can give ourselves up.*

"That's not happening," I say. "Hang on tight."

I pull the steering lever hard to one side and let up on the speed. The transporter turns sharply to the left and we do a 180-degree turn. I push hard on the speed lever until we are facing the transporter chasing us. The other vehicle rapidly approaches. Four hundred feet. Three hundred. Two hundred. I hold the steering lever steady.

Nooooooo! shouts Nebbish.

As we get close, I can make out the panicked looks inside the approaching transporter. Fifty feet in front of us, the other transporter dives straight down to avoid colliding.

"Oh baby!" I shout. "What a rush!"

I glance behind us, hoping I've shaken them, but they've only reduced the distance between us. Ahead of me is a group of about thirty transporters moving at uniform speed and distance, like a flock of birds. I maneuver my vehicle into the middle of the pack, hoping to confuse the transporter chasing us. The robotic operating systems of the other vehicles set off a chain reaction and the transporters scatter, as if a predator has appeared in their midst. That didn't quite work as I had hoped.

I look over and Nebbish covers his eyes with his hands.

Dix, are we still alive? asks Nebbish as he peers through his fingers.

"For now." I say. "But we're trying it again."

As the security agents recoup some distance, I slow down again and do another 180-degree turn. We are about two hundred and fifty feet apart, which provides them with less time to respond. The driver pulls hard on the lever while the passengers thrash their arms around. My hands shake, gripping the lever.

"Come on guys," I say. "You haven't got the nerve."

At about thirty feet in front of us, the other transporter dives again. The diving vehicle makes a beeline for a rooftop and only a last-minute turn avoids a crash.

I wipe my sweaty hands on my pants.

Nebbish whimpers, *Please let me live, please let me live, please let me live.*

"Okay, you dumb shits," I say. "Let's try this one more time!"

I try yet another 180-degree turn. I push the lever again to the left until we are facing the security agents' transporter. Then I pull hard on the speed lever for maximum velocity. Two hundred feet apart. One hundred. Fifty. I block out the screaming next to me. The front passenger in the approaching vehicle grabs the lever away from the driver. Fifteen feet away, they dive.

This time they don't pull out in time. Pedestrians scatter in all directions. The transporter crashes onto the ground and breaks apart. The three passengers bounce off the roadway and are flung into an adjacent building. They bounce off that building and into the next. It's like watching live pinballs. Parts of the disintegrated transporter thunk and ping into our vehicle.

I slump back into my seat as I put the transporter back in automated control. My clothes are drenched in sweat. I look over and Nebbish shakes from head to toe.

"You all right, buddy?" I ask.

That was the most terrifying experience of my life, says Nebbish.

"That's because you've never ridden on the 8th Avenue subway line in New York at night."

I look below, and the three agents are on their feet, waving their fists at us.

"Those guys should consider a career change," I say, grinning. "Like joining a sling team."

Where are we going now? he asks.

I reach over to the dashboard display and punch in new coordinates. "Back to Bleeker's place. I need to get my spacesuit."

* * * * *

When we arrive back where we started, Nebbish scampers out of the transporter. *I am never journeying with you again.*

As we approach the front door, Bleeker comes tearing out of the house with Seepa close behind.

I hope my transporter is intact, says Bleeker as he examines his precious vehicle.

"Yes, we're fine, thanks for asking," I say.

What happened to the agents who were chasing you? asks Bleeker.

"They ran into some problems with their transporter," I say. "Things are a little hot for me down here right now. I need to get my spacesuit out."

Yes, we can assist you with it, says Bleeker as he leads us into his house.

Tears run down Seepa's round cheeks. *We did not intend to betray you,* she says. *Bleeker had communicated to me that he had discussed this with you. It seems he had not selected the ideal opportunity to do so.*

Bleeker stares down at the floor. *I regret how this matter has developed,* he says. *We did not deliberate on this properly. We should have been more sensitive.*

"This isn't your fault," I say. "On dozens of occasions, my identity could have been exposed. It was through your efforts that I made it this far."

I grab them both and give them a big hug. "Thank you both for everything. You saved my life."

It feels like we stand there embracing for hours. But finally, I have to let go.

Hidden away in the back of my bedroom is my spacesuit, just as I'd left it almost twelve months ago. I pull it on and close all the buckles and snaps. Bleeker and Nebbish watch me in silence. The last items are the boots, gloves, and helmet. I discover Poof sleeping in my helmet and turn it upside down. She falls to the floor and runs away.

"Could you give me a ride to where the surface portal is?" I ask Bleeker.

Of course, Bleeker says with a long face. *This is very difficult for me. We will miss you.*

Let me go with you, Dix, says Nebbish.

"Your place is here," I say. "Besides, who will look after our thriving coffee business?"

Do you think Cheyhto will consent to me overseeing the cafés? asks Nebbish.

"Don't worry about Cheyhto. He doesn't know anything about growing or processing coffee. He'll have no choice but to keep you around."

I hope you are right, says Nebbish, his shoulders drooping.

At that moment, the door hummer goes off and Plinka waddles into the room.

When I saw Bleeker's transporter, I came rushing over, says Plinka. *Earth-being, were you just going to journey away on your spaceship without saying goodbye?*

I wrap my arms around her and embrace her. "I was going to drop by." I really don't want to leave her, but I don't see how I have a choice. My eyes well up.

"It is a shame that we did not have more time to develop our relationship. I will miss you, Dixon Jenner," says Plinka, blinking back tears.

"I will miss you, too," I say, wiping away a tear.

Plinka no longer holds back and tears flood her large black eyes. I put my arms around her and embrace her.

Dix, you need to leave, says Bleeker. *I anticipate more of Cheyhto's subordinates will soon arrive to detain you.*

I pull away from Plinka and lumber to the transporter. I climb in one last time to join Bleeker. He punches in the coordinates and we lift off. I peer out the window and wave. Within a minute, they are gone.

We ride in silence to the portal stairs. The scenery looks familiar to me now. The Martians walking down below no longer seem strange looking. Within minutes, we arrive at the stairs. I get out and grab my helmet. Bleeker joins me. I put my arms around him and give him one last hug.

"I can't believe I'm saying this, but I'm going to miss this crazy planet," I say. "You and Seepa are probably the closest friends I've ever had. I'm going to miss you two the most."

We shall miss you as well, says Bleeker as he squeezes my arm. *Have a safe journey home, my Earth friend.*

I make the long ascent to the surface. My legs feel so heavy as I struggle with each step. I stop to look back one last time. From high above, everything looks so small. Not nearly as real. In the distance I can make out the orange Assembly building, jutting out from the cityscape.

By the time I reach the top of the stairs, I need to stop to catch my breath before snapping on my helmet and activating the cooling system. I stand staring at the portal for the longest time, unsure whether to step on the mat or turn back. But is turning back really an option? And can I turn my back on family, friends, and my home?

I take a deep breath and put my foot down on the mat. The portal opens, and I step outside. As the portal shuts behind me, it's like a chapter of my life has also closed.

The sun is low in the horizon, but it's light enough for me to find the base camp. I'm hoping it's the same location as base last year. When I hike over to where I left my rover, it's gone. All that is left are tread marks in the sand. I need to hustle if I want to find the base camp before nightfall.

I trudge through the sand, thinking about what I will have to tell them. Not just about the past year, but about what happened to the colony. Those four hundred yards seem to take forever. Some vague figures pop up in the distance. At first, I can't determine if they are rock formations or people, but as I get closer I can make out six spacesuits. When I'm about two hundred feet away I turn on my communication system.

At one hundred feet, I raise my right hand and shout, "Live long and prosper. *Dif-tor heh smusma.*"

All six figures stop what they are doing and look at me.

"Holy shit!" shouts a female voice. "Jenner, is that you?"

CHAPTER THIRTY

Mars
Earth calendar: 2040-09-01
Martian calendar: 46-05-269

I feel like I've been riding a rollercoaster for two years straight. One day, I'm in small town Jersey, and then before I know it, I'm hurtling into space in a nuclear-fueled ship. Next, I'm making coffee for aliens.

Now, I'm back with humans and the culture shock is numbing. These people are all business. They don't have the charm of my Martian friends.

At breakfast, Sanchez and Chui pull me aside. "How was your first night back with humans?" asks the Commander. "We gave you a sedative last night, so you must have had a good sleep."

"Yeah I slept great and it's great to be back on dehydrated rations," I say, smirking. The two humorless astronauts ignore the comment. Welcome back to NASA.

"We didn't want to bombard you with questions yesterday evening, but we need answers. I hope you're ready for a debriefing," says Sanchez as she puts a hand on my shoulder. "If you have some insight as to what happened here, we can all head home that much sooner."

"Okay," I say.

"That's great," she says. "And Mission Control will be listening in."

I follow them into the Commander's quarters, which is no more than a nine-by-seven space filled with hardware and a few personal items, mostly clothing.

"Back home you are a hero," says Chui. "The media is saying it's a miracle you survived this ordeal."

"Believe me," I say. "I'm no hero."

We sit down on some metal seats that fold out from the wall. Sanchez pulls out a tablet. She and Chui put on headsets and she hands one to me.

She speaks into her headpiece. "Mission Control, this is Commander Sanchez, can you hear me?"

The response crackles in my headset. "This is Mission Control. Yes, we can hear you. We have with us, Dr. Charles Farley, who has asked to participate in the briefing."

"We have Dixon Jenner here now and are ready to begin," says Sanchez.

"Jenner, we're thrilled to know that you've survived this ordeal," says Farley. "You probably can't hear it, but everyone in Mission Control is on their feet applauding."

"Thanks. It's great to hear you," I say. "It's been a long time since I've heard other human voices."

"It's a miracle that you've been able to survive here on your own," says Sanchez. "We would like to hear your story. What did you do after the colony was destroyed? Last night you were mumbling something about aliens after we sedated you."

"You're going to be just a little shocked," I say. "I was saved by a Martian couple."

Sanchez and Chui look at me with mouths gaping.

"You're telling us there's alien life on Mars?" asks Chui.

"Yes," I say. "I lived with Martians this past year."

"Jenner, you may be suffering post-traumatic stress," says Farley. "I wouldn't be surprised if you've been experiencing hallucinations, the effects of shock and isolation."

"I'm feeling fine," I say. "I've not been hallucinating."

"I have to admit, I don't believe a word of this," he says. "None of our manned or unmanned Mars missions have ever detected any life."

"That's because they don't live on the surface," I say. "They live beneath the surface. There's this vast underground community made up of millions of Martians. It covers most of the planet."

"If it's true," says Farley, "can you show us some proof?"

"He can't prove it," says Sanchez. "We've been exploring Mars for decades and have come up with nothing to suggest any life exists on the planet, let alone an advanced society."

"I can lead you to the portal I use to get to and from the underground city," I say. "It's right next to where I left the rover. But I should warn you, we won't get a warm reception right now."

"Why?" asks Chui, rolling his eyes. "Do the aliens have ray guns?

"Knock it off, Walter," says Sanchez.

"Wait a minute," I say. "I just remembered I do have proof."

I run out to get my spacesuit. Out of a pocket, I pull out a smooth, brown sphere. When I return, I display it in hand. "This was a gift from Bleeker and Seepa."

Sanchez takes it from my hand to examine it. "What is it?"

"It's a sling alarm indicator."

"Commander, how far from the base is the site?" asks Farley.

"Only about four hundred yards."

"I want you to organize a party to investigate," insists Farley. "Nothing seems to add up here. Make sure to bring cameras and protection. But first, Jenner—how did you communicate with them?"

"Martians communicate through telepathy."

"You have telepathic powers?" asks Chui, smirking. "I don't remember reading this in your profile."

"It's not that *I'm* telepathic," I say. "It's just that Martians are able to transmit thoughts and read mine."

"This is Mission Control," says a voice coming through my headset. "When did you first make contact with the aliens?"

I tell them everything about Bleeker and Seepa. About how I was supposed to tell other Martians this ridiculous story about a rare disease and how Martians actually bought it. That I set out to make my mark—if only out of boredom. But after taking on schemes like the basketball league and the café, I started to notice that responsibility can feel good.

I speak for several hours. At some point, I have drawn in Sanchez and Chui to the point that they stop taking notes. Even Mission Control rarely interrupts.

The only thing I don't mention is Plinka. I doubt they would understand.

At some point Sanchez breaks in. "Let's all take a break. I'm sure you need one, Jenner. Let's reconvene at fifteen hundred hours. I also need to prep for our trip underground and our return mission."

Until she mentions it, I hadn't given much thought to my return to Earth. I guess I've been too caught up in my own stories.

"When will we be leaving?

Sanchez gets up to go to use the latrine. "In two days."

* * * * *

Later that day, I return to the Commander's quarters. Sanchez and Chui are present, and Mission Control is linked in again.

"Jenner, we want you to tell us what you know about what took place at the colony on September second of last year," says Farley. "The day the colony was destroyed."

I pause to reflect. I haven't thought about that day very much. Perhaps, subconsciously, that has been intentional.

I take a deep breath.

"This sounds like a cliché, but it started off as an ordinary day," I say. "I mean an ordinary day here on Mars. I began the day checking things in the greenhouse, which was part of my routine."

They respond with silence. I look down at my boots.

"After tending to the greenhouse farm, I planned the meals for the next few days. It was Dr. Markowski's birthday that day and I was going to bake him a cake. The oven and stove are shut down in the evening and restarted in the morning. This is a safety procedure."

"Jenner, we are aware of the procedures," says Sanchez as she looks up from her tablet.

I shift in my seat.

"I had problems running through the start up procedure. There was a dial that controls the heat coming from the nuclear reactor. It would get stuck from time to time. I would have to get the mission engineer, Tammy Spanner, to address the problem. On that morning, the dial got stuck again. I contacted Tammy, but she was outside the colony collecting rock and soil samples. I headed out for a ride in one of the rovers until she returned. She radioed me to let me know she was heading back, so I turned around. Then there was a massive explosion… and the colony was gone."

The room and Mission Control are silent. I avoid looking at Sanchez and Chui and instead look down at my boots again. Perhaps a minute passes, but it feels like a hundred.

Finally, Sanchez breaks the silence.

"It was fortunate that you were outside the colony," says Sanchez.

I look up at her. "It was me."

Sanchez puts down her tablet and leans forward to touch my arm. "What do you mean?"

"I didn't bother to shut down the power from the reactor. I know it was standard procedure. I was warned over and over again about it. I just didn't do it." I cover my face with my hands. "I killed the crew. I destroyed a multi-billion-dollar space colony. I was just being stupid and lazy."

A tear rolls down my cheek. No one says anything for a while until Mission Control responds.

"Jenner, sorry to break the news to you," says Farley, "but you didn't blow up the colony."

"What do you mean?"

"We've identified the source of the explosion to be the oxygenator," says Sanchez.

"It didn't start in the kitchen?" I ask.

"Incompetence was a factor in the explosion," adds Farley. "But not yours."

"Who was it then?"

"Tammy Spanner. It turns out we missed a few things about her in our vetting process," says Farley. "We recently discovered that she was a drug user in the past. There is a possibility that she had smuggled drugs into the colony and was high when the explosion occurred."

"That's shocking."

CHAPTER
THIRTY-ONE

```
Johnson Space Center, Houston, TX
Earth calendar: 2040-09-02
Martian calendar: 46-05-270
```

Farley stares at his desk phone.

Abe Tuff looks across the desk at him. "Chuck, why so glum? We've rescued Dixon Jenner."

Farley plays with the telephone cord. "I know. This has to be the worst event in the 82-year history of the agency and it happened on my watch."

"Yes, but you've been able to confirm that it was the negligence of Spanner," Tuff points out. "Not the agency."

"It makes no difference," Farley mutters, burying his face in his hands. "We picked Spanner. We trained her. We designed the oxygenator."

"There are always risks in what we do. Mishaps are going to happen."

"But this one was just plain stupid. We didn't properly vet the crew or test the hardware."

"What do you think will be the reaction from the White House?"

"Hold a parade or give him a medal," say Farley. "Maybe both."

"What happens to you?"

"I don't know. I'm likely to get canned. Maybe I can work with Jenner at some greasy spoon in Turd City, New Jersey."

The phone chirps but Farley continues to stare down at it.

"Aren't you going to answer it?" asks Tuff.

He pushes the hands-free button. "Chuck Farley."

"Good morning, Chuck," says Bronstein. "I hope this isn't too early in the morning for you?"

"I've been up for hours," says Farley. "Mission control runs twenty-four-seven."

"I'm in the Roosevelt Room," says Bronstein. "Joining me are the White House Communications Director, our issue management person, and one of the president's speechwriters."

"Good morning, everyone. I have my General Counsel here with me," says Farley, scratching his chin. "Ed, you caught me by surprise. I didn't realize this was going to be a group call."

"I told you I was going to speak to the President and get back to you," says Bronstein. "She asked us to develop a communications plan."

"Sorry, I'm a little confused," says Farley, looking across at Abe, whose expression is blank.

"Sit tight, Chuck," says Bronstein. "Let me walk you through the plan. The White House doesn't want the public to continue focusing on the colony disaster. It's a miracle that Jenner survived. That's what we should be focusing on."

"What do you mean? Doesn't the public have the right to know what happened?"

"We think the rescue mission will be more appealing to the public than a post mortem," says Bronstein. "NASA benefits from this."

"I don't like this at all," says Farley, shaking his head.

"Chuck, the President has already approved the plan," says Bronstein.

"I see."

"We need to discuss the details of the call," adds Bronstein. "We're working on some speaking notes for the President."

"What call?"

"We are scheduling a call between the President and Jenner tomorrow, late afternoon," says Bronstein. "We want to get maximum exposure during the early evening news slot."

"Sure," says Farley. "I'll let Mission Control know."

"Now, Chuck," says Bronstein. "We expect you to be at the White House when Jenner meets the President."

After the call ends, Farley slumps back in his chair. "Glad to see the circus is back in town."

CHAPTER THIRTY-TWO

```
Mars
Earth calendar: 2040-09-03
Martian calendar: 46-05-271
```

Looking through a porthole at the emptiness of Valles Marineris, I realize I will miss this place. Not living in the colony, that was harsh, but it's a totally different world underground. That's what I'm going to miss.

On Mars, I'm accepted for who I am. No expectations, no one judging me. That's not what it was like for me on Earth. Maybe that's why I've always been so rebellious. It was my way of rejecting the pressure. When I go back to Earth, everything will be as it was.

I'm not sure I want that anymore.

I realize Chui is calling me. "Jenner!"

"Sorry, Walter," I say.

"I just dropped by to see if you need any help packing your gear for tomorrow," says Chui. "As soon as we finish our underground tour, we'll head straight back to the ship and begin the launch."

"Why the rush?" I ask.

"We're told the window for a safe launch is short," says Chui. "The weather patterns will change in the next forty-eight hours."

"Um... yeah," I say.

"Are you all right?" asks Chui. "You seem preoccupied."

He reads my face like I'm a science experiment. These NASA types look at everything that way.

"Are you nervous about the call?" he asks. "I don't blame you if you are. It's not every day you get to speak to the President."

"It feels weird," I say. "I'm just a chef. I didn't do anything heroic. I was just lucky."

"I would say you'll become quite the celebrity," says Chui. "I think your life is going to change significantly. I can see a book deal, maybe a movie about your year on Mars."

"I don't want a reality TV show," I say with a sigh. "All I want is my own restaurant business."

Sanchez pokes her head in.

"The linkup to the White House has been secured," she says. "Dix, are you ready?"

I nod. We stroll over to the communication station. Sanchez puts on a headset and hands another one to me. I slip it on and hear static.

"Hello Mission Control," says Sanchez into the microphone of her headset. "Commander Sanchez from base camp in Valles Marineris."

"Hello Commander," says the voice. "We are ready to patch in the President. Is Jenner with you now?"

She looks at me and nods.

"Dix Jenner, here," I say.

"Madame President, Mr. Jenner is on the line now," says Mission Control.

"Hello, Dixon," says the President.

"Hello, Madame President," I say.

"So good to hear your voice. I understand you've had quite an ordeal," she says.

"Yeah, it was an adventure," I say. "It wasn't what I expected."

"We are saddened by the loss of your crewmates. Your mission is a reminder of the sacrifices made by very brave men and women in the name of science," says the President. "But we are thankful that you will be returning."

"Thank you, Madame President," I say.

"Dixon, the White House made a call to your family in New Jersey," she says. "They were thrilled to hear you're alive. Your mom sends her love."

"What about dad?"

"He is away on business, but I'm sure he is just as excited."

I doubt it. I'm sure I'll be getting some sort of lecture when I get back.

"I understand that you have made a major discovery while on Mars," says the President. "I am told you discovered there are aliens living on the planet and you were able to make contact with them. This likely ranks up there with Columbus discovering America."

"Maybe," I say. "I was just thankful to find them. I wouldn't have survived without the assistance of my Martian hosts. But they aren't the aliens here—I am."

There's laughter on the line, although it wasn't meant to be funny. You don't call the Germans foreigners when you're in Germany.

"We are looking forward to hearing your stories when you arrive safely home," she says. "NASA has already informed me of some of your activities on Mars. I understand you'll be leading a team underground to bring back photos. I plan to ask Congress to approve funding to send future missions to Mars, so that we can study the inhabitants."

Study the inhabitants. Her words strike a nerve. We aren't talking about rock samples here.

I realize, in the moment, that we don't have a great track record when it comes to indigenous people.

"Madame President," I say. "You don't study an advanced society. You learn from them. On Mars, there are no wars and no nuclear weapons. It's not a perfect society, but they do a lot of things right."

"Well, it seems you have experienced and seen a lot during your time there. I'll be looking forward to hearing more about it when you return," says the President. "I hope all goes well with the launch tomorrow, and that you have a safe journey home."

"Thank you, Madame President," I say.

"It was nice talking to you, Dixon," she says. "Goodbye."

CHAPTER THIRTY-THREE

```
Mars
Earth calendar: 2040-09-04
Martian calendar: 46-05-272
```

I'm seated on a large red boulder next to my rover, overlooking miles of red sand and rocks. The silence of Valles Marineris is broken by the sounds of my EVA's cooling system and my breathing.

What am I doing here? I'm a chef from Toms River, New Jersey. What do I know about survival on a barren planet?

But then it's not really barren. And I'm not just a chef anymore.

I've got a successful restaurant business here. My partner is the most powerful individual on the planet. I've made life better for the lower class too—and Cheyhto will never allow Nebbish and the others to manage the cafés.

I can't bring back the Futurum crew... but maybe I can make a difference somewhere else.

And isn't it funny how I never connected with a woman until I got to Mars.

Chui lumbers over to me. "Jenner, we need you to come inside to go over the details before traveling to your portal," he says. "We're heading out in twenty minutes."

I stand up and walk with him to the ship. The sunlight reflecting off the metal surface occasionally blinds me as we move. It's almost like a spotlight, and suddenly, I imagine myself being honored at a Knicks game. My parents proudly watching in the stands. Sitting in Olympic Grill, biting into a cheeseburger and washing it down with a beer. Walking on the boardwalk on the Jersey shore.

As we approach the airlock, I stop.

"I've changed my mind," I say.

"About what?" asks Chui.

"I'm not taking you to gawk at the Martians."

He grabs me by the arm. "Did you make up all the stories about the Martians?"

"No, it's all true. In fact, I've decided to stay here."

"You're talking crazy. You can't stay here."

"Sure, I can. I've been living here for the past year. I can continue as if you never found me."

Chui switches on his radio. "Ellen, we have a problem outside the ship," he says.

"What type of problem?" she asks.

"It's Jenner," says Chui. "He doesn't want to go home."

"I'll be right out," she says.

"Dix, you've been under a lot of stress," says Chui. "Maybe you're suffering from some form of Stockholm Syndrome?"

"Come on, Walter," I say. "I wasn't kidnapped. The Martians saved my life. They could have left me to die. I might have been a threat to them. You may think I'm crazy, but I'm not."

"How can you abandon your family back home?"

"I'm supposed to live on Mars for five years. I figure I have four years to go."

The airlock opens and out steps Commander Sanchez. She glares at me. "What's going on, Jenner?"

I walk in the direction of the portal. "I don't want to be part of a Presidential dog-and-pony show. I don't want to spend the next two years being studied by NASA scientists and poked and prodded by doctors. I have nothing waiting for me back in Jersey. My life is here now."

"But aren't you a wanted man here?" asks Chui.

"I thought about that," I say. "But I've got a relationship with Cheyhto. I hope that negotiating a bigger share of my café chain will persuade him to overlook the fact that I'm an alien."

"You know, as Commander I have the authority to have you strapped into a chair and delivered back to NASA."

Then a thought comes to me. "You're right. What was I thinking?"

I follow Sanchez and Chui into the ship. Inside, everyone is busy prepping for the launch. I stroll over to a supply cabinet and open it. Stacked on a shelf are just what I was hoping to find— several Sementric battery packs. I haven't forgotten about you, Todd. I slip them into a small case.

I head to the airlock and open it, setting off an alarm. As I close the door behind me I hear someone yell. "Jenner, what the fuck are you doing?"

I step out onto the surface and run.

I glance over my shoulder. Several crew members are chasing after me. Through my headset, I hear Sanchez ordering me to stop. When I check out my pursuers again, I find two crew members chasing me on the rover. My lungs and my legs burn but I can't stop. It's at least another five minutes until I reach the portal that leads to the stairs. I'm worried I can't keep this up that long.

But I don't stop.

When I reach the portal, I'm alone.

It's a perfectly clear sky today and when I look up I'm sure I can make out the Earth. Or am I imagining it?

My chest pounds, and I'm bent over trying to catch my breath. I stagger to the mat and watch the portal open. I step inside and remove my helmet, beginning my descent into the glowing stone city below. Once I step off the bottom step, I follow the route that I first took a year ago, past shiny stone buildings as transporters whisk by overhead. Martians carting provisions home bump into each other on the roadway. Children with toy slings chase each other.

I stop in front of a shiny, green building and push the door hummer. The door springs open, and Plinka beams when she sees me. I stoop down and step inside.

APPENDIX

Dixon Jenner's Martian Cookbook

SPAM SUSHI

Ingredients
2 cups of uncooked short-grained white rice
2 cups water
6 tablespoons rice vinegar
¼ cup soy sauce
¼ cup oyster sauce
½ cup white sugar
1 (12 ounce) can Spam
5 sheets sushi nori (dry seaweed)
2 tablespoons vegetable oil

Directions
1.   Soak uncooked rice for 4 hours; drain and rinse.
2.   In a saucepan, bring 2 cups water to a boil. Add rice and stir. Reduce heat, cover and simmer for 20 minutes. Stir in rice vinegar, and set aside to cool.
3.   In a bowl, stir together soy sauce, oyster sauce and sugar until sugar is completely dissolved. Slice Spam lengthwise into 10 slices, or to desired thickness and marinate in sauce for 5 minutes.
4.   In a large skillet, heat oil over medium high heat. Cook slices for 2 minutes per side, or until lightly browned.
5.   Cut sushi nori sheets in half and lay on a flat work surface. Place a rice press in the center of the sheet, and press rick tightly inside. Top with a slice of Spam and remove press. Wrap nori sheet around rice mold, sealing edges with a small amount of water. (Note: rice may also be formed by hand in shape of the Spam slices.) Sushi can be served warm or chilled.

DEEP-FRIED KOOL-AID

Ingredients
2 quarts vegetable oil for frying
3 cups all-purpose flour
2 cups white sugar
1 tablespoon baking powder
1/2 teaspoon salt
1 cup milk
2 eggs
3 tablespoons melted butter
1 teaspoon vanilla extract
1 envelope unsweetened Kool-Aid

Directions
1. Heat oil in a deep-fryer or large saucepan to 365°F.

2. Mix 3 cups flour, 1 cup sugar, the baking powder, salt, and 1/2 envelope of Kool-Aid together in a large bowl.

3. Whisk the milk, eggs, butter, and vanilla extract together in a separate large bowl until blended. Slowly stir in the flour mixture until entirely incorporated in a batter the consistency of a thick pancake batter.

4. Drop the batter by large spoonfuls, about 2 teaspoons in size, into the preheated oil; fry until deep golden brown on all sides, 2 to 3 minutes. Remove to drain on a platter lined with paper towels.

5. Mix together 1 cup sugar with the remaining 1/2 envelope of Kool-Aid in a flat-bottomed dish. Roll the drained donuts in the sugar mixture while still hot. Set aside on a fresh set of paper towels to cool slightly. Serve warm.

TRAILER PARK HASH

Ingredients
1 pound ground beef or turkey
5 large red, white or gold potatoes
2 garlic cloves
1 medium onion
1 large bell pepper
10 ounces beer
1 teaspoon salt
1 teaspoon cracked black pepper

Directions
1.   Peel potatoes and cut into 1-inch pieces. Place potatoes in a medium pot, fill with enough water so that there is 1 inch of water covering the potatoes and add 1 teaspoon of salt. Cover pot and turn up heat to high, until boiling.

2.   Once potatoes have begun to boil, reduce heat to a light boil to prevent potatoes from becoming mushy. Cook for about 10 minutes, until tender.

3.   While potatoes are boiling, finely chop garlic, onion and bell pepper.

4.   Put 1 teaspoon of oil in a large frying pan over medium high heat. When oil is hot, place ground meat in pan and cook until brown, breaking apart meat with a spoon.

5.   When meat has browned, remove with slotted spoon into a strainer to allow to drain. Leave fat in pan.

6.   When potatoes are tender, pour off water, cover to keep warm.

7.   Heat the fat in the frying pan over medium heat. When hot, add onions and sauté, until translucent, about 6-7 minutes. Add bell peppers three minutes after adding onions. Add garlic with about 1 minute remaining.

8.   Add meat back into frying pan. Over high heat, add beer to deglaze the pan, making sure to scrape the bottom of the pan to loosen grease.

9.   When sauce comes to a boil, reduce heat to medium, simmer uncovered until sauce is reduced, about 5-6 minutes.

10.   Serve meat with sauce over the potatoes in a bowl, mush all together. Top with ketchup, mustard, hot sauce and/or grated cheese.

CREAMY BURRITO CASSEROLE

Ingredients
1 pound ground beef or turkey
½ medium yellow onion, chopped
1 package taco seasoning
6 large flour tortillas
1 (16 ounce) can refried beans
2- 3 cups shredded Monterey Jack and/or cheddar cheese
1 (10 ¾ ounce) can cream of mushroom soup
4 ounces sour cream
Hot sauce, if desired to spice it up

Directions
1. Brown ground beef/turkey and onion drain.
2. Add taco seasoning and stir in refried beans.
3. Mix soup and sour cream in a separate bowl.
4. Spread ½ sour cream mixture in the bottom of a casserole dish.
5. Tear up 3 tortillas and spread over sour cream mixture.
6. Put ½ the meat bean mixture over that.
7. Add a layer of cheese.
8. You could put some hot sauce on this now.
9. Repeat the layers.
10. Sprinkle cheese over the top and bake, uncovered, at 350°F for 20-30 minutes.

DIX'S DELUXE BROWNIES WITH A SECRET INGREDIENT

Ingredients
1 stick of unsalted butter that's been infused with the 3.5 grams of the secret ingredient
¼ cup vegetable shortening
¾ cup of cocoa powder
1 cup cake flour
2 cups sugar
½ teaspoon salt
4 ounces bittersweet or semisweet chocolate
¼ teaspoon baking powder
⅛ teaspoon baking soda
2 jumbo eggs
Guts of one vanilla bean

Directions
1.   Preheat oven to 350°F. Spray Pam into a 9x7 pan and then line it with parchment paper.
2.   Leave butter out to soften until it reaches room temperature.
3.   Mix all of the dry ingredients together in a bowl – cocoa, flour, sugar, salt, baking powder, baking soda.
4.   In a second bowl, combine vanilla and eggs.
5.   Melt the chocolate gently in a microwave with short bursts.
6.   Stir in the shortening into the chocolate until it melts.
7.   Stream the chocolate mixture slowly into the eggs and mix with a spatula, then fold in infused-butter. Make sure everything is uniformly mixed without aerating too much.
8.   Fold the wet batter into the combined dry ingredients and stir again until it's just mixed.

9.   Pour mixture into the 9x7 pan. Smooth out the mixture and smack it flat on the counter a few times to make sure there is no air trapped inside.

10.   Bake for 15 minutes, rotate the pan, then bake for another 15 minutes.

11.   Remove from the oven and cool in the pan for at least 10 minutes. Use the parchment paper to take the brownies out of the pan and cool the rest of the way on a wire rack.

12.   Once cooled, cut into 1 inch by ½ inch squares. I don't recommend larger squares.

MISSISSIPPI MUD POTATOES

Ingredients
6 cups potatoes, peeled and diced
1 cup shredded cheddar cheese
¾ cup mayonnaise
1 cup bacon, cooked and crumbled
3 teaspoons minced garlic
½ cup onion, chopped

Directions
1.   In a 9"x13' baking pan, combine the potatoes, cheese, bacon, garlic and onion.
2.   Add in the mayonnaise and stir until all is coated.
3.   Place pan in a preheated oven, 325°F for 1-1 ½ hours or until potatoes are tender.

JERSEY SHORE HASH BROWN CASSEROLE

Ingredients
2 pounds frozen hash browns
1 can (10 ¾ ounce) cream of celery soup
1 medium onion chopped
1 green or red pepper, diced
2 ham steaks, cubed
12 ounces grated cheddar cheese
½ stick margarine, melted

Instructions
1.   Mix all ingredients except 4 ounces of cheese.
2.   Put in casserole dish sprayed with Pam.
3.   Spread evenly in dish and top with remaining cheese.
4.   Cover and bake at 350°F for 45 minutes.
5.   Uncover and cook another 45 minutes.
6.   Let stand for 10 minutes.

MAMA JENNER'S MASHED POTATO PANCAKES

Ingredients
3 cups mashed potatoes
¼ cup grated parmesan cheese
1 egg, lightly beaten
6 tablespoons flour
1 tablespoon onion, grated
1 tablespoon fresh parsley, chopped
Canola oil

Instructions
1.　　In a large mixing bowl, combine potatoes, cheese, egg, 3 tablespoons of flour, onion and parsley.

2.　　On a plate add 3 tablespoons of flour for dredging the pancakes. Fill an ice cream scoop or heaping tablespoons with the mixture, shape the pancakes in your hands and dredge them in flour.

3.　　Add 3 tablespoons of canola oil to a non-stick frying pan and sauté about 2-3 minutes on each side over medium-high heat or until golden brown. Add more oil if needed.

4.　　Remove mashed potato cakes to a plate lined with a paper towel to soak up excess oil. Service with a dollop of sour cream.

CREAMY AU GRATIN POTATOES

Ingredients
4 russet potatoes, sliced into ¼ inch slices
1 onion, sliced into rings
Salt and pepper to taste
3 tablespoons butter
3 tablespoons all-purpose flour
½ teaspoon salt
2 cups milk
1 ½ cups shredded cheddar cheese

Directions
1.   Preheat oven to 400°F. Butter a 1 quart casserole dish.

2.   Layer ½ of the potatoes into bottom of the casserole dish. Top with the onion slices and add the remaining potatoes. Season with salt and pepper to taste.

3.   In a medium-sized saucepan melt butter over medium heat. Mix in the flour and salt stirring constantly with a whisk for one minute. Stir in milk. Cook until mixture has thickened.

4.   Stir cheese all at once and continue stirring until melted about 30-60 seconds. Pour cheese over the potatoes and cover the dish with aluminum foil.

5.   Bake 1 ½ hours in the oven.

BERTHA'S DINER SCALLOPED POTATOES

Ingredients
4 cups potatoes, thinly sliced
3 tablespoons butter
3 tablespoons flour
1 ½ cups milk
1 teaspoon salt
1 dash cayenne pepper
1 cup grated sharp cheddar cheese
½ cup grated sharp cheddar cheese, to sprinkle on top
Paprika

Directions
1. In a small sauce pan, melt butter and blend in flour. Let sit for a minute.
2. Add milk, stirring with a whisk.
3. Season with salt and cayenne.
4. Cook sauce on low until smooth and boiling, stirring occasionally with a whisk.
5. Reduce heat and stir in cheese.
6. Place half of the sliced potatoes in a lightly greased one quart casserole dish.
7. Pour half of the cheese sauce over potatoes.
8. Repeat with second layer of potatoes and cheese sauce.
9. Sprinkle the remaining cheese on top. Top with some paprika for color.
10. Bake uncovered for about 1 hour at 350°F.

AUNT GINNY'S MAPLE-ROASTED SWEET POTATOES

Ingredients
2 ½ pounds sweet potatoes, peeled and cut into 1 ½ - inch pieces
1/3 cup pure maple syrup
2 tablespoons butter, melted
1 tablespoon lemon juice
½ teaspoon salt
Freshly ground pepper to taste

Directions
1.   Preheat oven to 400°F.

2.   Arrange sweet potatoes in an even layer in a 9"x13" glass baking dish.

3.   Combine maple syrup, butter, lemon juice, salt and pepper in small bowl. Pour the mixture over the sweet potatoes. Toss to coat.

4.   Cover and bake the sweet potatoes for 15 minutes. Uncover, stir and cook, stirring every 15 minutes, until tender and starting to brown, 45-50 minutes more.

5.   Make Ahead Tip: Cover and refrigerate for up to 1 day. Just before serving, reheat at 350°F until hot, about 15 minutes.

HOLIDAY GARLIC MASHED POTATOES WITH MASCARPONE CHEESE

Ingredients
3 pounds Idaho potatoes, peeled and cut into large dice
Kosher salt
1 ½ cups whole milk
6 cloves roasted garlic cloves, pureed
½ stick unsalted butter
8 ounces mascarpone cheese
Freshly ground black pepper

Directions
1. Place potatoes in a large saucepan, add cold water just to cover and 1 tablespoon salt.
2. Bring to a boil over high heat and cook until tender.
3. Drain well and run through a food processor.
4. While the potatoes are cooking, combine the milk, garlic puree and butter in a small saucepan and bring to a simmer over low heat.
5. Stir the milk mixture into the potatoes until combined.
6. Fold in the mascarpone and season well with salt and pepper.
7. Keep warm over in a double boiler until serving.

SANTA'S SAVORY TURKEY STUFFING

Ingredients

¾ cup unsalted butter plus a little extra for the baking dish

1 pound day-old white bread, torn into 1-inch pieces

2 ½ cups chopped yellow onions

1 ½ cups celery, cut into ½-inch pieces

½ cup chopped flat-leaf parsley

2 tablespoons chopped fresh sage

1 tablespoon chopped fresh rosemary

1 tablespoon chopped fresh thyme

2 teaspoons kosher salt

1 teaspoon ground black pepper

2 ½ cups low-sodium chicken broth

2 large eggs

Directions

1. Preheat over to 250°F. Butter a 13"x9"x2" baking dish.

2. Scatter bread crumbs on a rimmed baking sheet. Bake, stirring occasionally, until dried out, about 1 hour. Let cool, transfer to a large bowl.

3. Melt ¾ cup butter in a large frying pan over medium-high heat. Add onions and celery. Stir often until just beginning to brown, about 10 minutes. Add to bowl with bread, stir in herbs, salt and pepper, Drizzle in 1 ¼ cups of broth and toss gently. Let cool.

4. Preheat oven to 350°F. Whisk 1 ¼ broth and eggs in a small bowl. Add to bread mixture, fold gently until combined. Transfer to the baking dish, cover with foil, and bake until the center of dressing reaches 160°F, about 40 minutes.

5. To finish, bake uncovered, until set and top is browned and crisp, 40-45 minutes. Dressing can be made 1 day ahead. If chilled add 10-15 minutes.

ROASTED BRUSSELS SPROUTS AND APPLES

Ingredients
1 pound Brussels sprouts, trimmed and halved lengthwise
1 apple, cored and sliced (Fuji or Braeburn works well)
1 tablespoon olive oil
Salt and pepper to taste
¼ cup dried cranberries
¼ cup chopped walnuts
1 tablespoon maple syrup

Directions
1.   Preheat oven to 400°F degrees.
2.   Toss Brussels sprouts and apple slices with olive oil, salt and pepper on a rimmed baking sheet. Bake for 25-30 minutes or until Brussels sprouts are tender and browned on edges, stirring halfway through cooking time.
3.   Transfer Brussels sprouts and apple to large bowl. Stir in cranberries, walnuts and maple syrup.

SEASONAL CRANBERRY SAUCE

Ingredients
1 cup water
1 cup sugar
12 ounce bag fresh or frozen cranberries (3 cups)
½ teaspoon freshly grated orange zest.

Directions
1.   Bring water and sugar to a boil, stirring until sugar is dissolved.

2.   Add cranberries and simmer, stirring occasionally, until berries just pop, 10-12 minutes.

3.   Stir in zest, then cool.

DIX'S DECADENT PUMPKIN CUSTARD PIE

Ingredients
1 can (15 ounces) pumpkin
¾ cup packed brown sugar
1 ¼ teaspoon ground cinnamon
1 teaspoon ground ginger
½ teaspoon salt
¼ teaspoon ground cloves
¼ teaspoon ground nutmeg
4 large eggs, lightly beaten
1 ½ cups half-and-half cream
1 9-inch pastry shell
Whipped cream

Directions
1.   Preheat oven to 400°F degrees.
2.   Gently, line pastry with two sheets of aluminum foil, place pie weights over top. Bake for 15 minutes.
3.   Remove from oven and remove foil.
4.   Combine the pumpkin, brown sugar, cinnamon, ginger, salt, cloves and nutmeg in a large bowl.
5.   Add the eggs, beat lightly with a fork until combined. Add the half-and-half, mix well.
6.   Place the partially baked pastry shell on a foil-lined rimmed cookie sheet. Carefully pour the filling into the pastry shell.
7.   To prevent crust from over baking, cover the edge with foil. Remove the foil during the last 5 to 10 minutes of baking.
8.   Bake for 20 minutes. Turn pie to heat evenly. Bake about 25 minutes more or until a knife inserted near the center comes out clean.
9.   Cool on a wire rack.
10.   Cover and chill within 2 hours.
11.   Serve topped with whipped cream.

TRADITIONAL SHORTBREAD COOKIES

Ingredients
2 cups all-purpose flour
½ teaspoon salt
½ cup plus 2 tablespoons powdered sugar
1 teaspoon pure vanilla extract
1 cup (2 sticks) unsalted butter at room temperature
1 teaspoon water

Directions
1.   Preheat oven to 375°F degrees.
2.   Add the flour, slat and powdered sugar to a food processor and pulse to combine.
3.   Add in the vanilla, butter, and the 1 teaspoon of water. Pulse together just until dough is formed.
4.   Put the dough on a sheet of plastic wrap and roll into a log, about 2 ½ inches in diameter and 5 inches long. Tightly twist each end of the wrap in opposite directions.
5.   Chill dough in the refrigerator for at least 30 minutes.
6.   Slice the log into 1/3-inch thick disks. Arrange on parchment paper-lined cookie sheets, 2 inches apart.
7.   Bake until the edges just light brown, about 12 to 14 minutes, rotating cookie sheets half way through the baking process.
8.   Remove from oven and let cool on the cookie sheets for 5 minutes. Transfer to wire racks and cool until room temperature.

ACKNOWLEDGEMENTS

I never planned on writing a science fiction book. The genesis of this novel began two years ago in a humor writing course taught by Terry Fallis. As a joke, I introduced myself as a science fiction writer who had registered for the wrong course. I carried on that gag for several weeks and even wrote a sci-fi story for a class. I remember Terry saying that he enjoyed the story and suggested I consider turning it into novel. Thank you, Terry, for planting the seed.

There are so many people who helped me along the way. The frank guidance of Mica Scotti Kole was invaluable as I refined my manuscript and prepared to query publishers. She has this ability to be tough and kind at the same time. My good friend, Bonnie Swanson, who was always there to read another revision and believed so strongly in this book. To all my beta readers who took the time to read my draft manuscript – Sarah Smith, Karen Hubbard, Micah Chaim Thomas, Kyle Inge, and Larry Fox. To Deb Smythe and Chantal Saville for our monthly get-togethers to chat about our work and whatever else popped into our heads over glasses of wine.

I would also thank the people at Kyanite Publishing—B.K. Samantha, and Sophia—who took a chance on me and take such a strong interest in their authors.

Finally, I have to thank my wife, Mary Anne, for her support and understanding as I spent hundreds and hundreds of hours at my computer totally ignoring her. The pride she has in my achievements sometimes exceeds my own.

MEET THE AUTHOR

Author **Willie Handler** was a satirist well before he became a novelist. Hailing from Canada, where self-deprecating humor is part of the national character, he finds targets for his humor everywhere. His targets include friends, family, co-workers, politicians, farmers, subway passengers, bureaucrats, telemarketers, Martians and his barber, Vince. With his most recent work, he has crossed over to the world of speculative fiction.

CPSIA information can be obtained
at www.ICGtesting.com
Printed in the USA
LVHW081242100719
623488LV00003B/2/P

9 781949 645460